Doubt in the 2nd Degree

by

Marc Krulewitch

(Originally Published by Alibi/Penguin Random House.

All Rights Reverted to the Author on September 12, 2018)

Copyright © 2018 by Marc Krulewitch

Chapter 1

The mouse had been replaced by a penguin. An emperor penguin, to be exact. My jazz-themed coffee shop, Mocha Mouse, was now Penguin House. Since emperor penguins acquired tail coats at an early age, the penguin needed only a bow tie and top hat to complete the outfit. And like his mouse predecessor, the penguin played an alto saxophone. His name was Parker, as in Charlie Parker. Penguins were birds, after all.

I sat in Penguin House, reading about the latest unarmed African American shot dead by the Chicago police, when an unknown number appeared on my cellphone. Usually, I ignored unidentified numbers, thinking it better for the caller to leave a message than for me to appear as someone who jumped on the phone as soon as it rang. A sign of weakness, I thought. But today, I felt like talking.

"Landau Investigations, Jules Landau speaking."

"This is Debbie Lopez from the Cook County Public Defender's Office."

It took a moment to register what I heard. "Why does your name sound familiar?"

"I don't know—"

"Wait a minute! You got that guy out of prison. The one doing life without parole. You proved him innocent."

"I'm glad you pay attention to what's going on. But now I have a new client, Kate McCall—"

"Really? The one who murdered that auto-parts heiress in her apartment on East Lake Shore Drive?" I had not been following the story closely, but I did recall paparazzi photos of the victim, Jackie Whitney, stepping out of a limousine or laughing in a Michelin-rated restaurant. Late forties, fake blond, too much time under a sunlamp.

"Mr. Landau—"

"Jules."

"Jules," she said, a touch impatiently, "I really don't have a lot of time to talk right now, but my client has asked me to hire a private investigator."

"Doesn't the public defender's office have their own investigators?"

"We do, but she wants me to hire a non–state employee."

"Why me?"

"Apparently you've acquired a reputation."

"She can't even afford a lawyer. How's she going to pay me?"

"I have no idea, but if you're interested in the job, the three of us need to get together tomorrow, at the jail. You can discuss money with her then. So what do you think?"

Was it a trick question? "I'm interested, but if I start getting the feeling she's going to flake out on me regarding money, I'm gone."

"I'd expect nothing less from a PI. You and I need to meet tonight. I'll call you back with a time."

I didn't argue. She had the kind of all-business demeanor that said it was best to just agree then shut up.

In a thriving North Side neighborhood of various skin tones, creeds, and ethnicities, delicious smells emanated from the domed brick oven of the Kutaisi Georgian Bakery. Tamar Gelashvili, a petite woman with jet-black hair framing a beautiful, slightly Asiatic face, owned and operated the bakery. The previous owner, Tamar's "Uncle Gigi," had been arrested along with two Russian gangsters for their roles in murder, human trafficking, prostitution, and money laundering. Tamar's cousin had been killed by this cabal. In the course of my investigation, Tamar and I had become more than friends, but the demands of running a bakery necessitated a cooling-off period. Now, with the addition of some competent help and newfound confidence, we'd decided it was time to talk.

The late morning rush was winding down. I stood at the edge of the counter watching Tamar flit through the kitchen in a white V-neck T-shirt. When I caught her eye, she smiled warmly, disappeared into the prep room, then returned with a plate of flaky pastries. I followed her to a table. A glaze of perspiration spread down her lovely neck to the cleavage of her beautiful breasts. Butterflies swarmed my abdomen. Tamar put the plate down and gave me a vigorous hug.

"It's great to see you looking more relaxed," I said.

Tamar grinned. "You learn a lot in the first few months of running a business. Anyway, I spoke to my accountant and he said I should ask how you want the return on your investment structured."

After the arrests were made and the dust settled, seized assets and many years of unpaid taxes had put the bakery's future in doubt. Tamar desperately tried to raise enough money to satisfy all the statutory and municipal vultures flying lethargic loops around the North Side neighborhood, but the debt seemed insurmountable. Since I had inherited a 1933 Cadillac V-16, for which I would incur significant storage expenses, I sold the car and parked the money in the bakery.

"All I want is the principal back," I said. "Just pay at a pace that doesn't put the bakery under pressure."

"That doesn't seem right. . . ."

As Tamar struggled with my un-capitalistic tendencies, I wondered if our meeting was purely intended for business. Then I remembered the hug and foolishly read volumes into it.

Tamar stopped talking and waited for my response. She looked very intense. "I might have an interesting client," I said.

I sensed annoyance with my segue. "Okay," Tamar said.

"You heard about the Gold Coast murder? The suspect, Kate McCall, wants to hire me."

Crickets. Then, "The Jackie Whitney killer? You don't think she did it?"

"I don't know—"

"You'll take an accused murderer's money but not mine? Is she special for some reason?"

I searched her face. "What's this about?"

Tamar took her turn searching my face. "I'm not sure." She thought about it a bit longer. "Maybe it's the glee in your voice."

She was right. My speech did have an airy quality. "I suppose I'm feeling a little excitement at the prospect of a high-profile client."

"And you don't care if she's guilty?"

"Of course I care. But plenty of innocent people have been given life sentences, or been released from death row, or have died on death row. I want to believe the chances of that happening with Kate McCall are less if I'm involved."

Tamar's face softened. "I see your point—but wait a second. The Partisan did a profile on Kate McCall. They made her out to be this twenty-year-old dirt-poor Appalachian who has no choice but to use a public defender. How could she afford a private investigator?"

"Good question. After I meet her at the jail tomorrow, I'll report back with an answer."

I waited. Tamar said, "The article didn't include a picture. What does she look like?"

I cleared my throat. "After I meet her at the jail tomorrow, I'll report back with an answer."

"The Partisan kind of implied a hillbilly sex kitten—"

"What the hell is wrong with—"

"I'm working fourteen to fifteen hours a day. Down from seventeen to eighteen, although I've been training a manager who shows promise."

I gave her my raised-brow, wide-eyed look. "You need a better reason for me to get lost. How about telling me that only Georgian Orthodox boys stand a chance?"

"I'm just being realistic! This bakery's gonna dominate my life."

"Tamar, either you want to give something a chance or you don't. The demands of the bakery are just an excuse."

From Tamar's expression I anticipated disappointment. Then she said, "Maybe you're right."

"About what?"

"Using the bakery as an excuse." She reached over, grabbed my shirt collar, and pulled me into an extended kiss. After releasing me, she stood and said, "Let me know what happens at the jail. I'm really curious. And we're not done talking about my repayment schedule."

She walked back to the kitchen. I stayed put and called Debbie.

"Yes, Jules," Debbie said, still sounding testy.

"I know we just talked, but I was wondering if I could see Kate on my own, today?"

Dead air. "Why?"

"I thought meeting alone might give me better insight into her. There could be a different dynamic with you around."

Loud exhale. "Well, you can try if you want. You're supposed to fill out an application first, then wait three days for them to do a background check. I guess I could call and say it's an emergency. They probably won't buy that though. Either way, if you go, don't be in a hurry. You ever been to the maximum-security visiting area?"

"Your tone tells me it's joyful."

I thought, maybe, I heard the slightest mirthful snort. Before hanging up, Debbie emphasized that anything Kate talked about should be considered confidential. I assured her I understood, then drove home.

Once upon a time, a mostly black cat with a black dot of a nose inside a white mask climbed a dozen stairs, strolled through my open porch door, looked around, and adopted me. A few hours later, all my assumptions regarding cats as aloof creatures had been replaced with the knowledge that cats possessed human character traits making up distinct personalities. Not only did cats communicate with humans, they were happy to do so with an attitude. Within six months from the day she put down roots in my home, Punim's sarcasm had reached epic proportions.

Now, two years later, as I climbed a flight of steps to my apartment, Punim's paws touched down with an audible thump. Once inside, I noticed a morning spent in comatose digestion of chicken hearts had yielded to wild pouncing on imperceptible prey. Although she was not technically feral, Punim's domesticity was dubious at best. Weather permitting, the porch door was always open, yet she remained voluntarily homebound, venturing no farther than the landing, where she gazed into the alley of her untamed youth. Sitting on the couch, I ate a hummus sandwich and watched the beast claw her way up the red cedar cat tree, not stopping until she reached the top perch, where she began meticulously grooming.

I opened my laptop and checked the newspaper archives to review what had been reported on Jackie Whitney's murder. There were few details, only the basic facts that Kate McCall found Jackie Whitney dead in the bedroom closet of her Gold Coast apartment on May 19, three days after the victim returned from Palm Springs. An unidentified man had been renting the apartment during Jackie Whitney's absence, but had moved out several days earlier. The cause of death had not yet been revealed. Next, I found the Cook County Sheriff's Office website, filled out a visitor's application, then thought of those who endured the rigors and expense of law school only to take a job defending people too poor to afford a lawyer.

Chapter 2

At Twenty-Sixth and California, the massive Cook County Department of Corrections covered almost a hundred acres and employed more than thirty-five hundred civilian and law enforcement personnel. Conveniently attached to the jail was the Honorable George N. Leighton Criminal Court Building. On average, more than nine thousand men and women lived in the jail as guests of the county. Not long ago, a wrong turn resulted in a visitor spending thirty hours alone, locked in the maximum security visiting area. I didn't anticipate this sort of adventure, but one never knew.

Several months ago, during the murder investigation of Tamar's cousin, a misunderstanding obliged me to stand in a long line outside the jail's razor-wire fence, waiting to be processed into the bonding department. I recalled the stark reality of being given a number and put into a holding cell with eighty others awaiting their turn in bond court. Standing shoulder to shoulder with my cell mates, I was hit hard by the dehumanizing nature of penal systems, particularly the helplessness perpetuated by faceless bureaucrats controlling my fate. On the day I visited Kate McCall, it took forty minutes of waiting before I walked through a metal detector, got frisked, then showed my ID. "You're not on the list," the guard said. He appeared drowsy.

"I'm an investigator here to see my client. Her public defender called on my behalf."

The guard sighed, pretended to look through the list again. "You're not on the list."

I said loudly, "I have the right to see my client!" I showed him my investigator's ID. "It's an emergency."

The guard mumbled code-speak into his radio, then pointed at an undefined spot to my left and said, "Stand over there."

From my new location, I watched as a dozen or more visitors were ushered inside. A few minutes later, an African American sergeant appeared and asked me what the problem was.

"I need to see my client, Kate McCall. She hired me as an investigator. Her public defender called to make sure I could see her today."

"Which public defender?"

"Debbie Lopez."

The sergeant looked at something on the ground to his left and said, "What's she look like?"

"I've only spoken to her on the phone."

"Let me see some ID."

I handed over my driver's license, my FCC card, my PI card, and for good measure, my firearms ID. He gave each card a long, hard look before giving them back.

"Let him in with the next group," he said to the guard then walked away before I had a chance to thank him.

Half an hour later a group of us were herded into a hot, noisy room. A row of cubicles faced a wall of filthy Plexiglas. Round metal plates full of holes provided the avenue through which to speak. A group of women in tan jumpsuits filed in then dispersed to loved ones. Most of the communication was in the form of crying and swearing. A shapely, doe-eyed young woman with straight sandy blond hair tentatively approached the corresponding side of my cubicle and sat. She looked understandably sad. I guessed late teens, early twenties, and a bit below average height.

"Hello," I said. "I'm Jules Landau."

"How do, Mr. Landau. Ah thank you for comin'."

Her Appalachian lilt was unmistakable. "Kentucky?" I asked.

"Ahm tryin' to lose the accent. I know I sound hillbilly-like. Feel free to correct my talkin'."

I remembered Tamar's sex-kitten comment and agreed with The Partisan's description. Despite the unforgiving nature of harsh fluorescent lighting, Kate still looked cute as hell. I couldn't help but picture her with tight denim short-shorts and bare midriff. Her country-girl accent amplified her charm. But why did I feel a touch uncomfortable? "You sound fine, Kate. How can I help you?"

"Ah want very much to hire you. My friend will give you ten thousand dollars up front."

"That's a lot of money. The public defender has their own investigators—on the taxpayer's dime."

"My friend said they's all former criminals. He don't trust them much."

"Do I get to meet your friend?"

"I don't know."

"How will your friend pay me?"

"Through Debbie."

"She agreed to this?"

"Ahm sure we can figure somethin' out."

In the cubicle next to mine, a man started screaming in Spanish. I waited for the tirade to devolve into sobbing.

"How are you holding up?" I said.

Kate closed her eyes, shook her head. "Fair to middlin', I reckon."

"When did they arrest you?"

"Three days ago. You want to hear my story?"

"Not right now—"

"Can't say as I blame you, but I didn't kill nobody, I swear. It was that doctor, I'll bet. I had no reason to kill Jackie. I loved Jackie. She was the most wonderful person to me. All the evidence—"

"Tomorrow, Kate. You can tell the whole story tomorrow when Debbie and I are both here. I only came to meet you and let you know I'll do my best to make sure you get a fair—"

"Well, God bless you, Mr. Landau!" Kate said with an adoration that worried me. "Whereabouts are you from?"

Her sudden chumminess added to my discomfort, but didn't stop my curiosity from getting the best of me. I said, "I grew up in the northern suburbs. You said Jackie Whitney was a wonderful person. How exactly did you know her?"

She smiled. "Jackie come into the little grocery store where I work. Sweepin' and moppin' mostly. I see her out'n the aisles all the time. She never say nothin' 'til one day she come up and say, 'I'd never known you was a mushroom expert.' My boss, Mr. Chao, done told her that. I said I'm no expert, but I know some. And she say, 'I never seen one like this.' And then I 'splained what it all was and she liked that. From then on she come in and be real friendly and ask me questions 'bout me, you know, personally-like, and we become friends."

An obese woman holding a baby stood up and started shouting in a shrill, unidentifiable language. Her voice quickly became an ice pick stabbing my head. Two female guards tried to calm her, but by that time every baby in the room was crying. I stood and made some hand gestures indicating my intention to leave and mouthed that I would see her tomorrow. I think she got it.

Dad had been hallucinating about snakes since his dementia diagnosis. Through the oval glass of the door to my father's apartment, I saw Arthur, a husky man in his fifties, lumber toward me. I dared think the spring in his step and pleasant expression were good signs.

"Hey there, Julie," Arthur said. "C'mon in."

I followed Arthur into the foyer. "So how is he?" I said. "Snakes still bothering him?"

"You know what? I think the drugs are finally kicking in. I'm not saying he's back to his old self, but he's more like his old self."

We walked down the hall to Dad's bedroom where he sat next to his bed in his beloved swivel-rocker-recliner, bathed in the light of a Quincy rerun on TV. "Hey, Bernie," Arthur said. "Look what the cat dragged in."

Dad turned to us. "Hey! Waddya say, Julie? Come over here." Dad slapped the corner of his bed a few times. "Sit down, for chrissake."

I sat on the edge of the bed, next to his chair. "How're you doin'?"

"I feel okay. Arthur's taking good care of me. So what's new?"

That this could be the same man who only weeks ago saw untold numbers of snakes piling up in the corners of each room seemed unbelievable. I had given up on the idea of having a normal conversation, let alone discussing my latest case. But what the hell.

"You heard about the woman murdered in her Gold Coast apartment?"

"Of course. Auto-parts family. They've been around forever. They caught the guy, didn't they?"

"It's a woman. She just hired me."

Dad flashed me one of his ambiguous expressions, the kind that approved of getting a pile of cash but hated getting it from a drug dealer.

"What's with the look?" I said.

Dad snickered. "What look? She got the money to pay you?"

"She has a friend who's giving me a ten grand retainer."

Dad's face lit up. "No kidding? Good for you. You know how Frownie would approach a case like this, don't ya?"

My late mentor, Frownie, was a legendary hard-boiled snoop straight out of central casting.

"Everybody's a suspect," I said.

"You're damn right everybody's a suspect! But it's still about money. Somebody took it or somebody wanted it. Be careful. If you think she's got no case, don't go messing with stuff."

"What do you mean?"

Dad leaned forward then turned his body to me. "I mean, if it's nothing but dead ends, don't go making up shortcuts so it looks better for her.

Frownie used to do that. You know, try to plant seeds of uncertainty in the jury."

I couldn't believe my ears. "Bullshit! Frownie never made up evidence."

"Take it easy, will ya? It was a long time ago. I shouldn't have brought it up. Anyway, you think she did it?"

Maybe Dad seeing snakes was better. "I don't have any information yet. Only what's been on the news."

"What's your gut say?"

"It's hard for me to picture her killing somebody. But that doesn't mean anything."

Dad leaned back in the recliner and stared at the television. We sat in silence until I said, "Tell me more about Frownie messing with evidence."

Dad glanced at me then turned back to the TV. Then he looked at me again and said, "Do you know where my mother lives?"

I thought he was joking until the confused look on his face escorted reality back in. He waited for an answer.

"Nonny died a long time ago," I said.

Dad looked at me squint-eyed for a few moments then said, "That's right. What's the matter with me?" He leaned back in the chair, apparently thinking about something.

I said, "What do you think about the Cubs so far?"

His grimace was intensely familiar, the identical scowl I had known my whole life any time the Cubs were discussed, except his gaze remained in the distance alongside some blinking and mumbling. I walked out of the room and sat with Arthur at the kitchen table.

"Yeah, I should've been more specific," Arthur said. "He goes back and forth. But I swear he was with it all day yesterday."

With it. From now on, with it moments would be the best I could hope for.

Chapter 3

I lucked out finding a parking place on Bellevue then walked along Lake Shore Drive to Oak Street. It was one of those perfect days that one could legitimately say was not unusual for Chicago in early June. Sunny, light breeze, temperature in the upper seventies, negligible humidity. The sparkling lake gave the illusion of living in the most beautiful, perfect city, and reminded me why I endured the winters.

After crossing Michigan Avenue, Oak Street became East Lake Shore Drive, eight structures of neoclassical and Roman revival luxury on a quiet, orderly, urban streetscape. Residents of East Lake Shore Drive did not experience Chicago winters, but read about them in the newspapers of Palm Springs and Palm Beach. Three classical arches comprised the entrance to Jackie Whitney's residence, with the words "Kenilworth Manor" chiseled into the stone above the building's passageway. A plaque on one facade declared the street a landmark district. Another plaque paid tribute to the architect, Benjamin Marshall, who once hosted the Duke of Windsor at his Wilmette mansion. A third plaque displayed a heraldic shield with a red lion rampant. Prohibition-era pomp radiated from the succession of terra-cotta, brick, and limestone buildings, casting a spell, inspiring images of my great-grandfather's heyday as boss of the "bloody" Twentieth Ward.

"Can I help you with something, sir?"

Breaking the spell was a thickset man in a gray double-breasted jacket and military style officer's cap. Gold braids adorned his sleeves, his lapels, and the sides of his trousers. Below the M. Alvarez nameplate, the building's coat of arms adorned the jacket's breast pocket. Boyishly handsome in a clean-cut, Latin-looking way, he could've been forty years old as readily as fifty.

"Are you the doorman?"

"Yes, sir. Can I help you find something or someone?"

"It's part of your job to check on me because I look out of place hanging around this building. And you probably know everyone who lives here."

"It's sort of an unofficial duty," he said, appearing not the least put off. "I didn't mean to offend you, sir."

"I assure you, Mr. Alvarez, I am not offended. I was out for a stroll and realized I'd never been down this street. If I were you, I would've had me arrested by now."

Alvarez smiled and said, "Call me Manny." We shook hands. The sun reflected off his steel and gold watch. Rolex? A gold curb chain hung around his neck. "Have a nice day, sir," Manny said then turned to leave.

"Say, Manny, could I ask you a few questions about your job?"

His expression told me the question was unexpected. "Sure," Manny said then looked back at the entrance. "Are you a reporter or do you work for any news outlet?"

"No. I give you my word."

"Good enough. Would you mind stepping into the lobby?"

Initially, Manny's disinterest regarding what I did for a living seemed strange. But then I remembered the media frenzy surrounding the building in the days after the murder. Compared to all the newshounds trying to get past him to interview neighbors or get a look at the crime scene, a lone individual asking questions probably didn't worry him.

Two white vans decorated with the building's coat of arms pulled out from the valet station. I followed Manny into the lobby where the marble floors shined, the chandeliers glistened, and the heavy red velvet drapes with yellow fringe looked gaudy. Immediately to the left of the door, just off the main corridor, a round-headed man with a butch haircut and blue blazer sat at his post with a smile painted on his face. "Concierge" was written across the front of the desk in large cursive letters. A densely arrayed cluster of fig and rubber trees in an island of silk grass occupied the middle of the lobby. The doorman's desk was toward the back of the lobby near the elevators. It seemed odd to be stationed so far away from the door. Manny walked to one end of the desk and stood with his feet shoulder width apart, hands clasped behind his back, a pleasant grin on his face. Although he was short and stocky—maybe five-nine—his jacket fell straight over his waist.

"What questions do you have, sir?" Manny said.

"Call me Jules. What is a doorman's job description these days besides opening doors?"

Manny relaxed his posture but kept his vision down the lobby. He wore a silver wedding band, although it may have been platinum. "Maintain a friendly environment at all times," Manny said. "Greet residents and guests. If needed, help with luggage, accept packages, hail taxis, answer any questions."

"Wouldn't it be easier if you were located up front near the door?"

Manny smiled broadly. "One would think! It's a long story, but it has to do with cutting costs and an uncooperative concierge. But don't repeat that.

Basically, we are doormen, bellmen, and security all in one."

"Tell me about security."

"We're often told we are the front line for security. The co-op board voted to require all visitors to sign the guest book. We try to make sure that happens."

"How long have you worked here?"

"Since '92."

"Enough seniority to lock in the day shift, eh?"

"Yes, longevity has its privileges."

"It must be tough to find parking in this neighborhood."

"Yes, unfortunately my job does not include use of the building's parking facilities. However, the valet gentlemen take care of me." Manny winked at me. "If you know what I mean. I feel terribly guilty about it, although I'm told it's kind of an open secret and nobody cares." Manny coughed a couple of times. "Don't mention it, if you don't mind."

"Mention what?" I returned his wink. "Do the valets interact with the residents other than when parking their cars?"

"Yes, they pick up and deliver dry cleaning and groceries."

"In the white vans?"

"Exactly."

"What's changed regarding security since you first started working here?"

Manny's posture became a little less relaxed. He probably figured I wanted to know if the building had people undercover also watching over things. "Oh, they just want us paying closer attention. Like in an airport when they tell you to report people acting suspicious—whatever that means. I guess recognizing the building's tenants and making sure only appropriate people enter has more emphasis. Oh, and the board established a twenty-four-hour concierge/lobby-attendant position."

"Yes, I saw the man behind the desk when I walked in. What exactly are his responsibilities?"

"There's some overlap with my job, but they handle the regular mail, emergency help, getting a plumber or electrician. They're also supposed to keep up with what's going on in the neighborhood. New restaurants or clubs or what have you. We both help people who are locked out of their homes."

"So the doorman and the person behind the desk would have access to a resident's home?"

"Usually. Unless the resident requests that only their own designated friend or family member has access." Manny began pointing out cameras set up in different corners of the ceiling. Then a voice demanded our attention.

"There you are!"

A frail woman, smiling broadly and walking at an implausibly fast pace for her eighty-plus years, approached us with a shopping bag over one arm while waving to Manny with the other. Shoulder-length silver hair bordered oversized, orange-rimmed glasses. A flowing leopard-print skirt swished in time to the clomp of thick, low-heeled shoes.

Manny whispered to me, "Gloria is the eyes and ears of the building. She uses the lobby as a second living room so she can be around people. I adore her."

"Hello, my love," Gloria said to Manny, who bent down into an audible smooch on the cheek. "Thank you so much for taking care of my Louie."

"Gloria, you know how much we love Louie," Manny said. "But how are you feeling? Well enough to rejoin your bridge game?" Manny looked at me. "Gloria is a ranked Life Master of bridge."

Gloria waved him off. "I'm fine, and that was a long time ago." She looked at me. "Are you a dog lover like Manny?"

"Very much."

"What kind do you have?"

"I have a cat."

Gloria gave Manny a pretend dirty look. "Manny's little girl wants a kitty!"

"But you know she's not well," Manny said. He took out his wallet and produced a picture of a toddler sitting on the lap of an older brother.

Gloria frowned. She said to me in a lowered voice, "He could give a kitty a try, couldn't he? Happiness has healing properties better than any medicine." Manny shook his head. Gloria said, "You know, when I woke up in the hospital my first thought was Louie. Who would take care of Louie? But Louie was already with Manny and his wonderful family!" Gloria's eyes filled. A tear spilled out. "And because of Manny, a humane shelter will guarantee Louie has a loving home should something happen to me."

Manny put a hand on Gloria's shoulder. "C'mon, darling," he said then began walking her to the elevator. A minute later he returned looking somewhat misty-eyed himself.

"You have to like people to be good at this job," Manny said.

"Easier to like some than others."

His face lit up. "They're the ones who challenge me to like them. And you know what I do? I like the heck out of 'em. Kill 'em with kindness and watch 'em melt."

Manny struck me as a harmless, simpleminded guy. He oozed serenity. I envied his consciousness. "Did you like Jackie Whitney?"

This time Manny's brows jumped. "You're a private investigator, aren't you?"

I smiled. Scratch the simpleminded part. "You had me dead to rights the first moment you saw me. I never had a chance."

"Oh, gosh, I don't know about that. Although seeing you outside, I knew you were here for a reason."

"How did you know?"

Manny thought about it. "I can't say for sure. Something about your body language? The way you looked around? I've been doing this for a long time."

"A true professional."

"It's all attitude. A good attitude means you do a good job, which means you can earn a decent living."

"It's obvious you make an effort to get to know the residents. Do the residents get to know you too?"

"Oh, sure. They know me, my wife, my kids. They often ask me about my little girl, Alicia. She was born with a lung disease, so she needs lots of extra care."

"How does your son deal with his little sister's illness?"

Manny beamed. "Alberto adores her. He makes her oxygen therapy into a game so she'll relax with a mask on her face. He's quite a boy."

Manny stared at his feet. I wanted to get him back on track. "Did Jackie Whitney tip well?"

Manny gave me a curious look. "Do you have some kind of identification?" he said. I showed him my investigator's license then handed him one of my cards. He glanced at it then handed it back.

"Keep it," I said. Manny put the card into his jacket pocket. "Kate McCall hired me."

"To investigate?"

"I'm helping her lawyer construct a defense."

"You're working for the public defender?"

"Yes, but Kate McCall is paying for it. Do you know her?"

"Uh, no. She came and went visiting Jackie, but I didn't know who she was until I saw her picture in the paper."

"You simply knew her as someone who visited Jackie Whitney."

"Yeah. It's none of my business who she was. I never would've pegged her for a killer, though, but I guess you never know about those things."

"Did she visit often?"

"Quite a bit. In fact, she had a key to Jackie's apartment."

"Jackie gave Kate a key not for emergencies, but to come and go freely?"

"That might seem a bit strange. But Jackie had started renting out her place when she left town. The renters got a lower rate if they agreed to take care of her poodle, Trixie. Kate McCall was like her rental agent. So it made sense for her to have a key."

"Where's the poodle now?"

"The renter asked someone in the building to take her. I don't remember who it was."

"Kate McCall doesn't like dogs?"

Manny shrugged. "I never saw her taking Trixie out for a walk or anything like that."

"Did you ever take care of Trixie?"

"Oh, no. Jackie and I were friends, but not with that kind of rapport."

"What can you tell me about the most recent renter?"

"I didn't know anything about him at the time. He just came and went. The news said he was a doctor."

"Do you remember the last time you saw Jackie?"

Manny shook his head. "I hadn't seen her since before she left for California."

"Is it common for residents to leave for months at a time?"

"Our residents are wealthy enough to follow the sun, if they choose."

"You weren't on duty when she returned from Palm Springs?"

"No. Lenny works the swing shift."

"How can I talk to Lenny?"

"He comes in at three."

"Was Jackie Whitney already living here back in '92 when you started working?"

"No. My understanding is that she grew up in this building but moved out when she started college. After her parents died in a horrible car wreck, she moved back in. That would've been around 2002 or so."

"No highly publicized fight over inheritance?"

"She was an only child."

"I noticed you called Jackie Whitney by her first name."

"Everyone did."

"You were friends?"

"Like I said, she was my friend. And yes, she tipped well."

"Do you remember any strangers hanging around?"

"Nah. If anyone is loitering in the lobby, we ask if they have business here or know someone. If they won't leave, we call the police."

"But how the heck do you remember who lives here and who's a guest? Can you actually memorize everyone's face and name?"

Manny smiled. "Aha!" he said. "The secret to being a good doorman. Actually, it's not nearly as difficult as it might seem. You'd be surprised at how quickly your brain builds up a storage of faces and who they belong to. Kids, cousins, friends, everything gets associated. And you develop an instinct about who belongs here. Face it, the building is all rich white people. So their friends will most likely be like them."

"But not always, as in the case of Kate McCall."

"Exactly. And those are the kind of associations you remember the easiest, because they're so different."

"Could you recognize who Jackie's friends were? Enemies?"

Manny sort of laugh-scoffed. "The ones that visited the most often I assumed were friends of some type. As for enemies, I couldn't tell you."

"No, of course not. But if there was a long-standing feud with a neighbor, do you think you would know about it?"

Manny considered the scenario. "It's possible, but I can't think of a single example. The wealthy tend to isolate themselves in their own little worlds. Gloria is the exception, but there are longtime residents that I have no memory of ever seeing say so much as 'hello' to each other."

"How about strange behavior? Did Kate McCall act any different in the days leading up to Jackie Whitney's death?"

Manny shook his head. "Like I said, I didn't know her."

I didn't think he wanted to talk about it anymore. I said, "It must've been a tremendous shock when Jackie died."

Manny swallowed hard, blinked a few times, then ran the back of his hand across his eyes. "It's been barely two weeks. I still can't believe it. But I can't dwell on life's curveballs. The residents depend on me. They need a reliably smiling face."

A UPS man wheeled in a cart stacked eye-high with parcels. He greeted Manny as if previously acquainted. Something about Manny's single-mindedness compelled me to stay and observe. The delivery driver unloaded the packages on to the floor in front of the doorman's desk where Manny methodically arranged them. After saying goodbye to the driver, Manny opened a secret door that blended in perfectly with the wall. Inside the room was a chain-link pen. One by one, Manny phoned residents, verifying their expectation of a delivery then placed the deliveries in the pen before locking the secret door and returning to his station.

"Do you think anyone would mind if I spoke to the uncooperative concierge?"

"I, uh, I'm sure nobody would care. I'm sure nobody would notice. I certainly don't care."

"I detected the slightest reluctance. The uncooperative part won't be mentioned, scout's honor."

"Oh, no, no. Freddie is an interesting . . . guy. That's all. Please, go talk to him."

I thanked Manny for his time then headed toward the concierge station. Freddie was hunched over the desk scanning a map with two others. Three more people waited their turn for the concierge's attention. Freddie, the interesting guy, could wait another day.

Chapter 4

I stood on the pedestrian walkway behind Oak Street Beach, leaning against a tree while jotting down observations on a small notepad. Frownie had always told me to write down my thoughts after an interview. "Always, always include alleged statements of fact," he used to say. But I resisted at first. Something about carrying a notepad and pen hit me as shabby and obsolete, never mind uncool. Then I thought I'd give it a try, if only to see if I stopped getting up in the middle of the night to write things down. Frownie had died several months ago, at age ninety-one.

"Ikaria," I said to retired police detective Jimmy Kalijero when he answered the phone.

"What?"

"Ikaria. The Greek island."

"I know what it is. What about it?"

"That's where you should retire. They live forever on Ikaria. Don't you want to live forever?"

"What do you want, Landau?"

"Colorful" was the word I used when referring to Detective Jimmy Kalijero's relationship with my family. He had busted my father for running an illegal gambling operation when I was a teenager and still carried around some guilt for the harsh sentence Dad received. Since I'd become a private investigator, Kalijero had assisted me in three investigations—albeit grudgingly. I dared say our relationship had evolved to one of dubious respect.

"How are you, Jimmy?"

"What the fuck do you want, Landau?"

"How about a game of backgammon? Or what do you call it? Tavli?"

"Why?"

"I thought we were friends."

Kalijero expelled a loud, phony laugh. "When have we ever gotten together when it wasn't about a case you were working on, friend?"

"You're right, and I'm sorry about that. C'mon, give me a game of backgammon. You're retired, for chrissake! You got nothing else to do!"

Hearing only several seconds of breathing meant I had a chance. "You know, why not?"

"Seriously?"

"Sure, Landau. This is our chance to bond. We can become real pals."

Despite the unmistakable sarcasm, Kalijero agreed to meet me at Penguin House, where I found him sitting at a four-top with a backgammon board set up and nothing to eat or drink. His disrespect needed attention.

"I'll be right back," I said then got in line to order. Considering Kalijero had undergone prostate surgery the previous April, he looked rather perky for a working-class icon well into his sixties. His wavy salt-and-pepper hair, open silk shirt, and gold Parthenon necklace still gave him a slightly heroic flavor. I returned with two cups of tea.

"What's this?" Kalijero said.

"Mountain tea. It's Greek."

"I don't like tea."

I took a seat. "If you take up a table, you've gotta buy something. And you're taking up a four-top when there's only two of us." Kalijero didn't respond. I said, "Okay, you're right. I got another murder case. But this one I know you'll be glad I told you about." Kalijero took a die from his hand and dropped the other on my side of the board. I said, "You don't want to hear about the murder?"

Kalijero rolled a four then looked at me. I rolled a one. He moved two of his red checkers. I rolled a five and a three. Kalijero cloaked me in his oppressive gaze.

"What are you waiting for?" Kalijero said. I ignored him. Seconds later he said, "You don't know how to play."

"It's been a while—"

"Bullshit. You don't know how to play. You roll a five and a three there's no hesitation what your move is. Admit it. The only reason you called was to talk about a case."

I had nothing. "You got me, Jimmy. Busted. Is it really that big a deal?"

Kalijero had a way of staring I attributed to single, childless men unable to suppress the urge to shame a younger man. His vibe touched a nerve but I didn't ponder the psychological implications.

"Just say what the hell you're thinking already!" I said.

Kalijero began taking pieces off the backgammon board. I watched until he finished putting everything in its designated slot. I stood to leave. He said, "So who's dead?"

I sat back down. "Jackie Whitney."

"The auto-parts gal? What do you got to do with that?"

"The defendant hired me. Her lawyer and I are sitting down with her at the jail tomorrow."

"You doing pro bono work now?"

"She's got a benefactor. Have you been following the case?"

Kalijero shrugged, scratched his chin. "I know what's been reported. She left town, rented out her apartment, came back, got murdered. The judge sealed a lot of the court documents, you know."

"Why? We're not talking national security here."

"Family privacy."

"Since when is that a reason to seal an investigation?"

Back to the disapproving glare. "If you're a famous Chicago family going back a hundred years, that's what happens."

I guess it was a dumb question. Kalijero scratched his chin again. I said, "So whaddya think?"

He looked at me, then away. "I don't know."

"You want me to keep you updated?"

"I don't know," he said again then aimed his vision far afield, into some mental wonderland reserved for a big-city cop with forty-plus years of experience embedded into his awareness.

"Just say what you're thinking, Jimmy. Tell me to go fuck myself, but just say it already."

Kalijero looked at me. "I miss it," he finally said. "Investigating. I miss the hell out of it. Now get out of my sight."

From the sidewalk, the view of my apartment included a mound of black fur smashed flat against the window facing Halsted Street. Once I got inside, Punim observed me from her window perch.

"Miss me?" I said.

"Were you gone?" she replied.

I grabbed a bag of outrageously authentic tortilla chips—cooked in the carniceria that kept Punim well-stocked with livers, hearts, kidneys, and gizzards—then collapsed with my laptop into my lounge chair. It wasn't a deluxe swivel-rocker like Dad's, but a privilege nonetheless. I reclined forty-five degrees into a world of rhythmic crunching and thought about Kalijero. Police work was the only life he had ever known. I'd assumed that he would always enjoy dipping his toe in the waters of crime investigation. Perhaps I was being selfish. Maybe I shouldn't bother Kalijero. Maybe it would be healthier for Kalijero to retire in peace. The thought of leaving him alone unsettled me.

My angle of repose came with the inherent threat of drowsiness. Nickels formed on my eyelids. I thought about Manny the doorman's pleasant demeanor and his infectiously positive attitude. People felt good being around Manny. Intelligent, insightful, it was easy to see Manny as the building's shoulder to cry on. My doorman, my therapist. As the nickels were becoming half-dollars, Debbie Lopez called.

"Hi, Debbie."

"Okay, Jules," she responded amid the general sounds of shuffling papers and desk clutter. "How about seven?"

"Where?"

"I'm coming from Twenty-Sixth and Cal. I live northwest."

"Café Schmaltz. Logan Square. Know it?"

"What's the address?"

"California to Milwaukee, sharp right, down a block, on your right."

"Got it."

Chapter 5

Compared to the gradual reawakening of many Chicago neighborhoods since the 1980s, Logan Square's gentrification seemed to have happened at whiplash speed. No sooner had the artists started moving in than young professionals showed up, rehabbing commenced, and developers went on a buying spree. Industrial warehouses were converted to luxury lofts. Century-old brick and stone churches with handcrafted amber glass made way for condos and mixed use projects.

I arrived at Café Schmaltz about ten minutes early and looked around. The youthful faces and corresponding jeans and T-shirts told me Debbie was not among the crowd. Purple and violet gradients combined amazingly with the red, green, and blue mid-century modernist furniture. But it was the coffee shop's devotion to the warm, rich sounds of vinyl LPs that sealed the deal for Café Schmaltz.

As was my custom, I sat at a two-top against the back wall. A copy of The Partisan lay on the table next to mine. I read a few paragraphs of an article about Mayor Emanuel's outsourcing of the city treasurer's office to a private equity firm, then tossed the paper onto an empty chair. Something about coffee shops made me think about Frownie. Sometimes Frownie and I would be sitting around and he'd casually say something that only later on would strike me as intellectually profound. One time he said everyone's face had a story to tell and the best investigators knew how to find clues in those stories. I looked around. A twenty-something female sat by herself, sipping coffee, eagerly scanning Café Schmaltz. Something about her told me she was new to the city. She had that confident, optimistic look of one starting afresh after finally summoning the courage to leave childhood behind. From now on, life would be new, exciting, and romantic. Yeah, right.

A few minutes later, a stocky woman about five-five with short black hair walked in. The bulging leather messenger bag slung over her shoulder was a dead giveaway, although her gray skirt-suit and white blouse would've been enough. I waved. She walked over.

"Hi, Debbie."

She either didn't respond or I didn't hear her as she struggled to liberate the bag and let it drop. It hit the floor with a loud thwack.

"What do you want?" Debbie said.

Her question caught me off guard until I realized she had taken a couple of steps toward the counter. "Oh, uh, soy mocha." I moved an arm to my back pocket, but it was too late. She returned with our coffees and sat.

"Okay, first thing," Debbie said. "How do you operate? What's your initial approach toward an investigation?"

"Depends on the investigation."

"How about the investigation you just got hired for?"

"Everyone's a suspect."

"That's what I thought," Debbie said, not sounding pleased. "Let me be clear. We're not actors in a crime drama eliminating suspects one by one until the crime is solved. Presenting convincing, solid, reasonable doubt is our number-one priority."

"What's our number-two priority?"

"Presenting convincing, solid, reasonable doubt. Do you want to hear our third priority?"

"I think I got it."

"Okay, the second thing. I don't care if Kate is paying you, I'm in charge of this investigation." We stared at each other.

"Fine with me, boss."

"Third thing. The judge sealed the case. So you can't talk about it. Info will leak out, but it can't come from you." Her tone bordered on condescending.

"Check."

She began pulling files and other stuff from her bag. "The preliminary hearing is set for July seventh. Did you see Kate McCall?"

"Yes."

"What did you notice about her appearance?"

"On the small side but healthy looking. Somewhat depressed."

Debbie opened a folder. "Whitney was beaten to death on the couch with a hammer. On the table, two empty wine bottles and one glass. Only the victim's prints were found on the bottles and wineglass. Another glass was found in the kitchen sink. Blood alcohol level 0.139 percent, which means she was pretty drunk. The couch was in the living room, which looked out over the lake. This is a five-thousand-square-foot apartment, remember. Her body was found in the master bedroom at the opposite end of the apartment, sealed in a plastic garment bag and hidden on the highest shelf of the walk-in closet. The closet had a sliding ladder to access the top shelves."

I said, "How big was Jackie Whitney?"

"Five-six. One-thirty."

"I'll assume she wasn't drinking alone. Could a woman with Kate McCall's build, likely tipsy from wine, stuff one hundred and thirty pounds of dead weight into a bag, drag it to the other end of the apartment, then deadlift it up a ladder and jam it into a shelf, without someone helping her?"

"A deep shelf. The body was pushed back as far as it would go. The evidence against her is arguably compelling, but fishy. I think the cops jumped the gun. They're gambling she'll hand over an accomplice."

"Who found the body?"

"McCall."

"That's right. She had a key. They were buddies, although it's hard to believe they would've even known each other."

"Believe it. They were very good friends. Who told you about the key?"

"I had a nice conversation with the doorman at Jackie Whitney's building."

Debbie's eyes opened wider. "Did he tell you how Kate McCall and Jackie Whitney met?"

"Kate told me."

"What did she say?"

"McCall said she worked a few blocks away, at a specialty grocer for people who don't mind paying fifty bucks for a bottle of olive oil. Whitney befriended her over mushrooms."

Debbie started writing something on a piece of paper then double-checked the information against a page in the folder. "I want you to interview these two," she said. "Linda Napier and George Mason. Supposedly George was a close friend of Jackie Whitney. I'm not sure about Linda."

"What about the apartment where the renter dumped Jackie's dog? Were the residents there interviewed?"

"I don't know anything about a dog. The police report was absurdly vague about neighbors who were interviewed."

"The doorman said Whitney was friends with everyone and everyone called her Jackie."

Debbie had no discernable reaction, but handed me a packet containing the police report, coroner's report, and evidence photos. The first page was an outline of the basic events. "Okay," Debbie said. "Let's go over what the state's attorney thinks are facts. Jackie Whitney returned from Palm Springs on May sixteenth. Her flight landed around two forty-five in the afternoon. The doorman estimated she arrived home sometime between four and five o'clock. On May nineteenth, two thirty-three a.m., Kate McCall called 911, hysterical, said she found Jackie Whitney's body, and immediately fingered the doctor who was renting the place." Debbie looked at me.

"The doorman didn't seem that surprised Jackie Whitney gave a key to Kate McCall."

"McCall told the cops their friendship had grown into Kate becoming Jackie Whitney's personal assistant. And that included acting as a kind of leasing agent for when Whitney went out of town and rented her place to other traveling millionaires."

"The most recent renter was a doctor?"

"Dr. Joshua Kessler. Orthopedic surgeon at Rush. He moved out early, left a note complaining about the water not getting hot and an infestation of bedbugs, or something like that."

"Bedbugs? In that fancy building?"

"I didn't say it was true, only that he wrote it in a note. Anyway, after Whitney flew back from Palm Springs, she didn't phone Kate McCall like she normally would when getting back in town. And Whitney didn't return Kate's calls. Finally, Kate decided to check things out herself and that's when she found Whitney's body. The coroner thought she'd been dead at least thirty-six hours."

"Where's the doctor?"

"His number is on that list I gave you. He told the police he moved out on Friday, May fifteenth.. He left the key with the doorman."

"What's the evidence they're using against Kate?"

"Kate going over there in the wee hours, finding the body—i.e., knowing where the body was—and immediately blaming the doctor on the 911 call raised suspicion. Then Kate's grocery store boss finds a bloody hammer, Whitney's prescription pill bottles, her vehicle registration, and two keys, all in a plastic bag in the dumpster behind the grocery."

"Where she works? And why was her boss rummaging through the garbage?"

"He checks it to see if someone is illegally using it, then has the cops write them a ticket. One more thing. Kate's thumbprint is on the hammer."

"So Kate is stupid enough to hide incriminating evidence in the same dumpster where she knows her boss will find it?"

"One key was for the bedroom closet door, the other was for a safe-deposit box." The closet key struck me as odd. I wasn't sure why. "Is anything missing from the safe deposit box?"

"Jewelry and fifteen thousand in cash were found in Kate's apartment."

"How did anyone know about the safe-deposit box or what was in it?" Debbie reached into her bag without answering and began digging through it. I said, "Kate's being framed." Debbie straightened up with several folders in her hand.

"That's the route we're taking."

I waited for more. "And you feel strongly about her innocence?"

Debbie leaned a bit forward over the table, looked me straight in the eye. "Jules, my job is to provide the best defense possible for my client. If the state wants Kate to spend the rest of her life in prison, they better damn well prove their case. So until a jury decides she's been proven guilty beyond a reasonable doubt, she's innocent."

Her tone had officially become patronizing. "So what do you think of me working with you instead of a PD investigator? And don't hold back."

She was reading something but I knew she heard me. "I think it's great," she finally said sounding downright pleasant, but still studying a page from her folder. As I tried to gauge the sincerity of her statement, she put the file down. "You wanna know why?"

"I'd really like to know why."

"On any given day, I'm juggling at least twenty-five clients. That's twenty-five murderers, drug dealers, child molesters, rapists—you name it. If you're working with me, that frees up an investigator to help another lawyer."

Something about the unabashed logic of her words made me feel better. I guess I wanted to be wanted. I said, "So the cops really think they got the right person?"

"They think they got one of them. They're pretty convinced someone else helped her, maybe the doctor. I'm sure there's still a police detective on the case. He'll undoubtedly want to know what you're up to. They all hate my guts, by the way. And I hate their guts even more."

"Why can't we all just get along?"

The humor escaped Debbie. "After we meet with Kate, go have a look at the crime scene. I'll have an ID made up for you." Debbie took her phone and held it up. "Smile," she said simultaneously with the flash. "Then hunt down those friends of Whitney. Oh, and Whitney has a twenty-four-year-old son, Phillip. I'm still trying to locate him. He might only talk through a lawyer."

I cringed upon hearing his age, thinking Phillip a spoiled Millennial brat. "A lawyer? That would be kind of weird behavior, no?"

"I don't know if it's so weird. He's the sole heir to an auto-parts fortune. He was probably told to lawyer-up because that's what rich people do. But we still need to find out what kind of relationship they had.”

Debbie checked the time then started digging around in her bag again. I watched for a while then said, “So why hide the body there? I mean, if you’re going to hide it, wouldn’t you take it somewhere else? Away from the crime scene?”

She glanced up at me then turned back to the bag and resumed digging. “Hard to say,” she said. “A killer’s brain probably isn’t thinking rationally.”

Looking at the top of Debbie’s head was growing tedious. “I gotta go,” I said. “What time tomorrow?”

Debbie swore under her breath, but not at me, I assumed. “Just meet me in front of the courthouse,” she said, “around nine o’clock.”

Once back home, I ate a large bowl of spaghetti then plopped down on the couch. Punim settled across my thighs, her forelegs folded under her chest. The volume of the Cubs game was just loud enough to sound like muffled voices through a wall. I should’ve gone to bed since the effort to keep upright interfered with what little concentration remained. Slowly, I rotated to my back, careful not to upset Punim’s positioning. Once I was horizontal, thoughts of Tamar took over. I thought about our conversation earlier in the day. It was amazing how worries like Kate McCall’s overconfidence in my ability to get her freed, Dad’s deteriorating brain, and Debbie’s abrasive personality disappeared with the thought of a single kiss.

Chapter 6

The next morning I took the outer drive to the Stevenson Expressway and got to the Cook County jail in about forty minutes. A short flight of stairs led to three Roman arches not unlike the arches of Jackie Whitney's East Lake Shore Drive building. One could've drawn upon this similarity to contemplate the gateways to justice and the gateways to privilege. Instead, I stood on the bottom step watching for Debbie, marveling at the sheer number of government workers, lawyers, cops, associates, and their juvenile clients, all advancing on the building.

Debbie emerged with what I took for her signature look of preoccupation. Her first words, "If you want coffee, there's a roach coach over there," were spoken with the same charm as the previous night.

"I'm fine," I said.

"Here, put this around your neck." She handed me an identification badge with my picture. "Let's go," she said.

I followed Debbie into the jail. After going through security, we were led to a private interview room. A guard stood outside the door. Several minutes later, Kate McCall was brought in. Debbie and I sat on one side of the table across from Kate.

"Let's talk about the money," Debbie said.

"I'm fixin' to have an envelope brought to your office," Kate said. "And then you might could give it to Mr. Landau."

Debbie stared at Kate for a second. "I meant the money missing from Jackie Whitney's safe-deposit box. And the jewelry."

Kate looked at me. I said, "We'll talk about our arrangement later."

"The state's attorney will claim a financial motive," Debbie said. "The police said they found fifteen grand and Whitney's jewelry in your apartment. They said you took it from the bank the day after you reported finding the body. How did the cops find out about the box?"

"I was a signer on Jackie's safe-deposit box. I was sure the bank was going to tell them, so I done told them first. And they would've seen me on them spy cameras they all have anyhow."

"Did you really say you took the money and jewels to keep them safe?" Debbie said.

"I never did say nothin' like that! I said to keep the money safe for Jackie's son. I promised her the jewelry and cash would get to Phillip if anything happened to her."

"You had the jewelry and cash for almost two weeks before you were arrested—"

"I couldn't find the boy! I didn't know where to look."

Debbie sighed deeply as she read through some notes. "What's with all the cash anyway?"

"Rent for January, February, and March. The doctor paid cash. When Jackie returned, she was gonna spend it or deposit it slowly, so as not to draw attention from the tax man."

Debbie wrote furiously in her notebook. We watched her for several minutes. Still writing, she said, "Just jump right in, Jules."

"Can you account for your time on May sixteenth and seventeenth, the days Jackie Whitney was most likely killed?"

"I worked Saturday, six until two, then spent the rest of the day at home. I hadn't yet heard from Jackie since speakin' to her on Thursday. She was supposed to come back from Palm Springs that afternoon. Anyway, on Sunday I worked at the grocery from six to noon. We close at noon on Sundays. T'was a nice day. I went home, ate somethin', laid down, then walked a few blocks to Jarvis Beach. I followed the shoreline to Loyola Park beach, then spent a few hours just hangin' out in the sun, people watchin'. I stopped at the Heartland Café around five. Had a nibble, read The Partisan, home by six-thirty. In for the night."

"Can you prove any of this?" I said. "Can you prove you were home all night?"

"No," Kate said quietly. "I wish I had kept the receipt from the restaurant."

"On Tuesday the nineteenth you decided to go to Jackie Whitney's apartment," Debbie said. "Why at two-thirty in the morning?"

"I was worried. I couldn't sleep. I wanted to see for myself she had really come back."

Debbie said, "How did you find the body?"

Kate hesitated. Her eyes filled. She blinked a few tears down her face. "As soon as I walked in—there was a stink. All them windows in the front room were wide open, but the stink was still strong. As I walked to the back it got more powerful. The closet was open. I could barely keep from throwin' up. The smell had to be comin' from one of them shelves. There was no other place. I just started pushin' clothes and shoes away. On the top shelf I saw the tote—I mean bag. I touched it. I knew it was a body."

"You knew it was Whitney's body?" Debbie said in a way that would've pissed me off.

"'Course it was Jackie. T'was her apartment! I hadn't heard nothin' from her. Why wouldn't I think it was her body?"

"You said the closet was open, right? No need for a key?"

"Yes sir, the door was wide open."

Debbie took a deep breath. "Okay. How did your thumbprint get on the hammer?"

Kate frowned. "Oh, Lord, you'll find screwdrivers and a measurin' tape also with my fingerprints. I been doing all kinds of things for Jackie. The hammer was for helpin' her hang pictures."

Debbie continued writing. I said, "Who could've put Whitney's personal items in the trash where you work?"

Kate sighed. "It must've been that doctor. I think he come back to get some things. Jackie was there. They quarreled. He killed her then took those things to put in the trash. He knew where I worked because he met me there once, to give me the rent. He planned it all out."

"What was the doctor's motive?"

"He was fixin' to leave before the lease was up."

"That's not a murder motive."

"He stopped payin' in April. He was supposed to stay until October first. Jackie wanted to be around for the Fall and stay thru the holidays. Hopefully we'd find another renter if she decided to go back to Palm Springs. So Kessler owed six months of rent. Thirty thousand dollars. He said the hot water was broke. Then he said somethin' about roaches. All damned lies."

Debbie and I knew thirty grand for a surgeon wasn't worth killing for. I said, "Would the doctor have known your boss goes through the garbage looking for illegally dumped trash?"

Kate blinked her eyes repeatedly. "I don't rightly know," she said.

"What kind of person was the doctor?"

"A goddamn peckerwood."

"Okay," Debbie said as she stood up then knocked on the door. The guard entered. "We'll be in touch."

I followed Debbie out of the jail. Neither of us spoke. At the courthouse steps she stopped and turned to me. "You remember your assignment?"

"Don't you at least tell your clients to keep their chins up or something?"

Debbie remained agnostic. "Call me after you've checked out the crime scene and started tracking down those people. A child rapist and two murderers need my attention now."

This time a much older gentleman stood outside the door of Jackie Whitney's building. He wore a long red overcoat with black-trimmed sleeves and a black satin top hat. Two medals hung from ribbons pinned above his left breast. He remained stone faced as he held the door open, his vision locked straight ahead. Once inside the lobby, I watched Manny from behind as he leaned against the doorman's desk conversing with a dapper middle-aged couple I assumed were residents. The couple listened intently, occasionally nodding their heads and touching Manny's arm as he spoke. After a few minutes, Manny removed his wallet from his back pocket then laid out several photos on the counter. The couple spent time examining the photos, grinning, laughing. The woman looped her arm around her husband's arm then looked at her watch. They took turns embracing Manny and left. Manny returned the photos to his wallet, took off his jacket, then began sweeping it with a lint brush.

"You're back," Manny said, extending his hand. For a moment, I thought he might kiss my cheek.

I said, "If someone invented a brush that would take everything off a jacket like yours in one or two swipes, they'd be pretty damn rich."

"I know I'd buy one," Manny said then held up the brush. "A tool of my trade."

"I guess grooming comes with the job. How many residents' dogs have you taken care of?"

"Oh, just Gloria's. Of course, management insists on wool jackets—"

"Which are fur magnets."

"Exactly." Manny peered at the badge around my neck then glanced at my police report folder. "You want to go up to the apartment?"

"Yes, please. How long did the cops hang around?"

"They came and went for a couple of days. The crime scene tape is still up, but I'm authorized to give out keys with the right ID."

"The cops questioned you?"

"All of us."

"Were you told not to talk about it?"

Manny shook his head. "Nobody really knew anything, except what I told you about Jackie."

"What about CCTV footage?"

"They asked about our closed circuit video. I don't know if they looked at it or not." Manny gave me a key. "Don't leave the building with the key in your pocket," he said with a wink.

On the tenth floor, the elevator opened into a private hallway of polished granite and Persian rugs. Once through the apartment's door, I found myself standing on marble arranged in black and white diamond-shaped tiles. Queen Anne furniture and porcelain urns lined buttery yellow walls. A large brass luggage cart was also present. The wealthy traveled with lots of baggage, I thought, and knew a metaphor lurked close by. I turned right, followed the foyer to the dining room which also connected to a living room featuring a baby grand piano. Picture windows overlooked Oak Street Beach.

The back of the couch was flush against the wall. This surprised me. The killer would not have been able to sneak up on Jackie Whitney. The coroner cited death from two or three blows to the top of the skull, all striking within centimeters of each other. The victim was almost certainly sitting down. Blood had soaked thoroughly into the couch's leather upholstery, over the back of the cushions and down to the seat. Those stains were never coming out. More blood collected where Jackie Whitney's head came to rest. The coroner's report stated that blood had pooled into Whitney's lower extremities. This starts to happen about thirty minutes after the heart stops. The assailant must have come upon her suddenly and then let the victim sit around a while before moving her.

I took out the police photos of the hammer. Another photo encompassed the couch and surrounding furniture. The magazine on the coffee table was still there. It was opened to a display ad for Senior Tricks, a bridge club for old folks. A wrinkled piece of paper lay partly under the coffee table. I dropped to my knees then straightened it out enough to identify a few paragraphs of meeting proceedings. Another photo was enlarged to show Kate's thumbprint on the metal just above the rubber grip. The grip itself had no discernible prints. Also included was a photo of a plastic bag containing several tiny shavings of a substance that looked vaguely familiar. Maybe dead skin, I thought.

The body's path to the bedroom would've been the opposite way I had traveled to the couch, or via the media room, kitchen, and foyer. I walked both routes but found no blood on the tile or carpet, which suggested to me the victim was either carried in a position to keep her head from dripping or was dragged by the armpits with her head hanging forward. In the bedroom, the king size bed was undisturbed. A photo of a fairly large poodle laying on the floor with her head in Jackie Whitney's lap was on the nightstand. The shelves in the closet were mostly bare. A mess of clothing covered the floor. The ladder leaned against the top shelf where the body was found. Retracing my steps through the living room, I had somehow missed a photo of Jackie Whitney and another woman kneeling on either side of a large mastiff-type dog. I took a picture of the photo with my phone then headed back to the lobby.

From the doorman's desk, I watched Manny carry a couple of suitcases outside to deposit into the trunk of a taxi. An elderly woman clutching a small purse waited patiently in front of the open passenger door. When Manny slammed the trunk shut, the woman took some coins out of the purse and dropped them into his hand. Manny bowed deeply at the smiling, wrinkled face before backing away. Then he walked briskly through the lobby, shaking the coins in his fist as if about to throw dice at a crap table.

"Fifty-cent tip?" I said.

"Sweetest old lady you ever met," Manny said. "Ninety-six years old and still travels on her own— God bless her!"

I took out a picture of the murder weapon. "Does this belong to the maintenance people?"

Manny studied it a moment. "It looks like one of our hammers. Why?"

"I don't know. I just don't picture Jackie Whitney owning tools."

"Jackie would borrow a hammer or a screwdriver from time to time."

"Had she borrowed one shortly before she died?"

Manny thought about it. "I don't know. We haven't been keeping track of these things. But maybe we should."

"The old guy outside, dressed up like the Queen's Royal Regiment, I've never seen him before. Does he work inside too?"

Manny chuckled. "Marv's normal gig is the lobby's graveyard shift. "

"What's he doing here now if he works graveyard hours?"

"Just an eccentric old guy having a little harmless fun. He's eighty-two and has been employed here since 1954. Did you notice the medals? Silver Star and Purple Heart. A battle called Outpost Harry. Korean War. I thought maybe he was starting to lose it upstairs, but he's still sharp as a tack."

"You don't worry something unmanageable might happen while he's on duty?"

"There's not much to do overnight and the lobby is attended twenty-four hours, so help is nearby. A good thing too. Not long ago the front desk attendant found Marv unconscious. He was taken to the hospital where he spent a few weeks battling pneumonia. Nobody thought he'd recover, but he showed everybody how tough he is. Gloria organized a little party for him when he returned."

I smiled at the compassionate gesture. "Speaking of Gloria, I'm curious about her dog, Louie. What kind of dog is it?"

Manny looked puzzled. "Uh, I'm really not sure. One of those little curly white dogs you see everywhere."

"Like a small version of Jackie's poodle?"

"Yeah, but not a poodle. Maybe a mix. Sturdy little guy. Lots of spirit."

"Some kind of terrier?"

"Could be. Why do you ask?"

"I was just wondering what kind of dog someone Gloria's age would own. Have a great day, my friend." I bowed deeply while backing away.

Freddie slouched forward over the concierge desk, blue blazer hanging loosely over narrow shoulders. He looked a bit odd sporting a toothy grin while sitting alone behind a deserted desk. The nametag on his lapel said Frederick.

"May I help you, sir?" Freddie said. His voice registered deeper than I expected for a small-framed man.

"Hi, Frederick, Manny thought it was okay if I asked you a few questions regarding Jackie Whitney. I'm a private investigator."

The grin vanished. I took out my PI license and laid it on the desk. Freddie glanced down at it. "I really don't like to talk about it," Freddie said. His skin was a bit oily. Facial hair sparse. Something about his eyes seemed unnatural.

"I'm sorry. You were friends with Jackie?" Freddie nodded, his lower lip quivered. Both men who worked in the lobby had become emotional when talking about Jackie Whitney. I said, "I'm going to find out who did this horrible thing. You would be doing a great service to your friend if you talk to me a little bit."

"What do you mean, find out? That awful woman did it."

"Maybe. I just want to make sure it was her and find out if others were involved. When was the last time you spoke to Jackie?"

"A few days before she returned from Palm Springs."

"Really? So you two were good friends?"

"Yes. She called me at least once a week while she was gone." Freddie pulled a few tissues from a box on the counter, blew a loud honk. "She accepted me," Freddie said. "Jackie didn't judge me."

The comment's ambiguity was intentional. I thought I understood. "She didn't judge lifestyle choices you made. Is that what you mean?"

Freddie nodded and blew his nose again at the same time. "Jackie knew me before I started transitioning. When my name was Felicia."

My turn to nod, as if the Freddie/Felicia thing had been absurdly obvious. "How long did Jackie know you as Felicia before you started transitioning?"

"Around two years. She talked me through my fear. She helped me find resources, convinced me to come out, find the right doctors. My God, she paid for it! That's the kind of woman she was!"

"Did you know the woman they arrested? Kate McCall?"

"Of course not. Why would I know her?"

"Well, she was like Jackie's personal assistant."

"Jackie and I spoke only when it was just the two of us. That Kate woman was never around."

"Did Jackie ever talk about her personal life? Any conflicts she had with people?"

"She focused only on me. She was a giver. Give, give, give. That's all she ever did."

"Kate McCall had a key to Jackie's place. Did you also have a key?"

Freddie held both hands to his mouth and looked away. Through his fingers he said, "She had a key. Oh, my God!"

"Freddie, did you also have a key? Or access to a key?"

He turned to me, still covering his mouth. "No! I mean, if she got locked out or something, we were allowed to get a key. But for no other reason."

"Where would you go to talk?"

His hands came down. He swallowed hard. "Well, sometimes we'd get coffee somewhere. Several times she traveled all the way to my apartment in Pilsen to see me.. That's the kind of person she was. But often we just chatted right here, assuming there was nobody requiring my attention."

"Did you ever chat in her apartment?"

Freddie closed his eyes a moment, then looked around. "Oh, no. That would've been against the rules. Of the building, I mean."

"She could've invited you up, right?"

Freddie looked at his watch. "I suppose, but that's frowned upon."

"Do you work weekends?"

"No."

"Then you weren't here on May sixteenth or seventeenth, when Jackie—when it most likely happened?"

"No. I'm not sure anyone was working at the concierge desk."

"I thought it was manned twenty-four hours."

"When we're fully staffed, which is rare. It's difficult to find someone to work the overnight shift and stay longer than a month."

"Who can tell me if someone worked that weekend?"

Freddie gave me his supervisor's card. I thanked him for his time and left a card of my own.

Chapter 7

From the sidewalk in front of Kenilworth Manor, I called Rush University Medical Center.

"Orthopedic surgery. How may I direct your call?"

I asked for Dr. Kessler. Another phone rang then a recording offered me options. I chose to hang up and drive to the hospital. At the orthopedic building I showed my state investigator credentials to the front desk. The woman appeared unimpressed but wrote down my name and offered me her crowded waiting room.

I stood around for five minutes then started roaming past rooms of iced and elevated limbs. All I had to go on was Kate McCall's goddamn peckerwood observation. Several rooms had doctors beside patients or nurses conducting post-surgical mobility exercises. Then I came upon the backside of a man in Armani jeans and a powder blue sport shirt, leaning against the wall just outside a room. I walked past him. He was smiling broadly with a cellphone to his ear. Maybe if he hadn't been wearing a Vandyke beard, my hunch would not have been as strong. Inside the room, four young doctors—residents, I assumed—stood idly around a patient. I slowed down, hovered near the now giggling man, then entered the room.

"Is that Dr. Kessler?" I said pointing toward the doorway. All four stoically nodded. The patient watched television using earphones.

Back in the hallway, I slid my state investigator's ID into his line of vision. Without looking at me, he took the ID from my hand and continued his conversation. I stepped back to regroup. When he put my ID into his pocket, I tapped him on the shoulder. "Hang on," he said then looked at me.

"Can I have my ID back?"

His eyes plotted coordinates on my face. "Who are you?"

"You just put my ID into your pocket."

Kessler straightened up. "Let me call you back," he said into the phone. "Now what are you talking about?"

"Put your hand into your left pocket and you'll find my state investigator's ID."

He did as told then read it. "You're with the, uh, district attorney guys."

"No, I'm with the public defender."

Kessler smiled and nodded. "Oh, the other side. You're defending that cunt."

"Can we talk privately?"

Kessler looked at his watch then stuck his head into the room. "Hey, guys, I'll be back in ten minutes. Take a break or something."

I followed Kessler down the hall to his office. He plopped himself down behind a mahogany desk, put his feet up, then told me to pull a chair over from a table. A half-empty fifth of twenty-five-year-old Glenglassaugh sat on his desk.

"So what do you want to know that I haven't already told the cops?"

"How did you find out about Jackie Whitney's rental?"

"Through one of those agencies for people with a lot of money."

"You couldn't find a mortgage for less than that kind of rent?"

"I'm on loan from Stanford, through a private grant."

"Your agreement with Jackie Whitney was to pay in cash and take care of the dog?"

"Yep."

"Why did you move out?"

"What difference does it make?"

"I'm just trying to get the facts straight. You wrote a note saying the water didn't get hot and there were roaches?"

Kessler sighed loudly then lifted his feet off the desk. "I said bedbugs. An infestation and I had little bites all over me. All bullshit, but that's what I wrote. But it's true the water never got hot-hot."

"What about unpaid rent?"

"I told Jackie that Kate was keeping the money. I paid every month, including the month I left. Kate's a liar and a thief."

"What did you do with the dog, Trixie?"

"I left her with the lady who lived below Whitney's place."

"What was the apartment number?"

"I'm not sure. There are only three apartments on that floor."

"When did you and Jackie Whitney last speak?"

Kessler rubbed his forehead. "She called me in early May to see why I had supposedly stopped paying."

"And you told Kate about this phone call?"

"I left messages. She never returned my calls. But I'd decided to move out, so I didn't care anymore."

"Why did you bother writing the note?"

"Just to fuck with Kate. I was hoping she'd freak out over the bedbugs."

"Did you move out in one day? I mean, did you come back for anything later?"

Kessler scratched his head. "No. No. I just packed my things and left."

"On what day?"

He laced his fingers over the top of his head and looked at the ceiling. His Adam's apple bobbed. "Whatever day I told the cops. I don't know. The fourteenth? Fifteenth?"

"Whitney's closet. Was it open?"

"How the hell would I know? I stayed in the guest room."

The doctor glanced at his watch then leaned forward in his chair. I said, "Okay, I guess that's it. You won't mind if I contact you again—if I have any other questions."

"Of course not. Hang on." Kessler opened a drawer, rummaged around until he found a card, and handed it to me. I returned the gesture with a card of my own.

From the sidewalk in front of the hospital I dialed the next name on my list.

"Verkakte Fashions," a male voice answered, and I laughed at the somewhat off-color Yiddish word. The voice said, "Hello?"

"I'm sorry, can I speak to George Mason?"

"Who's calling?"

"Jules Landau. I'm an investigator with the public defender's office."

Silence, then, "I already spoke to the police."

"I'm working for the defense."

"Why don't you just ask the police what I had to say?"

"Because it doesn't work that way. Both sides get to talk to character witnesses."

George blew his nose. "How can you defend those people?"

"You're supposed to say that to the public defender, not the private investigator."

"Well, who do you work for?"

George would require gentle handling. "I work for myself." Technically, I wasn't lying. "I'm in the business of truth, George. I give you my word, I just want to find out what kind of person Ms. Whitney was."

"She was my best friend," George said, his voice cracking.

"Then just tell me about your best friend. Honestly, George, that's all I'm asking."

Sometimes it's the phrasing that gets you in the door. George agreed to meet me in an hour.

The store was located on North Halsted, close to The Chicago Diner. I parked near my apartment then walked six blocks to the restaurant, arriving light-headed with the kind of hunger that reduced people to behaving like their primitive ancestors. While I ravaged the diner's trademarked vegetarian Radical Reuben, I thought about the guy lost in the Australian outback, mad with hunger, who happened upon a baby kangaroo, tore it apart, then devoured Joey raw. The man later reported how satisfying the animal tasted.

I looked over George's police report statement. It revealed his dislike of the defendant, and when he last spoke to Jackie Whitney. Then I entered Verkakte Fashions, a boutique specializing in women's mod clothing. Everything was boldly colored, sharp, hip, and streamlined. Vespa scooters were strategically parked around the shop. Neon signs advertised nightclubs. I asked a young woman hanging black A-line skirts if George was around. She pointed to a man sitting behind the counter paging through a magazine. He had short, spiky golden blond hair with black roots.

"Hello, George," I said. "We spoke on the phone."

George closed the magazine and motioned for me to follow him to an office at the back of the store. He sat at his desk in a steno chair, I took a seat on a small couch.

"Okay," he said. "Ask me your questions."

"How long were you and Jackie close friends?"

"Since high school."

"Wow. So tell me about your best friend."

George breathed in deeply then let it out. "Even in high school she was her own person. I give credit to her wonderful parents. Pretty, lots of money, brains, and as many friends as a teen girl wanted. But she wasn't a princess-bitch like so many others. She befriended me. Accepted me when my own parents wouldn't." George grabbed some tissues from a box on his desk then dabbed his eyes.

"Junior year, I moved into her parents' apartment. Besides being a homophobe, my father drank. I showed up at her door with a black eye and fat lip."

"How long did you stay with her family?"

"Until I went to college."

"Did she have other close friends?"

George paused. "Well, there was Linda Napier. At one time they were like sisters. You could say the three of us were like sisters." George giggled. "We partied together, well into adulthood. Just alcohol and pot. Then one winter Linda slipped on the ice, broke her leg in three places, shattered her ankle. Horrible. She mostly recovered but got addicted to Oxy in the process. She discovered that heroin was cheaper and more easily obtainable, and we watched her drift into hell."

"But she got help?"

"Yes, she got somewhat clean a couple of years ago, or at least enough to get back in touch with us. She says the only drugs she takes now are the ones her psychiatrist prescribes. I don't believe her. It's obvious she still drinks."

"Did she ever introduce Jackie to anyone from this dark period of her life?"

"Jackie never said anything to me about it."

"What was Jackie and Linda's relationship like after Linda returned?"

"Well, we both saw that she was trying to put her life back together—bless her heart. And that's what Jackie focused on. We couldn't save her from herself, but as long as Linda was trying, Jackie would be there for her."

"Financially?"

George paused. He seemed conflicted. "Yes. Jackie owns the townhouse where Linda lives, Jackie owns the Lexus Linda drives, and Linda's brother sends her money every month. She's very humiliated being so dependent on others. I promised I wouldn't tell anybody, so if you talk to her, please don't mention any of this."

"Agreed. How's your relationship with Linda these days?"

"We talk a lot on the phone. Sometimes she stops by the store. She's not as forthcoming as she used to be, but barely a day goes by when we don't at least text each other."

"What does she hold back about?"

"Who she hangs out with. I think she's afraid of being judged."

"So she may be concealing people from her past?"

George considered the question. "I suppose."

The saleswoman I had seen earlier appeared in the doorway holding a dress. "Hey, girl!" George said. "Hannah, meet Jules. Jules, meet Hannah."

We exchanged smiles then Hannah walked to George and pointed to something on the garment. "Damn her!" George said. "Send it back to that shrew and tell her to use a lockstitch, which is exactly what I told her to do." Hannah turned to leave, then George said, "Great job catching that, Hannah. I love you! If you ever quit, I'll hunt you down and kill you!" Hannah laughed then walked out.

"I'm sorry," George said. "What were you saying?"

"Linda came back into the picture before Jackie met Kate McCall?"

"Oh, yeah. A couple of years, I would say."

"Do you have Linda's number?"

George took out his phone, scrolled though his contact list, then wrote Linda's number on a notepad and gave it to me.

"What about a boyfriend for Jackie? Any love interest?"

"Uh, not really—or not lately, I should say. She was dating this rich lawyer for a long time. I don't remember his name, but I do remember he was somewhat older. She brought him into the store once. I didn't like his vibe and warned her not to trust him. Boy, did I call that one exactly right."

"What happened?"

"He turned out to be a sneaky little weasel. They had a huge fight. When she called me to vent I could tell she was getting all choked up, but wouldn't allow herself to cry. I kept saying, 'Just let it out, girl!' but she saw crying as the weasel winning."

"How long ago did this happen?"

"Around the holidays. Before she went to California."

"When did she leave?"

"Uh . . . shortly after the new year."

"Would you say she was vulnerable to men?"

"Vulnerable?" George said, almost shouting. "Lord, no. She liked men but she didn't need them. This lawyer worked his butt off to break through Jackie's shell and win her over. She made him wait a good three months before sleeping with him. And that's when the trouble started. She gave the weasel her heart and he stepped all over it."

"Was he abusive? Did he threaten her?"

"She never said anything like that. But Jackie became blind to what a slimeball he was. Even though she found out he defrauded his own niece's estate just to pay his taxes, she looked the other way because the charges were dropped. Now he supposedly rips off elderly people—legally—or something like that. It wasn't until she found out he was having an affair that she finally woke up."

"Anyone else close friends with Jackie?"

"There was someone from that dog and cat place, her name escapes me at the moment."

"An animal shelter?"

"Yeah. I forgot what it's called, but I know it was very important to Jackie. I think she gave them a lot of money. And Jackie has an adult son, Phillip."

"Are you in touch with Phillip?"

"I saw him at the funeral, all grown up." George's lip started quivering. "But I was too much of a mess to talk to him."

"What was Jackie and Phillip's relationship like?"

"She did her best, for who she was."

"Meaning what?"

"She loved him but mothering didn't come naturally to her."

"She didn't want children?"

"Phillip was not planned."

"So she hired a nanny."

"Of course. She still had too much partying to do. He was a precocious kid, always way ahead of his years in maturity. One day a teenager showed up. He decided he wanted to live with his daddy, the punk-rock drummer."

"How can I get in touch with Phillip or his father?"

"The father OD'd on heroin. Phillip works at that animal shelter I mentioned."

"He works there?" The image shattered my spoiled brat assumption.

"Yes. He organizes the volunteers or something like that."

"Interesting. So I guess it'll be up to Phillip whether Linda can stay in the townhouse and keep driving the Lexus."

"I suppose."

"Jackie made friends easily?"

"That's a complicated question." George looked away with a wry smile. "The short answer is yes. But a lot of them didn't hang around long. Jackie was very possessive of the people in her life, be it friends or lovers. Her brutal honesty got on people's nerves. She was just trying to help, but it had to be her way. She acted like you belonged to her. Jackie knows best, I used to say."

George was giving me a lot to consider. I took out my notepad. "I hope you don't mind if I make a few notes."

"Not at all," George said then chuckled. "My, aren't we low-tech these days."

"I know, I know," I said. "Did Jackie get on Linda's nerves?"

"Linda never said that."

"What did you and Linda think of Kate McCall?"

George shook his head. "Oh, God, please. I feel sick just thinking about her."

"Do you know the story of how Jackie and Kate met?"

"Kate worked at this little gourmet grocer where Jackie bought her fancy specialty cheeses. Kate stocked shelves, swept floors. That's all white trash like her is good for."

"Easy, George."

"I'm sorry. I struggle with defending that hillbilly bitch."

I had anticipated this reaction. "Look at it this way. You're helping me ensure the prosecution will prove her guilt. That's really all we're trying to do at the public defender's office. The evidence against Kate is overwhelming. We're just going through the motions because someone has to do it. Why not me? I'll take the money."

My semi-bullshit response had the desired effect. "Jackie was the type to take in stray animals. She seemed charmed by Kate's humbleness, her enthusiasm to help Jackie get something off the shelf or ask the boss about something Jackie needed. She works so hard and never complains, Jackie would say to me. She's not dumb, just ignorant. And it went from there."

"Jackie wanted to better Kate's life."

"She saw potential in Kate. God only knows what that was."

"She became Jackie's personal assistant?"

George rolled his eyes. "She did. And no, I wasn't jealous. I didn't have time to be anyone's gal Friday. I own this place, you know."

"When did you last speak with Jackie?"

"I think Wednesday evening she called me from Palm Springs—the week she came back. She was really pissed off because the renter had moved out."

"She told you he had already moved out or was going to move out?"

"Uh, no, I think she knew he had already moved out."

I wrote down George's response then underlined it. "Did you know anything about this renter?"

"Nothing. I really had no interest in Jackie's little scheme."

"What do you mean scheme?"

"Oh, you know, the way rich people are always thinking of ways to get extra cash to stick in a safe. I thought Jackie was above that obsession to have more money."

"So you knew she had a cash arrangement with the renter."

"Yep."

"Okay, if Kate is the killer, what was her motive?"

George's face darkened. "I told her not to trust those people. They live by different rules. I'm sure Kate got sick of Jackie bossing her around and

Kate's redneck brain took over. Maybe Jackie lost her temper and reminded Kate of her white-trash stock."

"Ouch. Jackie really used those words?"

"Probably not."

"Oh, uh, what about that guy at the concierge desk—"

"The transman."

"Yeah. Freddie made it sound like Jackie had been a close friend. Before and after the transitioning started."

George sighed. "You know, when Jackie first started talking about Felicia and the whole transitioning thing, my first thought was why would you want to get involved with this? Then I finally recognized this compulsion Jackie had to help people. But I think she saw it more as fixing them. Either way, Jackie must've sensed I didn't care to know about her new Felicia/Freddie friendship, because she stopped talking about him and I didn't ask."George squirmed in his seat, glanced out the door. I said, "One more thing. How did you come up with the name Verkakte Fashions?"

George laughed. "That was Jackie's idea. It means, 'crazy, mixed-up fashions,' she said. I could tell she really wanted me to use the name, so I did."

Other definitions of "verkakte" included "crappy," but I didn't mention it.

Chapter 8

On the way home, Tamar called. "Oh. Em. Gee," I answered.

"Dinner tonight, my place."

"How's that possible?"

"I decided to give the new manager a chance to close by herself. Be there around seven." She hung up.

I had mixed feelings. Tamar lived with her ancient aunt, who scared the shit out of me. The poor woman fled Eurasian civil war only to have her son murdered in Chicago by Russian mobsters. Ever since, she's spent her days staring at a candle illuminating an icon of St. Andrew beside a photo of her son. An equally ancient Georgian woman took care of her and kept the flame burning. On one occasion when I was convinced the aunt had died, my closer inspection provoked a guttural, prehistoric screech worthy of a Hollywood special effect.

I dialed Linda Napier's number. A raspy voice answered on the first ring. Like George, she initially resisted meeting me.

"I was just at Verkakte Fashions. We had a great conversation."

A long, wheezing smoker's laugh prefaced Linda's response. "I bet you did. You must be handsome. What did Georgie say about me?"

"He told me your name."

"Uh-huh. And now you want to come over."

"I don't like to play hardball, but if you spoke to the prosecution, you have to speak to me. That's the law."

She fell for it. "Okay, whatever. Come over." She gave me an address. "I'm home all day."

The East Lincoln Park neighborhood shrieked stunning, coveted, hot! A small sign pushed into a flower bed announced Linda's home security system. She seemed a touch unsteady standing in the doorway of her townhouse. Wedged into distressed acid-washed jeans, brassy-haired and leather-faced, she was beautiful but her beauty had a toxic quality. She welcomed me in with an exaggerated sweep of her arm. I didn't notice any track-mark scars.

"Sit anywhere."

I picked one end of the white couch; she slouched into the other end.

"How long had you known Jackie?"

"From day one."

"Always close?"

"Always."

"Were you friends with Kate, the woman arrested?"

Linda closed her eyes. I thought she fell asleep. "Kate scared me. I told Jackie I didn't trust her. We tolerated Kate—barely. For Jackie's sake."

"We? You and George?"

"Me, George, everyone."

"Why would Kate kill Jackie?"

Linda stared straight ahead. Even from the far end of the couch I could see her eyes filling. "She was a crazy hick who figured out where a bunch of cash was, and that was that."

"Do you have any proof of what you just said?"

"She was always taking advantage of Jackie."

"How?"

"Jackie paid for her apartment. Paid her to be a personal assistant."

"That was Jackie's choice, wasn't it?"

Linda frowned. "She's a sucker for pitiful creatures. The animals I understand. But that ignorant bitch wasn't helpless. What a waste."

"So why would she kill someone who was giving her all this money?"

The question annoyed Linda. "I told you! Kate saw a lot of cash in Jackie's apartment, in Jackie's safe-deposit box, the cash the renter gave her, the cash Jackie paid her. Jackie finally caught on that Kate was stealing."

"How did you know the renter was paying in cash?"

Linda hesitated. "George must've told me. I can't remember for sure."

"How do you know about Jackie's safe-deposit box?"

Another hesitation. "Because she told me about it. She said she kept cash in it."

"I've met with Kate twice. Yeah, she's not educated but she's not stupid. She could've found ways to hide the money or move it around without drawing Jackie's attention. The Kate's-a-thief-scenario you describe just doesn't make sense to me."

"You met Kate twice? While behind bars? Big deal. I have no doubt she had a vicious, unpredictable streak. She reminded me of a wild animal, skulking around. You didn't know what could provoke her to attack."

"And how would Jackie have incensed her?"

"Jackie was a very controlling woman. She didn't just give you her money, she was buying you. But you can't control a wild animal like Kate. Money to Kate was red meat, and she turned on Jackie just like I warned her she would."

"How well do you know Jackie's son?"

Linda's face softened. She looked ten years younger. "I adored Phillip. He was so sweet. And so smart! An old soul, I used to tell Jackie. His father lured him away as a teenager, to hang out with his rock band. I saw him for the first time as a grown man at the funeral." Tears spilled down her face.

"Tell me about Jackie's love of animals."

"Furry Best Friends Forever, the humane animal shelter. She gave them a lot of money. Volunteered, fundraised, whatever they needed."

"Had she developed any close friends at the shelter?"

"Lucille. One of the execs."

"Do you know anything about Jackie's friendship with the concierge at her building?"

"I know only the little that George told me. And that includes George telling me that Jackie didn't want to talk about her friendship with her—or him. We both thought the concierge was just another of Jackie's little projects."

"When did you last talk to Jackie?"

"Around Thanksgiving. Then she stopped talking to me. George told me she was leaving for Palm Springs after Christmas. I called her and left a message, but she didn't call me back. It was her way of saying she wasn't happy with me."

"Why was she unhappy with you?"

"She didn't approve of my life choices."

"Did you know she was coming back early?"

Linda nodded. "Only because George told me. George kept me updated about Jackie."

"Did she ever give you money?"

Linda didn't like the question. "What difference does it make?"

"You said when she gave someone money, she bought them. Wanted to control them. It's only natural a private investigator would want to know if you'd experienced this firsthand."

"Yes, she was helping me financially. In fact, this is her townhouse

"What are you really saying, detective?"

Linda's attitude was getting the best of me. "Did she try to buy you, Linda? Control your life? Did she piss you off?"

"A friend never pissed you off?"

"Not enough to kill."

Linda struggled to straighten up from the couch then grabbed a small glass bowl from the coffee table and threw it at me. I lifted my arms just in time to deflect the bowl off my wrist before it struck above my right brow.

"You fucker!" Linda screamed. "You think I killed my best friend?"

I touched my forehead. Blood covered the tips of my fingers. Linda sat upright at the edge of the couch.

"I need a Band-Aid."

"You bastard! Do you think I killed Jackie?"

"No, Linda. I was just trying to make a point."

Linda walked away then returned with a handful of Band-Aids and dropped them on the coffee table. I grabbed a couple then started walking around looking for the bathroom.

"When you're done, just go," Linda said. "And you're crazy if you think I'd ever go to bed with you!"

Huh? I got the hell out of there. The rearview mirror worked fine for placing a Band-Aid over the cut. I couldn't wash the blood off my fingers, but I didn't care. Go to bed with her? Wrestling an alligator sounded more appealing.

I stood in the shower, hot water pounding my head. It was stupid of me to provoke Linda like that. Why couldn't I resist being an ass? George and Linda were prejudiced against Kate's Appalachian background. Dr. Kessler was slippery, but maybe that was my bias. Pretentious pricks like Kessler were great liars. I needed confirmation he hadn't returned to Jackie's apartment between Thursday and Monday before giving him the benefit of the doubt.

The phone rang shortly after I dressed. "I got a break in the action," Debbie said when I answered. "Got anything?"

"Yeah, first I went to Jackie Whitney's apartment—"

"Whoa, whoa, whoa. Just give me yes or no. We'll meet later tonight."

"I got a date at seven. Can you meet earlier?"

Debbie sighed audibly. "When?"

"Penguin House. About five?"

Prolonged silence. "Where is it?"

I gave her directions; she mumbled something then hung up.

Laptop over my thighs, I looked up the Furry Best Friends Forever website. I was familiar with the shelter because I had set up a pet trust for Punim using one of their brochures. As if on cue, Punim's paws hit hard on the bedroom floor. She trotted toward me down the hall, the small pouch in front of her rear legs swinging side to side. I clicked on the link Purrfect Pusses, which opened to rows of cats waiting to find homes. Punim jumped up to the arm of the recliner and slowly hunkered down.

"See how lucky you are?" I said.

"No," she said. "You're the lucky one."

Penguin House's mix of older hippies, post-hippies, hipsters, yuppies, muppies, and brogrammers slowly dissipated between four-thirty and six, leaving behind a kind of sad, abandoned atmosphere. As one of the few patrons still remaining—all of us sitting alone—it occurred to me that I belonged to a yet-to-be-named cultural stereotype. Maybe it was the image of the proverbial outsider looking in that kept me coming back to Penguin House.

Not until seven or so did the evening crowd arrive and renew the familial energy coffee shops craved. As planned, Debbie arrived during the lull. As she had at Café Schmaltz, she appeared as the picture of preoccupation, messenger bag slung over her shoulder. A few heads turned when the bag thumped to the floor. The Band-Aid above my brow went unnoticed.

"Okay," she said. "Talk."

At that moment I really disliked her. "Has the state's attorney ordered DNA tests on the skin shavings I saw in one of the crime scene photos?"

"I don't know."

"I want to see the lobby's CCTV video from Thursday to Monday. I didn't see it listed in the police report."

Debbie nodded then scribbled on her notepad. I felt better about her. "What else?" she said.

"The couch was flush against the wall. So there was no sneaking up on Whitney. The hammer must've been on the killer or lying nearby. Three blows to the head, all striking within centimeters of each other. I think the assailant came upon Whitney suddenly, completely unexpected."

"The killer was known to the victim. Old news."

She annoyed me again. "The thumbprint on the hammer was on the metal shaft above the rubber grip. That's how you would hold a hammer to carefully tap in a nail for hanging pictures. You don't choke up on the grip if you want to smash someone's head in."

Debbie started scribbling again then looked up. "Although they could argue she grabbed the hammer high on the shaft, then adjusted her hand to the rubber grip."

"No blood on the floor. The murderer either dragged or carried the victim at least fifty feet to the bedroom closet while taking care to keep the head in an upright position, so it wouldn't drip."

"Dead already," Debbie said as she got to her feet. "The blood stops flowing. I need caffeine. You want the mocha-soy-thing?"

"Sure."

After she returned with a large black coffee and my mocha I said, "Dr. Kessler thinks McCall was stealing his rent and telling Whitney he wasn't paying."

Debbie thought about it. "Yeah? I say Kessler's a thief. Maybe we can dig up some dirt, like gambling debts."

I couldn't tell if she was serious. "I want to confirm Kessler didn't return to the apartment after May 15th.

"You told me that already. What about Whitney's friends?"

"George Mason and Linda Napier both hate McCall. Apparently Jackie Whitney was supporting McCall financially. In exchange, Kate had to endure Jackie Whitney's controlling behavior. They think her hillbilly side eventually snapped—maybe after a condescending remark—and she killed Whitney."

Debbie began bending her neck at different angles, then held up her arms as if imitating a chicken. She finished her calisthenics with torso rotations before pulling a FedEx envelope from her messenger bag and handing it to me. Inside was a manila envelope containing several stacks of banded cash.

"It arrived this morning," Debbie said then started gathering her belongings. "I'll look into getting the closed circuit video."

"Jackie Whitney was a big animal lover who spent a lot of time and money at a humane shelter. Usually, the big donors have lots of ass-kissers sucking up to them. I thought I'd go there."

Debbie appeared confused as she tried to find a comfortable position for the messenger bag to lay against her side. "Okay," she said then walked away.

Chapter 9

A Georgian bazaar came to mind as I entered Tamar's apartment and took in the aromas of onion, garlic, walnut, and spices. I presented her with a small bouquet of red and pink roses and daisies. She kissed me, led me to a love seat where two plates with fruit pastries waited on the coffee table, then put the flowers in a vase. That the pastries most certainly contained butter was the farthest thing from my mind. She wore slim-fitting, tapered jeans with a willowy blue camisole. Her black hair fell silky clean over her shoulders. Near the corner of the room, the buzz-kill better known as Whistler's

Mother from Hell rocked quietly in front of St. Andrew and her deceased son.

"Sorry," Tamar said. "I'm on my own with Deida tonight. Sit." I obeyed. She walked to the kitchen then returned with two glasses of red wine.

"How can you have such a beautiful body and own a bakery?"

Tamar smiled, maybe a little embarrassed. "I'm too busy to think about the food."

"How does it feel to be a woman of leisure for eight hours?"

We both sipped. She said, "I guess I'll get used to the pressure and responsibility. At least I hope so."

I wanted to say something that didn't sound trite. Instead, I took a bite of my pastry. Tamar said, "You don't like wine, do you?"

"Why do you say that?"

"Involuntary facial contractions then a large bite of the khachapuri."

"It's all cough syrup to me."

Tamar laughed. "You met your new client?"

"Yes. She has a mysterious benefactor paying for my services."

"Hmmm. Interesting, but sounds fishy." Tamar took a healthy sip then said, "You're thinking about something. I can read you like a book."

"There's this—person. A man—a woman transitioning to a man—"

"A transman."

"Exactly. Jackie Whitney had a close relationship with this person before and during his transition. I'm just wondering how close they actually were."

Tamar stared at me with her tired brown eyes. "You mean did they have a sexual relationship?"

"Yeah. There's always that physical attraction issue I have to consider. Signals crossed, signs misread, friendship misinterpreted as something else. You know what I mean?"

"Anything's possible," Tamar said as she tried to suppress a yawn. "What else is on your mind?"

"The public defender I'm working with is intense. Her name is Debbie Lopez. A true believer with no sense of humor. She's obsessed with filling a jury's head with reasonable doubt. She doesn't give a damn who the real killer is. This approach conflicts with my natural tendency to solve a crime."

"You have conflicting goals."

"Mos def. I think I have a better idea of the victim's personality."

"Jackie Whitney the socialite."

A short, gravelly screech ensued, sending a shiver through my heart. Tamar walked to the old lady, knelt down, then said something quietly in her ear. The replying noise was low and groaning, like a creaking door. After a few exchanges Tamar returned to the love seat.

"What did she . . .?"

"I don't know. Something about her uncle who used to sleep with his Caucasian shepherd dogs—I think."

I tried not to laugh. Tamar said, "Just like the wine, your face gives you away. Go ahead and laugh. It's okay." Tamar wasn't smiling.

I said, "Back to Jackie Whitney. She liked giving people money and friendship, but expected obedience in return. And she was brutally honest to her followers. If you wanted to stay in her good graces, you'd better follow her advice."

Tamar bit into her pastry. I finished mine. "I hate people like that," she said with a bitterness that transformed her personality. "She must've been a seriously double-edged sword. Some people can only take so much abuse. They stuff down the resentment because they want the money, but they're having violent fantasies. I bet somebody snapped and that was it. Killed her."

"You're not the only one who thinks that."

Tamar lit up. "Really?"

"Yeah, really. Don't be surprised how clever you are."

"How many suspects do you have?"

"How many is everyone?" I wanted to sound funny, but it was true.

"Everyone? Even me?"

"Sorry. Not you. But I've become pretty cynical about human motivation. Anyone is capable of crossing lines we were taught not to cross. It just depends what pushes your buttons. Everyone has a dark side. I don't care who you are."

Tamar averted her gaze, took another sip of wine. Then she brought our dishes to the kitchen and returned with two bowls and a plate of bread.

"Spiced bean-veggie soup with corn bread."

Relaxed yet exhausted, we made refreshingly animated small talk. Reflecting on the state of the bakery and her role as leader, she laughed at quirky employees, bizarre customer requests, and how petty Georgian rivalries traversed two continents and an ocean, only to surface in her prep kitchen. Our dialogue became an effortless give-and-take of humorous, ironic, and philosophical anecdotes, the kind of conversation that squashed the concept of time into a single moment. Even the old lady's shrieks sounded less fiendish. Tamar checked her watch.

"I need to get Deida to bed," Tamar said.

I watched her gently coax the old lady out of the chair before leading her away. Fifteen minutes later, Tamar reappeared, gave me a knowing look, then walked to her bedroom.

As enjoyable as the evening had been, so was the three a.m. alarm unpleasant. How can you live like this? I thought as my eyes struggled with the ceiling light. On the way out, Tamar deadpanned, "I brush my teeth and eat breakfast at the bakery, which allows me to sleep in a bit."

No surprise Punim stood wild-eyed in the middle of the room. Three-thirty a.m. was dash-around-chasing-invisible-prey time in her untamed circadian rhythm. I dozed off as she finished her rounds.

At nine I stood in the shower, vaguely aware of having slept. During breakfast, I looked at the Furry Best Friends Forever website again. Animal sheltering had become corporate. Furry BFF had a CEO, president, treasurer, secretary, board of directors, and development board. The fundraising boss would know someone as wealthy as Jackie Whitney. They opened at ten.

I took the brown line to Armitage then walked about five blocks to Furry BFF. The sleek, two-story, concrete and steel building reminded me of an architectural design firm. The lobby was bright and airy with blond bamboo flooring and had the feel of a modern library reading room. Humans and dogs occupied U-shaped sectional sofas. Oversized chairs surrounded a large fountain of rustic mosaic stone with terra-cotta spill pots. The animals lived in roomy, naturally lighted condos where they stretched out across wooden tables or curled up on chairs or giant pillows. Mobs of puppies and kittens wrestled, played tug-o'-war, chewed toys, or slept partially visible in little houses. A section of one wall was designated for thanking benefactors. Below an older, white-haired gentleman deemed the Francis of Assisi Champion, was a headshot of "patron saint" Jacqueline Charlotte Whitney.

I asked a woman behind the reception counter who was in charge of fundraising. "Her name is Lucille Mackenzie," she said. "You'll find her on the second floor where all the admin offices are."

"Do I need an appointment?"

She laughed. "No. Just go up and ask around."

A flight of stairs led to a large room with offices spaced along the perimeter. A few people worked at desks within the periphery but most of the space was occupied by dogs, sleeping or playing. None of the offices had nameplates. A young man asked if I needed help.

"I'm looking for Lucille Mackenzie," I said.

He began counting offices, moving clockwise from the entrance. "That one," he said. "Sixth door down."

Lucille Mackenzie's door was wide open, as were all the office doors. I lurked near the entryway a few moments then poked my head in. She looked familiar sitting behind the cherrywood desk talking on the phone. Mid-thirties, with flowing honey-blond hair, she spoke teasingly in a contrived childlike voice. "Of course I love you, silly boy!" she said. "Cha-cha-cha later?" Her large brown eyes looked crazy with excitement, like a little girl just given a pony for her birthday.

A colorful horse-motif scarf adorned her neck over a low cut blouse displaying more than a peek of cleavage. A small red Chanel handbag lay on her desk next to a fruit basket mixed with a colorful floral arrangement. On the walls, Picasso, Warhol, and Hockney displayed their modernist dachshunds alongside leaps and lunges of modernist dancers. I was about to back away when she smiled and waved me forward, as if delighted to see me. She emphatically pointed at the chair in front of her desk.

I sat then leaned forward to read the card attached to the fruit basket. May our Rest-in-Peace basket ease the pain of your loss. Your friends at Youji Lu Grocer. "I lost one of my kitties just a few days ago," she said, startling me with the sudden transformation into an all-business voice. "My grocer heard about it and sent me this condolence basket. Now that's what I call customer service." She laughed. "What can I do for you, sir?"

I introduced myself and handed over my ID. Her smile wavered then disintegrated as she handed it back. I said, "Did you know Jackie Whitney well?"

Lucille nodded. "Yes," she said. "Jackie was a special person around here. Especially to me."

I realized why Lucille looked familiar. "You were personal friends, weren't you?"

"Yes. How did you know?"

"In her apartment. I saw a picture of you and Jackie kneeling on either side of a very big dog."

Lucille grinned. "Buttons. A big, sweet old girl. Jackie and I were so happy to find her the best possible home."

"Do you know the woman they arrested?"

"Do you think she did it?"

"I don't know. Do you know her?"

"I know only what I've heard on the news or read in the papers."

"What about Jackie's old friends Linda Napier and George Mason? Do you know them?"

"My God, are they suspects?"

"Investigations usually start with friends and family. It's really just routine."

Lucille sighed. "Linda was a lost soul. My heart goes out to her."

"Care to share?"

"About two years ago she started volunteering. Unfortunately, she kept showing up drunk or spaced out like she forgot where she was. I spoke to her several times about her behavior. She promised to shape up, but nothing changed and she made the other volunteers nervous. Finally, I had to tell her she couldn't volunteer anymore."

"Jackie knew what was going on?"

"Oh, yeah. She supported my decision."

"What about George?'

"I don't know George. Jackie talked about him and I knew they were very close, but we were in different circles."

"You were in the fundraising, gift-giving, donor appreciation circles?"

Lucille hesitated. "Yes, but not in the snobby way you're suggesting."

"I'm sorry, I didn't mean—"

"No, no, you're fine. It's my fault. I'm overly protective of my donors."

"Jackie is the patron saint, I noticed."

"She's been a godsend for the shelter to achieve its vision. And our wonderful volunteers are the heart and soul of the shelter."

"Would you say Jackie built this place?"

"Well, that's probably over the top."

"Do other officers or VIPs get involved with donors?"

Lucille tapped the eraser end of a pencil on the desk a few times. "Follow the money! That's what you're doing, right?"

I pretended to think about it. "Unconsciously, maybe. But I'm a very curious person. I like to understand how organizations operate."

"The paid staff is small, so many of us do a lot of different jobs. I'm the primary fundraiser but I also work closely with the treasurer. Unfortunately, as is the case for most nonprofit treasurers, Elaine has lots of demands on her time." Lucille sighed. "She's very overworked. There, I said it. Anyway, I help Elaine by taking care of various admin tasks so she can focus on financial reporting."

"You must be good friends, working so closely together."

"Yes, Elaine and I have become very good friends. I think you'll find people who choose to work for a humane animal shelter often share common values. And making our biggest donors feel special and appreciated is also a crucial part of my job. If they want to be my friend, I'm thrilled."

"You must be doing a hell of a good job. I mean, this is an amazing, modern, high-tech facility. It must've cost a fortune."

Lucille blushed. "Our capital campaign was a great success. But it still takes lots of money to maintain the building and provide quality care for the animals."

"I heard that Jackie Whitney could be a challenging friend."

"What do you mean?"

"Quick to welcome you into her world but brutally honest. Happy to help a friend out with money, but she acted as though the money gave her the right to control you."

"Oh, I don't agree. Not in my experience."

"Can a donor stipulate how the money should be used?"

"Yes, they can put restrictions on their donations. It can be tricky sometimes."

"When was the last time you spoke with Jackie Whitney?"

"In May, before she came back."

"Do you remember the conversation?"

"Oh, just that her renter was being a pain in the tush and she was cutting her vacation short, and that we should get together. That kind of thing."

"But she never mentioned Kate McCall?"

Lucille cocked her head. "Oh, no, no. Like I said, I never heard anything about Kate McCall."

"Did you spend much time at Jackie's apartment?"

"I never went to her apartment."

"I thought she was a personal friend."

Lucille sighed. "Well, yeah, but of a type. We'd meet at a restaurant and waste the afternoon with drinks and gossip. But that was the extent of our socializing. You could say we were daytime gal-pals."

I thought I understood. "And the renter in question, the doctor—"

"Did you know that the doctor dated Jackie's friend Linda Napier?"

I kept my focus on Lucille while digesting the new information. "I did not know and that is interesting. How did you find out?"

"Before Jackie left town, she told me about Dr. Kessler, that he might be worth developing as a donor. I told her the key was to get him here to see the facility. Jackie said she would work on it and let me know, but I never heard anything. Then one day my phone rang. Linda and Dr. Kessler were in the lobby. She wanted me to give him a private tour."

"Had Jackie introduced the two?"

"I guess so. I didn't realize who he was at first. Linda introduced him as Josh. They definitely acted very cozy, bordering on inappropriate."

"I get the feeling you didn't approve of the match."

"Well, it was the middle of the day and they were acting drunk. I don't think Linda needs a boyfriend who parties like that, doctor or not."

"When did you realize it was Jackie Whitney's renter, Dr. Kessler?"

"I bumped into them a few times on North Michigan Avenue. She introduced him again as Dr. Kessler, and laughed. Another time I saw them go into Jackie's building together. That's when I realized who he was."

"But you never discussed their relationship with Jackie?"

"No, Jackie and I were not in touch when she was in Palm Springs. And I didn't feel comfortable reporting on Linda's love life."

"Do you know Jackie's son? Phillip?"

Lucille began stroking the scarf with her fingers. "He's our assistant volunteer coordinator. I adore him. He's so smart and way overqualified for his position. He has an MBA. I don't expect him to stay very long, but he does an excellent job. I know he made Jackie very proud. And Phillip shared Jackie's deep love of animals."

"How is he handling his mother's death?"

"He seems really calm, but I'm worried he's keeping his emotions locked up. I want him to go to therapy, but he won't."

"Maybe introspection is just what he needs—"

"Stuffing emotions is very destructive to the human body. The heart especially. He should take time off and allow himself to properly grieve."

And who are you to tell someone how to grieve? I wanted to say. "Can I meet Phillip?"

Lucille's face clouded over. "Oh, I think you should leave him alone for now. His mother was just murdered and you want to start peppering him with questions and make him relive the whole thing over again? The police already spoke to him, I'm sure they'll tell you what he said."

I did my best to look hurt. "Lucille, all I want is justice for Jackie Whitney—and for Phillip."

"I'm sorry, I feel a little possessive of him after what happened. I know he's a grown man but like I said, I worry about him. Anyway, he's usually out and about with the volunteers. His schedule is erratic."

"Well, thank you—"

"Have you taken a tour of the shelter, uh, Mr. Landau?"

"A little bit. In fact, I was here a few months ago, to get information on setting up a pet trust."

Lucille beamed. "Wonderful! What kind of trust? Who are you using as a trustee, if I may ask?"

"Revocable. I'm the trustee."

"Good. But you've made provisions for a successor trustee, I hope, just in case you are incapacitated or—"

"My credit union will administer the trust if I die first. And when Punim dies, whatever is left will go to Furry BFF."

"Very nice. How did you come to set up the trust?"

"Punim's young and I'm all she has."

"I understand your feelings. But you're still so young yourself. Remember, the trust is subject to estate taxes. While you're alive it's treated like any other asset."

"You know a lot about pet trusts."

Lucille laughed. "My background includes an estate and trust certification specialty, which plays an important role in our long-term fundraising goals." She looked at her watch. "Before you go, why don't you check out the volunteer opportunities?"

Chapter 10

I walked a mile down Clybourn to North where I took the red line to Chicago Avenue then walked another mile to a blind alley off Delaware Place. The alley ran behind the Youji Lu Grocer and was clean and tidy like a fancy suburban cul-de-sac. When a pound of mushrooms costs a thousand dollars, your customers expect no less. Even the dumpster looked regularly scrubbed clean. I lifted the lid. Only a quarter full. A woman smoking outside the back door to the adjacent boutique watched me. She looked flawless in her black pencil skirt, white tailored jacket, and red lipstick.

"It's not what you think," I said.

"What am I thinking?"

I walked over to her. "Have you worked here a long time?"

"Ever since I opened the place three years ago."

"And you come out here for a smoke several times a day?"

"Yep."

"Have you ever seen a guy rummaging through that dumpster looking for some special garbage?"

She laughed and blew out a lungful. "Oh, I've seen him all right," she said. "Chinese guy. He wears waders up to his chest."

"I get the feeling you have some history with the guy."

"A pipe burst in our basement, ruined a box of gift bags. I tossed it in the dumpster and ended up getting a $200 fine for illegal dumping."

"Ooh, that hurts. Not very neighborly. Do you sell women's accessories? Handbags and stuff?"

"I do. Thinking about buying something?"

"How about a Chanel handbag? The little ones. A clutch, I think they're called. Red leather with a metal bracelet."

"That's called a wallet on a chain. They start at around three thousand dollars."

My turn to laugh. "Okay," I said. "I guess a dozen roses will have to do. Hey, what about scarves?"

"What about them?"

"How much for the really colorful ones with horses on them?"

"If it's the kind I'm thinking of, they start around two hundred and fifty."

"Okay, then. Thanks for your help."

The woman dropped her cigarette, snuffed it out with her toe. "Have a nice day," she said then returned to her boutique. As I retraced my steps, a hulking figure entered the alley from Delaware Place. His lumbering gait, protruding stomach, and cue ball head could've represented any ex-cop stuffed into a polyester sport coat with shoulder seams riding up their collarbones. But I knew this ex-cop.

"What's up, Landau?" Detective Brookstone said. "Still playing junior G-man? Making the city safe?"

"You mean safe from people like you, Brookie?" I said. "Is that the same jacket you wore on that CCTV video? You know, the one where you beat the hell out of that female bartender because she cut you off?"

Brookstone's eyebrows lowered. Tiny muscles clenched up the side of his head. "You want to see a replay of that, smart guy?"

"Okay, chill out. I deserved that. But help me understand something, Brookie. From the day I started investigating, you made it really clear that you don't like me. But we don't even know each other! You just came out swinging as soon as I hit the street. Why? What did I ever do to you?"

"I'm surprised your pal Kalijero hasn't sat you on his knee and told you the facts of life already. Maybe he'll also teach you to keep your big mouth shut and save your pretty little face from getting bashed up."

"Too late, Brookie. Been there, done that. Several times, in fact. And it was worth every bruise and welt. So what are you doing in this alley?

I'm fresh out of crack, if that's what you're looking for. Or are you on your way to high tea at The Drake hotel?"

"You're helping that public defender get that bitch off murder."

"What the hell do you care?"

"Someone else cares."

I took a moment. "What? You're somebody's muscle? What're they scared of? The DA is prosecuting. If she's guilty they'll prove it in court."

"That isn't always the case and you know it. Just take it easy on the reasonable doubt crap. Let justice be served. Got it?"

I didn't like his tone. "Sounds like a threat. What're you going to do, beat up my mother?"

Down went the brow again. I imagined the bartender's overwhelming fear just before he tore into her. I stepped back then took a circuitous path around Brookie, back to Delaware Place.

This unexpected encounter caught me off guard. Not until I had reached Superior Street did I emerge from a daze to find myself wandering down Michigan Avenue. Leaning against Neiman Marcus, I called Kalijero.

"What?" Kalijero said, answering the phone.

"Remember Tommy Brookstone? Brookie? The off-duty cop who beat up that woman bartender?"

"What about him?"

"Out of nowhere, he just shows up in an alley and tells me to lay off investigating the Jackie Whitney murder. And why the hell haven't you told me about some grudge he's been holding against me? I assume it has to do with my dad."

"He told you he had a grudge?"

"He didn't have to tell me. He's been going out of his way to be a prick since day one. I finally said something about it and he told me to talk to you."

Silence, then a loud sigh. "You already know about me busting your dad's gambling operation, but you don't know everything. It turned out a young detective was working as an enforcer for one of the sub-agents, squeezing money out of gamblers not paying their debts. Sometimes, he went around collecting while on duty. His name was Tommy Brookstone."

"Holy shit."

"Frownie still had connections to the cops back then. He got wind of Brookstone's little side job and told your dad to watch it. Bernie Landau was smart enough to know that if Brookstone was actually beating people up, he was doing it on his own and not as part of a sting operation. He was also smart enough to recognize Brookstone as a kind of insurance policy. So when your dad got busted, he played the Brookstone card to get a better deal from the DA. That's how your dad got to do his time in a medium security prison instead of going to Stateville."

"But Brookstone got to stay a cop?"

"Nobody would testify against him except your dad. Internal Affairs insisted there be some consequences, and since Brookstone wasn't well-liked, the brass busted him back to patrolman with rookie pay. He stayed there for ten years. That's a lot of money. He blames me too, by the way."

"What did you do?"

"It's what I didn't do. I was a respected veteran by then. I could've found a way to get your dad's deal with the DA to go away. But like I told you before, I had already turned down Frownie, who begged me to get Bernie a lesser charge—for your sake. Now I'm supposed to put the kibosh on his chance to do his time in medium security instead of a shithole? I couldn't do it."

"I need to find out who hired him. Got any info on Brookie since the feds skewered him?"

Another round of silence, then, "He's back on the force, you know."

I didn't know. "How is that possible? He—"

"He beat the hell out of a woman half his size and only got probation and anger management classes. Anything is possible in Chicago. I would've thought you knew that by now. I'll make some calls. But don't count on anything worthwhile."

"One more thing. Why would a killer move a body from the living room to the bedroom closet to hide it on a shelf? I mean, the body's still in the apartment so what's the point?"

"You're talking about Jackie Whitney's body?"

“Of course.”

“You just unlawfully disseminated sealed court records. You could go to prison for that.”

“Oh, c’mon! Aren’t you working with me?”

Kalijero laughed. “It means the murder wasn’t premeditated. Moving a body out of the apartment would require planning. The killer panicked and thought hiding the body would buy time, put more space between the killer and the cops.”

“Not premeditated. Now it seems obvious. Thanks, Jimmy.”

“Hopefully I won’t slip up and tell someone you leaked info on the case,” Kalijero said. “But you never know.” He hung up.

Kalijero and I had too much history for comments like that to worry me. And he knew something trivial like an alcoholic cop with a bad temper wouldn’t scare me off. I sat at a patio table outside of Gino’s East and called Furry BFF. Lucille had acted like she wanted to be Phillip’s guardian, but she didn’t mention having to communicate with him through a lawyer.

“This is Christie,” a woman’s voice answered.

“Can you tell me if Phillip is working today?”

“Uh, who’s calling, please?”

“My name is—George. I’m an old friend of Phillip’s mother.”

"Okay, why don't you give me your number, George, and if I see Phillip, I'll have him call you back."

I gave Christie the number to Verkakte Fashions then called George and told him what I had done. "That puts me in an awkward position," George said. "Wouldn't you agree?"

"You'd be doing me a great service if you could get him to talk to me. Or find out when he's walking dogs at the shelter, then I can take it from there."

"I'm uncomfortable being sneaky."

"George, I promise you I have Phillip's best interest at heart."

"Fine, I guess."

"One more thing. Did you know Linda was dating Jackie's renter, a Dr. Kessler?"

"That's news to me. But as I told you before, Linda was pretty close-mouthed on her personal life, so I didn't push it. Why?"

"Just curious. Thanks for your help."

Running on fumes for having walked over two miles on four hours of sleep, I grabbed a taxi back to Furry BFF, bought a veggie burrito, then hung around trying to get a visual of volunteers walking dogs. There wasn't a whole lot of grass in the immediate neighborhood. Locust trees were scattered here and there, offering small islands of green vegetation, but not much else. I leaned against a bicycle rack, ate, and waited. Soon a gray-haired woman wearing a green waist-length smock appeared, walking a yellow Lab mix. The male dog utilized buildings or telephone poles when a tree wasn't available, eventually disappearing down a side street. A few more volunteers came along, then several more, all taking the same route, the dogs logically following the messages left behind by their fellow shelter mates. What started as a trickle turned into an army. Senior citizens, middle-agers, young couples, parents with pre-teens, all appeared with dogs at their sides. When my phone rang, some of the dogs barked.

"He's there," George said over the phone. "He just called me from the shelter."

"What does he look like?"

"Oh, my gosh. Well, thin, fairly tall, dark straight hair, nice looking."

"Did you have a conversation?"

"Yes, he was very pleasant. I told him how sorry I was. He was very appreciative."

"Thanks, George. I owe you."

Lagging toward the rear of the procession, I followed the dog-walkers to a vacant lot full of mown weeds and gravel, surrounded by a deteriorated chain-link fence. The sagging posts and broken links had been jerry-rigged to maintain a degree of stability. Some dogs ran off-leash while others were led around by their masters. Volunteers lined up at the vulnerable parts of the fence to prevent escape attempts. Several people scoured the area picking up dog waste and putting the larger stones into a pile in the corner of the lot. The people were having as much fun as the inmates.

I joined the crowd, engaged in conversations about their assigned dogs, petted many of them, and considered the possibility of structuring my life to accommodate a deserving dog. Punim, of course, would have to be consulted. A couple of volunteers fit George's description of Phillip. Then a man confirmed that Phillip was indeed kneeling down, rubbing the belly of a German shorthaired pointer. I walked over.

"Can I pet him?" I asked.

Phillip glanced up at me. His face was slender with delicate features. A prominent brow ridge gave him a deep-in-thought look. "Of course," Phillip said. I took a knee and began scratching "Bo" behind the ears. The dog slurped my face. "Adopting?" Phillip said.

"Not now," I said, wiping my mouth. "I was hoping I could talk to you."

Phillip straightened up. "Reporter?"

"Private investigator."

I took out my ID and handed it to him. He studied it, handed it back, then said, "Kate McCall didn't murder my mother?" His lack of emotion was a bit creepy.

"I want to make sure the police got the right person, that's all."

Phillip nodded. "Interview friends and family first," he said then stood up. "Walk with me."

I followed him and Bo out of the de facto dog park. "That's a beautiful dog," I said. Phillip voiced no opinion.

Once we reached the sidewalk Phillip said, "What gives you doubts?"

"Your mom was supporting a lifestyle beyond what Kate could've achieved on her own. Why kill her?"

We continued in silence until he said, "Why kill her? Really good question." His sincerity caught me off guard.

"What do you think about Kate McCall's guilt, Phillip?"

Phillip didn't hesitate. "No opinion."

She might have murdered your mother, for fuck's sake!

"My dispassion puzzles you," Phillip said. "Is he normal? Pathological? Philosophical? Nihilistic?"

Nihilistic? I said, "Who am I to say what someone should feel?"

"Good answer."

His clipped manner of speech was peculiar. "Do you mind telling me what you thought of Kate McCall as a person?"

"Never met her. Didn't know she existed until the arrest."

I stopped. Phillip continued a few feet then stopped and looked back. I said, "You didn't know your mother had a personal assistant?"

"The format of her day-to-day life was not discussed."

We resumed walking. I remembered Kate McCall's excuse for keeping jewelry from Jackie Whitney's safe-deposit box. I said, "Did you know anything about jewelry in a safe-deposit box that Kate was supposed to give you?"

"Mom had jewelry. No idea where."

"What did you and your mother typically talk about when you got together?"

"How I was doing, did I have a girlfriend, what I did for fun, if I liked my job."

"Did your mom tell you about her personal life? What kind of a social life she led?"

We came to a four-way stop. Phillip adjusted Bo's collar then told him to sit. We watched several other volunteers and their dogs walk past in the opposite direction. Phillip said, "Cursory accounts of activities. Who she accompanied to a party, the opera, the fundraiser. She'd admit only to friendship."

"Speaking of friends, others have suggested your mom had high expectations of her friends. Especially those she gave money to."

"Mom knew best and wasn't afraid to say so."

"Kate McCall had become very important in her life. Why do you think she didn't tell you about her?"

Phillip stopped in front of the door to the shelter. I sensed he didn't want me to follow him inside. "Can't say. Probably thought Kate had no relevance to me."

I gave him one of my cards. "Listen," I said. "I hope you'll give me a call if you think of something that might be important. You never know about these things."

Phillip gave me a thoughtful expression and nodded.

Chapter 11

Maybe it was a change in atmospheric pressure, but from the downstairs lobby I always perceived when someone was waiting outside my office. Today was no different. When I reached the third floor, Linda Napier sat in one of two club chairs I'd put on the landing to serve as my waiting area.

"Why didn't you call and set up an appointment?" I said.

"I was afraid you'd hang up on me. My behavior was abominable." She looked closely at the scab above my brow. "I'm so sorry."

I unlocked the door then picked the mail up off the floor. Linda didn't wait to be invited in. By the time I sat, she was seated in front of my desk.

"So what can I do for you?" I said.

"The murderer. If it wasn't Kate McCall, who? Why?"

"I don't know, and money."

"I'm just confused. I—I don't understand who it could've been if not Kate McCall."

"Worried about something?"

"I'm not worried, just confused. Why would I be worried?"

"Hey, catch me up on something. When did you and Dr. Kessler start dating?"

Linda abruptly stood then walked to the room's only window. She spoke while looking out over busy North Avenue. "I decided to surprise Jackie by showing up at her place to wish her a good trip. I wanted to be on speaking terms again before she left. But I was too late. Josh—Dr. Kessler—invited me in for coffee. You're probably wondering why I didn't tell you this yesterday."

"Probably."

Linda turned around and walked back to the chair. "Anyway, it's over."

"When did the relationship end?"

"I don't know. It changed. We're still friends."

"Were you seeing Dr. Kessler when he supposedly wasn't paying his rent?"

"He paid every dime! That trashy bitch was keeping the money."

"Did you tell your friend George about your relationship with Kessler?"

"No."

"Why not? Weren't you close?"

"Very close. But things had changed. I had been away for some time, and I thought it better to keep my intimate life private."

I still wondered what she was doing in my office. "There was a time when you were more forthcoming with George about your personal life."

"I see you've been discussing me with him."

"It's just odd to me that you would keep secrets from your oldest and closest friend."

"How is that any of your business?"

"I'm a private investigator. When people appear to be hiding something—anything—it's my job to become suspicious."

Linda shifted in her seat. "It would've been too easy for me to become dependent on Jackie and George to tell me what to do about men. Or about anything. I had to make up my own mind and not look for their approval first."

"You think Kessler had any reason to kill Jackie?"

Linda flinched. "No! Of course not. Why would he?"

"Did you help him move out?"

"A little. So what?"

"Was it done all in one day?"

"No. Well—no, because I started moving smaller things a week or more before he was completely out."

"Were you with him when he finished packing up and left the key with the doorman? What day was it?"

"Um," Linda said, then reflected long and hard on my question. She either knew what I was getting at or was replaying the events in her head. "I think so—I don't know. I can't remember."

I stood. "Anything else?"

Linda remained seated. "I thought maybe you'd let me buy you dinner, as a way of apologizing for my behavior yesterday."

I hadn't seen that coming. "That's not necessary," I said. "I forgive you. But feel free to get in touch again—should you feel the need."

At one o'clock, it had already been a long day. I needed a nap. Instead of going home, I locked the office door, adjusted my ergonomic high-back chair, and luxuriated in the pressure releasing from my lower spine and thighs. The ensuing dreaminess involved Dr. Kessler's possible guilt and Linda Napier's role, if any. The CCTV video of May 16 and 17 would determine the direction of my investigation.

My phone rang about two-thirty, rousing me into a dopey kind of wakefulness.

"Did I wake you?" Kalijero said.

"Huh? No. What's up?"

"Brookstone. He's working for a lawyer named Henry DeWeldt."

I needed a moment. Then it came back. "A lawyer? What kind of lawyer?"

"I don't know. Supposedly he's pretty rooted into our city government."

"A big payroll to meet, I bet. How did you find out about Brookie?"

"Cops who beat up women have big mouths. They can't help themselves. Like the drug dealer bragging about a big score. Only Brookstone was bragging about the easy money this lawyer was paying him just to act tough. Dumbass started dropping his name."

"What's Henry DeWeldt's connection to Jackie Whitney's murder?"

"That's your job, Mr. Private Investigator. Remember?"

"Oh, yeah, I forgot. Anyway, thanks for the tip."

"Hang on. You need to expect Brookstone to keep finding you. He's got a whole network of cops he kicks back to when he's working a side job. As you keep digging, he's going to want to know what you know."

"I'm working for the other side. Fuck him."

"Don't be an ass. We both know you're not gonna be satisfied playing the reasonable doubt game. You'll need him if you find real evidence against someone else." Kalijero hung up.

I splashed cold water on my face, made a peanut butter sandwich, then drove back to Michigan Avenue. By some miracle, I found a legal parking place on East Lake Shore Drive. Manny walked out the front door just as I stepped out of my car. From the trunk of a taxi, he lifted two very large suitcases then took one in each hand—luggage cart be damned. Since Marv was not present, I held the door open and followed Manny all the way to the desk where a luggage cart waited. I barely kept pace. Also waiting was a young man in a doorman's uniform.

"Thanks for getting the door, Mr. Landau," Manny said.

"So that's how you keep so fit and trim," I said. "Power walking with a suitcase in each hand is like a whole body workout. You don't need no stinkin' luggage cart."

"Manny's a salsa athlete," the young man said. "You should see him hoofin' on the dance floor."

Manny laughed. "Meet Lenny, Mr. Landau. We're just about to change shifts."

I looked at my watch. "The swing-shift man. You like those hours?"

Lenny shrugged. "It beats graveyard or being a floater who never knows when they're going to work."

"Mr. Landau is a private investigator," Manny said. "The real deal. I bet you've never met a private investigator."

Lenny didn't share Manny's fascination. "Actually, I have. He told me it's really boring work."

"Do you mind if we chat a little bit?" I said to Lenny. "I promise not to be boring."

Lenny stepped back, gave me an incredulous look, and said, "It's about time!" His reaction confused me.

Manny put his hand on Lenny's shoulder. "Well, have a good night, sonny boy," he said.

"Before you leave," I said, "I got a question."

Manny stepped a few feet away from the desk. "What's up?"

"Can I have a peek at the guest sign-in book you mentioned?"

"I guess so. Why, may I ask?"

"Just the pages that cover May sixteenth and seventeenth."

Manny hesitated. "When Jackie was supposedly—"

I nodded.

"Wait here," Manny said, walked back to the desk, then said something to Lenny who handed him a book from under the counter. "Here you go. Take a look."

The possibility of a signing in to kill somebody should not be overlooked. Stupidity was the downfall of many a murderer. The book was a common daily journal with lined pages. I looked through the last names of visitors from the morning of the sixteenth to the evening of the seventeenth, but did not see Kessler's name. "Thank you, sir," I said to Manny, handing him the book. After Manny handed it back to Lenny I tried to slip a ten-dollar bill into his pocket but he refused.

"No, no, no," he said. "That's completely unnecessary."

Once again, I bowed to the man in the officer's cap then turned back to Lenny. "What did you mean a minute ago when you said, 'It's about time'?"

"Well, from what I've read, I might've been one of the last people to see Jackie Whitney alive."

"Is that a confession?"

"Not funny."

"Did you know her at all? Did she talk to you much?"

"Did I know her in what sense?"

"What was her mood like? Her attitude if she spoke to you?"

"Witchy."

"Was she always witchy to you?"

Lenny thought about it. "Well, at least always crabby to some degree."

"Does it bother you when people are nasty?"

"Nothing bothers me here."

"Do you know the concierge, Freddie, very well?"

Lenny began to smile then pursed his lips. "He's an interesting guy," Lenny said.

"Funny. Manny also used the word 'interesting.' Why do you think that is?" I watched Lenny struggle to think of something to say that didn't sound insulting or politically incorrect. I decided to help him out. "I get it," I said. "He's a transman. Big deal. But is he a nice guy? Friendly? I heard he and Jackie Whitney were friends. Did you see them together?"

"She used to hang around at the concierge desk. They giggled a lot. Sometimes, she would sit behind the desk and they would talk really intensely, you know what I mean? Like eyeball to eyeball."

"This was only as Freddie . . . ?"

"I didn't work here when he was Felicia. So I don't know if they acted weird then."

"Weird? You think the eyeball-to-eyeball talking was really that weird?"

"Not only that. I mean, it just seemed weird how Jackie Whitney acted around him. Maybe a little too comfy? But that's just me. What do I know?"

"You're wondering how intimate they really were?"

"Yeah, I guess that's it. But I'm not saying they were intimate. I don't know anything for real. Although sometimes Freddie would leave his desk to help her carry packages up. That's my job."

"To her apartment?"

"Where else? Maybe he just dropped them at the door? I don't know. He'd spend fifteen or twenty minutes up there. Where else would he be all that time?" A limo driver stood in the lobby waving at Lenny. "Gotta go," he said then ran off pushing a luggage cart.

I headed toward the concierge desk. Through the front windows, I could see Lenny pulling suitcases out of the limo's trunk. I said to Freddie, "Why do you think the building doesn't have a full-time doorman stationed at the actual door?"

"Because the concierge is supposed to help unload luggage. But I don't help unless a couple of cars pull up. Screw it. They don't pay me for two jobs; why should I work two jobs? Manny and the guys don't seem to care. More tips for them."

A man and woman in their sixties approached the desk accompanied by a younger man looking dapper in a fine suit. I stepped back and watched Freddie graciously provide sightseeing pamphlets, draw circles on areas of small maps, and write down detailed directions to a specific location. Parents sightseeing while their successful son went to work, I imagined.

When they walked away I said, "What if a resident comes back with lots of packages?"

Freddie hesitated. "That's the doorman's job."

"So you never lend a hand with something that?"

"I'm not supposed to. During the day, the concierge desk should always be manned."

I nodded, as if it made perfect sense, then excused myself and walked back to the doorman's desk.

"Did you have a nice chat with Felicia—I mean Freddie?" Lenny said.

"You mind if I pay a visit to the ninth floor?" I said.

"For what?"

"I just want to chat with whoever took care of Jackie Whitney's dog after her renter moved out early."

"I might catch some shit for it, but I'll just say I thought you were a cop."

Unlike Jackie Whitney's palace on the tenth floor, on the ninth the elevator opened to a common hallway servicing three apartments. As luck would have it, I thought I heard something resembling a dog's high-pitched bark coming from behind the middle door. I knocked, which left no doubt as to where the dog lived. An older, female voice exclaimed several "shushes" before the door opened and a kind, elderly face appeared behind a chain lock.

"Yes?" she said, sounding surprisingly pleasant considering a stranger stood at her door in a building with a doorman.

"I'm very sorry to bother you," I said then explained why I was there.

"I already told the police I didn't hear anything," she said.

"Do you recall on what day Dr. Kessler brought Trixie down to you?"

"Oh, heavens. The middle of last month some time."

"That must've been quite a surprise to see this man standing here with a dog."

"She seemed quite comfortable at his side. I could tell he felt guilty about handing her over. I told him he was lucky that he knocked on my door. My neighbors don't like seeing animals in the building. They complain about noise and such."

"Did you hear a lot of noise from Jackie Whitney's apartment?"

The lady unhooked the door and stepped into the doorway. Behind her I could see a standard poodle wagging its tail.

"Oh, once in a while Trixie would bark a little bit. My neighbors are just old, that's all. Always looking for something to complain about."

"Did Jackie come down to get Trixie when she returned on the afternoon of the sixteenth?"

"Yes, but we weren't here. I often spend the weekends with my son and his family. They live in the suburbs. My granddaughters love Trixie. On Sunday I returned to see that Jackie had taped a note to my door. I brought Trixie up Monday morning, but nobody answered. When I tried again on Tuesday, there were police everywhere and I found out what happened."

"Did you know Jackie Whitney very well?"

"I remember the parents but the kids keep to themselves once they grow up." She described how the character of the building had changed over the decades as the old money passed down to the younger generations. "When I was a young woman, many in the building would organize progressive dinner parties where each floor would open their doors and serve different foods. Truly amazing, now that I think about it. Imagine, all twenty floors open to any resident who felt like stopping by. Unthinkable nowadays."

I thanked her for her time then hung around the lobby trying to get someone to talk about Jackie Whitney. Among the dozen or so residents that gave me the time of day, most remembered her, but none claimed her as a friend or admitted to any relationship beyond that of an acquaintance.

Punim paced and whipped her tail. I had been gone all day. She was not happy. I dropped a liver and two hearts into her bowl and she tore into them, shredding the organs into chunks small enough to swallow. A real piranha-puss. I knew all would be forgiven.

I made a three-veggie-patty sandwich then fired up my laptop. Kalijero's somewhat conciliatory tone regarding Brookstone troubled me. Cops and ex-cops, I thought. God help us. For the first time, I wondered if I could completely trust Kalijero. Henry DeWeldt was a principal partner in the law firm DeWeldt, Van Buren, & Associates, PC. His photo spoke loudly of the sober corporate lawyer never happier than when sitting in front of an opened book of intellectual property law. He sat on various boards of directors, including Furry BFF. Why would he be associated with a semi-literate ape like Tommy Brookstone?

Chapter 12

The next morning a woman's pleasant voice thanked me for calling DeWeldt and Van Buren.

"I'm interested in meeting with Mr. DeWeldt regarding a will," I said.

"Have you worked with Mr. DeWeldt before?"

"No."

"Hold, please." Then, "This is Nancy. I understand you'd like a will executed?"

"Yes, I'd like to work with Mr. DeWeldt."

"Mr. DeWeldt usually hands these types of requests off to associates like myself—unless he makes a personal decision."

"How about I make an appointment with Mr. DeWeldt?"

"Okay, I'll transfer you back." Once again I was welcomed to the DeWeldt and Van Buren law firm.

"I'd like to make an appointment with Mr. DeWeldt, please."

"And what is this regarding?"

"Estate planning."

"Hold please." Then, "This is Nancy. I understand you're interested in estate planning?"

I hung up.

A little hardball might be in order. I found a website for the Attorney Registration & Disciplinary Commission, plugged in the name Henry DeWeldt, then hit search. Up popped two men by that name, one with the designation "Jr." It turned out DeWeldt Junior had an integrity problem, allegedly bilking an old lady out of a bunch of money. This activity sounded familiar. Time to call "Johnny Bail Bonds" Duggan.

"Johnny Bail Bonds. How may I direct your call?"

"Jules for Johnny," I said, knowing those three words were the same as Chief O'Hara shining the bat signal into the sky.

"Hey, Mr. Jules!" Johnny said. "What can I do you for?"

"You got any contacts over at the ARDC? The lawyer discipline people?"

"I've pawned a lot of shysters, so I'm thinkin' mos def, my friend."

"We're talking starched white collar. Henry DeWeldt, Jr., pillaged an old lady's trust instead of managing it. Only got a suspension. How does that happen? Whose palms got greased, that kind of thing."

"I just got a lead on a skip, so give me a few hours to do a little hound doggin'."

What a decade ago had been the Illinois Central rail yards was now Millennium Park, a civic center of lawns, gardens, public art, and music. Dressed in my finest gray worsted wool suit, I walked among the native grasses, deciduous shrubs, and blooming perennials, deep in thought about murder. I was still stuck on motive. Linda and Kessler both insisted Kate McCall was stealing from Jackie Whitney, but neither claimed Jackie Whitney herself told them about it. That didn't make sense. And if Kate McCall was getting away with stealing golden eggs, murdering the goose would've been the last thing on her mind. Money assuaged all bitterness, after all. Establishing Dr. Kessler or Linda Napier lying about their whereabouts played well for Kate's reasonable doubt defense. But who was it that couldn't resist crushing Jackie Whitney's skull?

Johnny Bail Bonds called back. "Okay, my sources say DeWeldt's got lots of suction. Junior was gonna be disbarred. DeWeldt got to the review-board dudes, made offers of cash and entry into some private clubs, that kind of thing. It's the old boys' connection hard at work."

"What about the old man? DeWeldt Senior. Also caught milking an old lady's trust?"

"Nobody said anything about the old man."

"Okay, Johnny. Thanks a billion!"

Four blocks away, DeWeldt, Van Buren, & Associates loomed over the neighborhood from the forty-ninth floor of Brandt Tower. Two layouts of luxurious furniture worthy of a statesman's living room served as the firm's waiting area. Apart from the receptionist's gaze, I felt quite comfortable on the couch in my beautiful suit reading Forbes magazine.

"Can I help you with something, sir?" she finally asked.

I looked at my watch. "I'm just killing time before my appointment."

"May I ask who your appointment is with?"

"Uh, one of the associates. I forgot her name. It's just a will." She smiled and returned to her duties.

While I was engrossed in an article describing the improbable comeback of the Hostess Twinkie, two young lawyers appeared from an inner hallway.

One looked neatly pressed and tailored, the other I gave props for trying to look comfortable in a gray flannel suit. His hair also looked too long for the clothes and his voice was too loud for his profession. As they passed me and exited the office, certain characteristics about the guy's face struck me as familiar, then I remembered the photo of Henry DeWeldt from the website. On the wall, other headshots were mounted showing the various partners through the years. I walked over and studied DeWeldt the Elder's face. The pale blue eyes, strong chin, and high cheekbones told me the disorderly looking man was almost certainly DeWeldt the Younger. Another photo caught my eye, this one of DeWeldt the Elder shaking hands with a woman while handing her a check. I looked closer. The check was a ten-thousand-dollar donation to the Senior Tricks bridge club's general fund. The ad in the magazine on Jackie Whitney's coffee table came to mind.

"Is Mr. DeWeldt in the office today?" I asked the receptionist. "I wanted to say hello from my father. They knew each other a long time ago."

"Oh? You didn't mention that before."

"I thought maybe I'd run into him while waiting for, uh, Nancy. I think that's her name."

"Well, he'll probably be going to lunch soon. I didn't think Nancy was in the office today."

"Uh, maybe not. But I was supposed to meet her here first."

"You want me to check—"

"No, no, that's okay. I'll just wait around a little bit and call her if I get concerned. I'm curious. How many lawyers in this firm?"

"About two hundred," she said, a little puzzled by my question. I returned to reading about Twinkies but my attention was soon drawn behind the reception desk where two large conference doors opened. Several men appeared, including Henry DeWeldt, Sr. He spoke cheerfully with his colleagues a bit before saying goodbye and walking toward the elevators.

Before I could make a move, the receptionist jumped in with, "Mr. DeWeldt, this gentleman has a message from his father he'd like to relay."

DeWeldt looked at me suspiciously. "Oh? Who is your father?"

"Can I walk out with you, sir?"

"I suppose. I don't own the hallway. At least not yet." He smiled and waited for me to reciprocate, which I did. We stood in front of the elevator.

"Tom Brookstone—"

"Brookstone has a son? I didn't know that."

"No, I'm wondering why you hired him to intimidate me."

DeWeldt's eyes narrowed. "Intimidate you? I don't know you."

"I'm investigating Jackie Whitney's murder."

DeWeldt looked stricken. The elevator dinged. He stepped in, I followed then said, "Brookstone warned me about getting in the way of a jury finding Kate McCall guilty. Care to comment?"

DeWeldt stared at the numbers lighting up with each floor. As more people boarded, I remained close to my partner. "You already acknowledged that you know Brookstone," I said, ostensibly talking to no one in particular, which elicited curious glances.

"I don't know what you're talking about," DeWeldt whispered.

I slipped a business card into his jacket pocket. "I know the strings you pulled for Junior," I whispered back. "He should've been disbarred, dontcha think?" I thought I felt heat radiating out of DeWeldt's collar. When the door opened to the lobby, I grabbed his arm as the others walked out. "Think about it. I have subpoena power, you know. And rumors can run like wildfire in this town about why Junior got off so easy. What if the media started investigating? A lot of questions would arise. So what the hell are you doing with an ass-clown like Brookstone? I look forward to your call."

I started walking away. This time DeWeldt grabbed my arm. The color had returned to his face. "Go ahead," he growled. "Say all you want about my son. Nothing will be proven and I'll sue you for slander."

His surge of confidence bothered me. I watched him leave the building then dialed Debbie's number. She answered with her usual sweetness.

"What do you need, Jules?"

"I'd like to get together again and talk about my latest findings."

"That penguin place, same time."

It was an order, not a suggestion. "I can't wait to see you," I said. She hung up.

Chapter 13

The Youji Lu Grocer's trickling fountains, natural light, and bamboo floors emanated warmth. Faint smells of oil and incense, torchiere lamps, and wall sconces added to the elegance. People spoke quietly as they shopped. A Chinese man smiled broadly while walking the aisles. People stopped him, bowed, then spoke. He showed them where products were, explained ingredients.

The Chinese man finished with a customer then walked directly to me. "May I help?" he said in heavily accented English. His name badge read Mr. Chao.

"Kate McCall worked here?" I said then gave him my ID. I thought he smiled knowingly as he looked at it and handed it back, but I couldn't be sure.

"You Kate friend?" Mr. Chao said.

"I want to help Kate," I said. "I think Kate is innocent."

"Yes. You help Kate. Kate a good worker. Kate know much about Kentucky mushroom. I show you."

Mr. Chao led me to one of the produce displays. He pointed to a bin of yellowish mushrooms. "Morel," he said. "Oldham County, Kentucky. Good for iron and vitamin D." He brought me to another basket. "Agrocybe mushroom. Big for copper nutrition." Mr. Chao showed me several more varieties and described their nutritional profiles. "I not know big information for mushroom. All this knowledge from Kate."

"But Kate cleaned for you, no?"

"Yes. She good cleaner." Mr. Chao raised a closed fist. "Strong woman. I know Chinese mushroom. She go home to Kentucky, bring back mushroom, teach me for Kentucky mushroom."

"Do you think Kate could kill that woman?"

"Yes," Mr. Chao said without hesitating.

I waited for him to elaborate but he just stared at me. "Why do you think yes?" I asked.

"I think because I also kill. You also kill. All person also kill."

"But did Kate kill this woman, Jackie Whitney?"

Mr. Chao shrugged and said, "Who know?"

"Kate knew you looked through the trash?"

"No. I don't think. Kate not stupid. Kate very smart."

"The prescription bottle, the car registration, the keys. Kate put them in your garbage?"

"No. I say already Kate not stupid."

"Any guess who put them there?"

Mr. Chao appeared deep in thought a few moments, then said, "Maybe you put."

I would've laughed, but I got the feeling he was making fun of me. "Did you know anything about Kate's life outside of the grocery?"

Mr. Chao nodded, stared straight ahead. A smile crept over his face. "Kate love children with disable. Wheelchair, crutch. Kate bring children here, she teach about garden. Then she go to garden place and show to grow plant . . ."

Mr. Chao thoughtfully described what I interpreted as a community garden designed so handicapped children could get their hands dirty while learning to grow vegetables, herbs, and flowers. Several times he paused to dab his eyes when describing the faces of joyful children and the pleasure Kate derived from their happiness. Verb-subject disagreements and missing articles did nothing to diminish Mr. Chao's enchantment.

He continued to stare straight ahead after he stopped. I waited for him to look at me and said, "You knew the victim, Jackie Whitney?"

He nodded. "She good customer," he said quietly.

"Did you know her at all? Was she someone you would talk to?"

"I know only she buy much cheese and olive oil. And she like Kate. Very sad."

I thanked Mr. Chao for his time then bowed before leaving.

I arrived at the Kutaisi Georgian Bakery in the last throes of its lunch chaos. Tamar had a table reserved for me with a piece of notebook paper she had written "reserved" on. Also waiting for me was a portobello sandwich with roasted garlic.

"Portobello doesn't sound very Georgian to me," I said.

"I know a lot of hungry Georgians who would be glad to have that sandwich," she said. "And that's just the crew in the prep room."

"My apologies," I said and took a bite. The sandwich was amazing.

"I saw a picture of Kate McCall in today's Chicago Post," Tamar said.

I waited for more but that's all she had. "Don't waste your time with that rag," I said.

"You don't want to tell me about the article?"

"What article? I don't waste my time with tabloid stupidity."

"You forgot to tell me how cute she was."

"I didn't have to tell you. You had already read of her described as a 'sex kitten.'"

"But you saw her in person and didn't say one way or the other."

The tone was unmistakable. I stopped eating, pushed the plate aside, leaned forward on my elbows. "You mind telling me what's going on?"

"Who's Li'l Abner?"

"A character in a hillbilly comic strip from a long time ago. Why?"

"What about Daisy Mae?"

"Abner's hillbilly girlfriend. What're you getting at?"

Tamar pulled the Post out from under the table. The headline read, "There's No Need to Fear! Private eye Li'l Abner Landau is here to save his beloved Daisy Mae McCall." I closed my eyes then opened them. It wasn't a dream. There I was, my cartooned face on Li'l Abner's muscle-bound body. Sitting on my shoulder was Daisy Mae's voluptuous form with Kate McCall's face.

At that moment, I truly understood what being speechless meant. "You mind giving me a summary?" I said. "Or are you going to make me read it?"

Tamar held the Post up and began reading. "Superman, Batman, Spiderman, y'all ain't got nothin' on Chicago's coolest private eye, Li'l Abner Landau. Even that Royal Mounted Canadian

Dudley Do-Right can't rescue Nell enough times from imminent dismemberment to compare to good ol' boy, Li'l Abner Landau. In fact, you can plumb take the whole dad gum Justice League of 'Merica and it won't mean diddly squat compared to . . ."

The author could only be Ellis Knight, a twenty-something journalist who once had the potential for respect when he wrote for The Partisan, but had apparently swapped his soul for a Post front page byline. Knight's style was smartass, while hinting of some greater truth. I doubted many readers picked up on the truth part. Aside from describing my role in solving two murders and locating a missing person, I heard nothing resembling truth. But who cared about truth when Ellis Knight could spin a tale suggesting city-boy-country-girl love that had no basis in reality?

"Okay, I've heard enough," I said. "It's all fiction, Tamar. My motivation has nothing to do with Kate McCall's looks and everything to do with making sure the DA has arrested the right person. And the money Kate McCall is paying me helps the motivation too."

Tamar said nothing, dropped the Post on an empty chair. "So what are you allowed to tell me today about Kate McCall's guilt or innocence?"

"Well, I have people unsure about their comings and goings around the time of the murder. That could mean everything or nothing. Jackie Whitney apparently had been dating a corrupt lawyer who hired a goon to discourage me from investigating."

"Huh? What do you mean 'discourage'?"

"He's a cop who flat out warned me off. I have an inkling why."

I purposely took my time eating until Tamar said, "Oh, c'mon, tell me."

"First, say you believe me about my motivation . . ."

"I believe you. Tell me."

"Jackie Whitney may have discovered this lawyer was bilking money out of an old lady or two. But get this. His son did the same thing, and got just a slap on the wrist."

"And if Jackie Whitney and the lawyer were dating?"

"Then I have a connection between the lawyer and the victim and maybe the defendant sitting in jail."

"By threatening you, the lawyer only brings to light that he may have some involvement with the crime. Why would someone be so stupid?"

"Scared people often do stupid things. A lot of crimes are solved because of stupidity."

I changed the subject to life at the bakery. Tamar sounded fairly optimistic. She seemed to be relaxing much more into the role of owner and operator. Then she surprised me with an envelope.

"What's this?" I said tearing it open. Inside was a check for ten thousand dollars and a loan statement.

"That's the first installment of what I owe you. And it's an amount the bakery can comfortably afford—as you put it a few days ago."

I sensed her mood had lifted. "You had a good month, I guess?"

Tamar smiled. "Not bad. Thirty-four more months like the last one and I'll be free and clear of you."

"I don't like the sound of that. Maybe you should keep the money."

Tamar giggled, grabbed my collar like she did the last time I was in the bakery, then pulled me into a prolonged kiss. "I gotta go," she said and was off.

I watched her disappear into the prep room then grabbed the Post off the chair, exited the bakery, and walked around the corner to Fairfield Ave. I had my car in sight when a voice shouted, "Hey!" The ungainly figure of Brookstone lumbered toward me looking quite joyful.

"How did you like the article?" Brookstone said. "You're famous! I'm like your press agent."

"You sold Ellis Knight a load of crap."

"Sell him? I just told him about you coming to a murderer's rescue and he took it from there. I remembered he wrote those other articles about your fine detective work."

"Tell me, Brookie. Do you really think I owe you because my father squealed about your little side job breaking thumbs?"

"Ah, you talked to Kalijero. You're goddamn right you owe me. You're his blood, and now you want to ruin my chance to make up for all that lost pay? Ten extra years on patrol?"

"Don't forget all that potential thumb-breaking pay too. How did you track me down so quick?"

"What did I say, Landau? Yesterday, what did I say? Stop the poking around."

"No, you didn't. You said stop looking for reasonable doubt."

"You know what I mean, asshole. You was at that broad's building yesterday, talking to that doorman."

"How did you know that?"

"Same way I knew you were here. We're watching you, Landau. It ain't just me. Just leave it alone, for chrissake."

"Okay, Brookie, level with me. I'll pay you to turn on DeWeldt. How's he connected to Jackie Whitney's murder?"

"He isn't connected to any murder."

"Then why does he want to see Kate McCall take the rap?"

"Because she's guilty. Doesn't matter anyway. My job is to make sure you stop your poking around. If you start behaving maybe DeWeldt will give you a little present. You know?"

Brookstone rubbed the tips of his fingers together. I inspected his large face. His chin looked as if all the bones in my hand would shatter against it. I said, "Talk to Kalijero. He'll explain I don't let threats stop me from pursuing a case."

Brookstone sighed. "I'm gonna tell you one more time to quit it. After that, you could really get hurt."

Brookstone turned to leave then reversed course and gave me a left jab square in the nose. Even before he connected, I sensed him holding back, that he intentionally avoided crushing my face with that concrete block of a fist. Either way, I found myself sitting alone on the sidewalk in broad daylight on a beautiful day, my eyes teary from intense pain throughout my nose and eye sockets.

I drove home then spent an hour on the couch, ice pack on face, cat in lap. Thanks to freakishly soft cartilage, my nose wasn't broken, just red and swollen. More ice-time was probably a good idea, but I had someplace to go.

Chapter 14

The Attorney Registration & Disciplinary Commission was located just a few blocks from Henry DeWeldt's law office on East Randolph Street, and was where the clerk's file room database would contain all the commission's disciplinary decisions. I searched by law firm and came up with eighty-three initial complaints of fraudulent or deceptive activity filed against attorneys at DeWeldt, Van Buren, & Associates. More surprising than seeing forty percent of the law firm represented was that the board found none of the complaints as having enough merit to advance to the next disciplinary level. I looked into ten individual cases and found an amazing coincidence. All victims were elderly residents of various senior housing facilities all owned by a corporate entity called Contentment. I walked out of the commission's office, wondering how Jackie Whitney's death could be connected to a scumbag law firm and corrupt commission members. Who among that crowd lost their temper within arm's reach of a hammer?

I went straight to the Cook County jail, this time with my state identification. Apart from waiting in long lines, the ID worked much better than my private investigator's ID had, and even allowed me to obtain a private interview room. I'd never felt so official.

Kate looked tired and depressed but managed to flash me a small smile. "How are you holding up?" I asked.

"Ah-ite, I guess. Your nose is all swelled up. You gotta head cold?"

"Allergies. Listen, I've got kind of a strange question. It has to do with Jackie's friendship with the concierge in her building."

Kate nodded. "Yeah, I reckon I know what you're gettin' at."

"What makes you so sure?"

"Because Jackie done told me folks was givin' her strange looks when talkin' to Freddie. And she knowed some would go a-gossipin', 'specially 'cause Freddie sometimes helped tote packages up to her apartment."

"They were good friends, right? Nothing beyond friendship?"

Kate closed her eyes, nodded her head several times. "I can assure you, Mr. Landau, they was just friends, nothin' more."

"Okay," I said then held up the front page of the Post. Kate leaned in, putting her face close to the Plexiglas. I watched her brown eyes bounce around the page. Despite the fact she was in jail, her skin looked clear and bright and her hair had a lovely shine.

I said, "It's really just a feature story about me helping defend you."

"Them cartoons say it all," Kate said, wiping a tear off her cheek. "I'm just dumb hillbilly trash. So I must be guilty."

"I know that's not true," I said, her guilt or innocence now beside the point as I succumbed to my overwhelming attraction. "And when you're proven innocent, the whole city will know."

"Thank you, Mr. Landau," Kate said, then smiled sweetly.

"But now I need to ask you a question," I said. "Do you remember Jackie dating a man named Henry DeWeldt?"

"There was a Henry, but I don't know his last name."

"What did he look like?"

"White-haired gent. Older but plucky. Still had a spring in his step."

"What did Jackie tell you about him?"

"She never done speak of him, not really. Only, 'I'm a-goin' out with Henry tonight,' or 'Henry's a-takin' me to the opera.'"

The disappointment hit hard. I wasn't sure what I was hoping to hear. "But Jackie never confided in you about him? Maybe said some pretty unflattering things about the kind of lawyer he was?"

"No, sir, Mr. Landau. Like I said, Jackie didn't never speak of Henry in no personal way. Although—" Kate stopped. She stared up and to the right as she tried to recall something. "She told me one morning when she come into the grocery that they done had a big ol' fight. She wouldn't tell me nothin' what they were fightin' over, but she plumb wore herself out tellin' me what a corrupt piecer shit that Henry was."

"Think hard. What was the basis of the rant? Was there some conclusion she came to?"

"Well, I do remember her a-sayin' somethin' like, 'Men are lyin' pigs, can't trust 'em, I hate 'em.' That kinda talkin'."

"How long ago did this happen?"

"Um—not long before she was fixin' to go to Palm Springs."

"Around Christmas."

"Yes, sir. In fact, they was at a Christmas party the night before she come into the grocery and chewed my ear."

"If I only knew what they were arguing about," I said out loud.

"I'm sorry, Mr. Landau. I wish I could tell you more about that fight, but I just don't got nothin' else."

I was about to tell Kate not to worry about it, then something clicked and I remembered the magazine advertisement on the coffee table in Jackie's apartment.

From an Internet listing I found a downtown bridge club with the innocent name Senior Tricks,. Stopping there would make me late for Debbie's meeting, but I didn't care. The wealth that the near north address implied did not prepare me for the nineteenth-century Renaissance revival country house, once owned by the McCormick family and now an exclusive gaming club for the well-born Chicagoan. Bridge was played in one of the "staterooms." Lavishly decorated in the gothic style, the walls featured hangings of gilded leather, bolts of sapphire-blue French silk, and an enormous equestrian portrait of an English king.

Amid this royal backdrop, silver-haired citizens, mostly women, huddled around wooden felt-covered gaming tables. Seated alongside many of them were much younger men and women, some looked to be in their twenties. I recognized Manny's friend Gloria standing at one of the tables, observing the action.

"Hello," said a woman with the name tag Lois. "Do you have an elderly parent looking for a bridge partner?"

"I have an elderly parent but he lacks the patrician bloodline and he's slipping fast up here." I pointed at my head.

"The aristocratic connotation is really just a relic of the past, assuming one has the finances to join. And some of our members are also in various stages of dementia."

"They can still play a complicated game like bridge with dementia?"

"They've been playing their whole lives. The oldest memories are often the last to go."

I nodded, genuinely fascinated by this fact, then introduced myself and handed her a card. "I'm investigating a pattern of fraud perpetrated against the elderly."

"Oh, that's terrible! I hate hearing such stories."

"I have a hunch that this club is used to fish for potential marks." I showed her the list of names I had written down at the disciplinary commission. "Everyone on this list has filed a complaint against the same law firm. Do you know if any of these people are part of this club?"

Lois looked them over. "I recognize several names."

"I see Gloria is here," I said.

"Oh, you know Gloria?" Lois pointed to the name Seymour Steinberg on the list. "That's Gloria's husband. Sy passed away a few years ago."

"Gloria and I have a mutual friend. Maybe I'll talk to her about this later."

"Gloria's here almost every day. She's an unofficial teacher and coach. Everyone adores her."

"It's still a pretty posh club, eh?"

"Traditionally, yes. Many of the members have famous surnames. But the demographics are working against the club. The board is trying to recruit younger players, although the game isn't as popular as it used to be."

"Younger players from the same social class."

"As I said, it's not about class anymore. If you have the money, you can join."

"That's nice. It's all about the game."

"It really is. In fact, if you observed the interactions, you would notice how the game of bridge itself is a kind of equalizer. You'll also notice the members are not dressed as you would imagine people of their backgrounds would dress for a place like this. It's more important to be comfortable than covered in clunky jewelry."

"Those younger people sitting with them—new recruits? Grandchildren?"

Lois laughed. "You've heard of golf pros? Those are bridge pros partnering with their benefactors. It's very common nowadays at fancy clubs like this."

"Have you noticed people coming here not to play bridge? I mean, they just want to talk to a certain member?"

"Uh, yes, that seems to be happening more and more. The members give us their names in advance, so we allow them to sit and wait. But a game can never be interrupted."

"Do they leave cards? Do you know where they're from?"

"No, but they're usually well-dressed men with briefcases. I assume they're money managers or salesmen of some type."

I thanked Lois for her time then headed to Penguin House, where public defender Debbie Lopez would be waiting.

"You sick or something?" Debbie said, referencing my nose. "You better not be contagious."

"How does this sound: Jackie Whitney was dating a high-powered lawyer named Henry DeWeldt. She threatened to blow the whistle on some of DeWeldt's very unethical activities. That's why Henry had her killed."

Clearly underwhelmed, Debbie said, "Care to share some evidence?"

"Eighty-three complaints in the last year alone filed against DeWeldt attorneys with the ARDC. Not a single one advanced beyond the inquiry board. I took a sampling of ten cases. All were charges of fraud from elderly plaintiffs."

"None of the charges stuck, you just said that."

"But that's the point. DeWeldt must have cronies on the commission getting payoffs."

"Jules, I can't just make up a story and claim it's a motive for someone to kill Jackie Whitney."

"You asked me if I was sick. No, DeWeldt hired someone to warn me about looking for reasonable doubt and punched me in the nose to prove he meant it."

For the first time, I saw Debbie smile. "No shit?"

"It's true. And I'm kind of shocked you believed me so quickly."

"What? You think this kind of intimidation is unheard of in Chicago? Someone with your bloodlines—"

"You know about—"

"Of course I know. You come from a family of political hacks and petty hoodlums starting with Great-Granddaddy Morris."

"Why, thank you, Deb, my cup runneth over."

Another laugh, only this time louder. "Oh, c'mon, have a sense of humor. What else do you know?"

"What about DNA tests on those skin shavings?"

"The state's attorney isn't interested."

"Then shouldn't we file a motion to have it done independently?"

"Who's going to pay for it?"

"Why doesn't the state want to do it?"

"You should know by now about shoddy police work and overzealous prosecutors. If they think they have a good enough case as it is, why jeopardize it with risking someone else's DNA being at the crime scene?"

"How much does it cost?"

"Around eighty-five hundred to get the job done right."

"I thought costs of DNA testing had come down."

"They have for a single test. But you also have to take into account multiple rounds of testing on different pieces of evidence."

I swore loudly. "The renter, Kessler, didn't sign the visitors' logbook at Jackie Whitney's building during the coroner's murder window. But I still want to see any CCTV video."

"I'll bet the cops didn't bother checking the surveillance video just like they often don't follow up on leads."

"But the CCTV is mentioned in the police report."

"Doesn't matter. It's not like crime dramas where detectives view dozens of hours of footage hoping to see a car pass by. Unless they're sure the camera was pointed at the crime scene, they might just lie and claim to have looked at surveillance video. And if the video was going to be marked as evidence, the building wouldn't have to keep the video on their server. See if your doorman knows how long they archive video."

"Jackie Whitney's friend Linda Napier was dating Kessler. She swears he was paying his rent but she can't say whether Kessler returned to the apartment after move-out day—during the time Jackie Whitney could've been murdered. She seemed nervous, as if afraid of incriminating someone."

"Incriminating herself or Kessler?"

"Maybe both. And I met Jackie Whitney's son. He's pretty much sold on Kate McCall's guilt."

"Okay, keep digging on that lawyer and Kessler and Linda Napier. Sounds like they might have something to tell us—in their own way. Leave the son alone unless something comes up."

"You're in a good mood," I said.

"You getting punched in the snout—that says this lawyer is scared. You might be onto some legitimate reasonable doubt. We can get Kate out of there."

"But who's the killer?"

For the third time, Debbie laughed, although this time it sounded forced. "Don't care. Doesn't matter. Someone else's job."

"What do you mean it doesn't matter? Doesn't justice matter? An innocent woman is dead."

I'd hit the proverbial nerve. "Hey!" Debbie snapped. "Don't lecture me about justice! Ricardo Martinez. Know him? That's what I thought. Doing life without parole for murder. I decided to look into it and found out the eyewitness was legally blind and not wearing his glasses. And I had a taped confession of the killer. It still took me two years to get this guy out of prison. That's justice, setting an innocent person free. That's my job. The other side's job is to put the right people behind bars without fucking it up. But they fuck it up a lot more than anyone realizes."

Debbie collected her belongings and walked out.

Chapter 15

Brookstone leaned against a parking meter with his arms crossed. "I take it back about having anything against you, Landau," Brookstone said. "This whole business with your old man. You shouldn't take it so personally. In fact, I even have fond memories of your old man, before he screwed me over. He was kind of a nice guy for a two-bit con."

"Punching someone in the nose is a little hard not to take personally, dontcha think?"

Brookstone nodded his head in an exaggerated display of penance. "You're right. And I'm sorry about that. I was just trying to get a message across. I really don't want to hurt you or nothing, but we know you was meeting with the public defender in there. That tells us you're still snooping. Okay, we give. How much do you want so you walk away?"

He asked the question without the least bit of cynicism or mockery. "I swear, corruption must become part of a cop's DNA as soon as they put on the badge."

Brookstone stared at me, shook his head. "Why you gotta make things so hard for yourself?"

"Why be a cop, Brookie, if you're just a criminal at heart?"

Tiny spasms resurfaced along the side of Brookstone's head. "I hear your old man's got that brain rot disease."

His words inspired loathing, but it was his grin that truly inflamed me. "An innocent person is in jail," I said.

"Pretty soon you'll be changing your old man's diapers, won't you?"

Like a fool, I stepped toward him. Men approached from both peripheries. I stepped back, bumping into another guy. I should've been scared but what could happen on a sidewalk crowded with pedestrians?

"Why don't you take a ride with us," Brookstone said. A sedan had pulled up.

"And if I say no? You're all gonna beat me up or shoot me right here in the middle of the sidewalk around all these people?"

Laughter from around me. "Just go for a ride," Brookstone said.

"I'm not going anywhere." When I moved to leave someone's knee drilled into my thigh then a fist bore into my lower back. I crumpled into supporting arms that escorted me to the waiting car.

Brookstone rode in front while I was in the back flanked by my new friends. Nobody spoke. Residual pain demanded most of my attention but I could tell we were headed west on Belmont. A few minutes later, we parked in front of a one-story nondescript building across from an enormous radio tower. My chaperones guided me inside where a bunch of small offices abutted a warehouse. Brookstone held the door open to one of the offices but didn't enter. Henry DeWeldt sat behind a desk, looking worried.

"I won't take up too much of your time," DeWeldt said. "How much do you want to quit working for your client?"

"How much are you paying Brookstone? You realize he moonlights for the Chicago Police Department, right?"

"That's all the more reason to take a gift, investigate something else, and get on with your life."

It hurt to laugh. "Okay, I see the light. And I'll sell myself real cheap. Just give me plenty of truth. Kate McCall didn't kill Jackie Whitney. I want to know who did."

DeWeldt studied me. "How do you know she didn't kill her?"

"She had no reason. Kate McCall never had it better than when she worked for Jackie Whitney."

DeWeldt didn't respond, just stared at me. "Why would you think I had anything to do with her death?"

"Just a wild hunch."

DeWeldt leaned back in his chair, studied his fingernails. I guessed paraffin manicure. "Tell me," he said. "This hunch of yours. Was it influenced by your probing for truth? Did you come across some information that's causing you to assume things?"

"Not that I'm aware of. Can you be more specific?"

"If you know how to get this information, returning it to me would make you a wealthy man."

"What does this information have to do with Jackie Whitney?"

"It has nothing to do with Jackie Whitney, which is why the information is of no use to you. I was simply Jackie's lawyer, in charge of her estate."

"Give me some credit, Henry. It didn't take much investigating to learn you and Jackie had evolved beyond simple lawyer-client rapport. Too much pillow talk, is that it? It that what you're afraid of?"

DeWeldt sighed then said, "Please understand something, Mr. Landau. I don't enjoy employing mobster-like intimidation tactics. I'm just a businessman protecting myself and everything I've worked for. These men keep telling me that only acts of violence will make someone understand how serious I am. And I'm supposed to emphasize that each painful incident will be more painful than the one preceding it. The thought of playing that kind of hardball makes me sick. But I'll try it out if I have to."

DeWeldt crossed his arms against his body, closed his eyes, then dropped his chin to his chest. He was either a fabulous actor or genuinely sincere.

I said, "All I understand is that you have a fondness for paying off people so you can screw the elderly out of their money, and that you were an unfaithful boyfriend."

DeWeldt lifted his head then barely glanced at one of the goons before a slug to the back rocked me, sent me to my knees. A moment later, two pairs of arms lifted me, dragged me to the door, then tossed me to the sidewalk.

A cab dropped me off at Penguin House. By the time I found my car and returned home, it was dark. The previous four hours had been excruciating. Punched in the nose and back, kneed in thigh. I felt strangely fortunate that the pain in my back came from the muscles above the kidney. If DeWeldt was really the murdering type, I reasoned, would I be alive no less worrying about pissing blood?

An hour later a knock on the door got me off the couch. I opened the door and was met by Tamar's lovely dark eyes. She had a small backpack slung over her shoulder.

"Surprise," she said. "Irina is proving to be a more reliable assistant manager every day. That means more time for me to get away."

"No phone call?" I said. "Just stop by and assume I'm available?"

Tamar sauntered past me, dropped her backpack on the recliner, then walked into the kitchen and said, "Do you call your jailhouse sweetie before visiting? What do you got to eat?"

I walked over to her, unable to hide my physical discomfort.

"What happened to you?" She put her arm around my waist.

"Don't overreact. I got roughed up a bit. Nothing serious, just deep bruises."

"Your nose is swollen!"

"A little swollen. My wounds are superficial, I swear. Just aches and pains, really."

Tamar's anxious eyes darted around my face. "I'd feel better if you'd tell me more."

"Let's sit and talk awhile." We walked back to the couch. Tamar leaned into me then put her arm around my shoulders. "This morning I told you about a dirty lawyer who possibly dated Jackie Whitney. His law firm seems to specialize in preying upon wealthy elderly. The firm's lawyers get caught, but the agency that checks up on unethical behavior shrugs it off. If Jackie Whitney had evidence linking the lawyer to corrupting disciplinary commissioners, his life and the lives of others could certainly be ruined. That's an obvious motivation for murder."

"But how do you prove it?"

"I can't, at least not yet. As it stands, it's useless for the trial."

"And if you get killed, you'll also be useless for the trial."

"If I was going to get killed, I'd be dead by now." I had tried to sound funny, but Tamar missed the humor. "On the coffee table," I said and pointed to a menu from Tasty Harmony, the restaurant down the block. "Pick something off the menu and order two of them. Tell them you're with me and they'll bring it to us."

Tamar did as directed and within a half hour two wraps with tortilla chips arrived. I asked what her overall feelings were about owning a bakery. She bit off a chunk of her wrap and thought about it. "I have a confession," she said. "Apart from the early hours, owning a successful bakery has started to give me great satisfaction—like I've never felt before."

The sincerity in her voice thrilled me. I was about to gush over how much she had accomplished when Tamar suddenly turned the conversation back to my investigation.

"Who else would benefit from Jackie Whitney's death?" Tamar said. "I mean, maybe you're too quick in assuming the lawyer saw his corruption exposure as worth killing over."

"Maybe. But why is he so hot for me to stop helping Kate McCall?"

"I bet there's a connection between Kate McCall and the lawyer."

"It's hard to picture, considering their different backgrounds. Although they did have the victim in common, so it's possible." Neither of us spoke for a few moments, then I said, "I guess there's really two questions that need to be answered. Who benefits from Jackie Whitney's death? And who benefits from Kate McCall taking the blame?"

Tamar nodded enthusiastically. I really wanted to talk more about her life, but she wouldn't cooperate. "Was Jackie Whitney into anything illegal? Like drugs?"

I thought of Linda Napier then said, "Not that I know of."

"You hesitated," Tamar said.

"Whitney had a friend who was a recovering drug addict. But it was the drugs that pushed them apart. At least that's what I've been told."

Tamar tried to suppress a yawn. The demands of her sleep cycle could not be ignored, nor should they be.

Chapter 16

The next morning I awoke with a vague memory of Tamar's travel alarm going off at three a.m., and then a kiss goodbye. My aching muscles made for a painful walk to the bathroom, but the hot shower was well worth it. When I shut off the water, my ringing phone compelled me to spatter water the length of the hall and into the living room, where I arrived too late to catch George's call.

"You rang," I said when George answered the phone.

"Yes, I just got a strange call from Linda. She wanted to take me to meet someone. She was acting real paranoid, saying she couldn't tell me who it was over the phone. I told her if it had something to do with Jackie she should tell you—and that I preferred not to know."

"Call her back and tell her you'll be right over—"

"I can't just leave the store! I'm the only one here."

"You're not leaving. It'll be me going over there. If she calls you back to see where you are, just apologize and say you have too many customers."

George agreed to cooperate but he wasn't happy. I dressed and headed back to East Lincoln Park.

Idling patiently on a narrow one-way alley, my growling stomach reminded me I hadn't eaten breakfast. Surveillance only lasted a few minutes before Linda's garage door began opening. Her white Lexus SUV backed into the alley and sped off, coming to a screeching halt at the sidewalk before peeling out as she turned on to Belden. I followed as she zigzagged her way to Clark and then headed south. When she continued on to North LaSalle I had an idea where she was going. When she turned onto East Oak, I knew exactly where she was going.

Linda parked in a loading zone in front of Jackie Whitney's building, turned on the flashing hazard lights, then ran to the revolving door and pushed her way through. I parked illegally at the end of the block, followed her into the building, then stood behind the cluster of fake trees. Linda stood close to Manny, leaning forward a bit, clearly violating his personal space. Manny stood his ground, casually grabbing glances in the lobby to see if anyone had taken notice of his activity. I studied his face trying to gauge emotions. He appeared not to mind Linda's company and even seemed somewhat concerned with whatever she was talking about. At one point Manny put his open hands together in front of his chest as if in prayer, and spoke slowly with a kind of helpless, beseeching expression. When he stopped talking, the two kept their eyes zeroed in on each other for several awkward moments before Manny walked away to the implied safety of the doorman's desk. Linda started talking again. Manny busied himself with some kind of paperwork. Finally, Linda turned and fast-walked her way back through the lobby. Manny put a cellphone to his ear. I ran through the lobby and got to my car in time to follow Linda back to the townhouse. To my surprise, she answered the door almost immediately. She looked groggy, like she'd been up all night drinking.

"What do you want?" she said.

"I couldn't help but notice your little discussion with the doorman."

"Yeah, so what? It's a free country."

"I also couldn't help but wonder what you were talking about."

"Why don't you ask the doorman?"

"Because I'm asking you."

"I don't have to answer any more of your questions, detective."

"Once again, I'm a private investigator, and you should answer my questions unless you want me to think you're hiding something."

Linda closed her eyes, took a deep breath, then walked into the living room, leaving me standing in the doorway. I interpreted this as an invitation to enter. We sat at opposite ends of the couch, as we had during our first visit.

I waited. She said, "After Josh—Dr. Kessler—ended our relationship, I was upset. Manny—the doorman—had always been very friendly to me. I confided in him. He was very sweet. We became friends, but he wanted more. I succumbed once, but that was it. I told him we could only be friends. But he kept calling me, stopping by at odd hours. Finally, I had to face him and tell him to leave me alone. That's all I was doing."

"Why did you call George before going to confront Manny?"

"George? George told you this? George is an old friend. I wanted a friend with me in case Manny reacted—you know, in a scary way."

Linda was a good storyteller, very breathy and dramatic in her delivery. I said, "It's hard for me to picture Manny getting angry, no less acting scary, in a lobby full of people."

"He's still a man."

"Your conversation had nothing to do with Jackie Whitney?"

Her face morphed into something angry and scary. "Oh, no you don't, you shit! I'm not going to let you get to me. I had nothing to do with Jackie's death."

"I'm not saying—"

"I wouldn't do anything to hurt her! You're just like the cops, treating everyone like a criminal. And I'm not going to let you twist my words around to try to incriminate me!"

I stood. Linda looked baffled. "I didn't mean to be rude," she said. "Sit down, please. Do you want a drink?"

I declined the offer then departed, sufficiently creeped out.

First stopping at El Desayuno Loco, I fudged my vegan principles and ordered an egg and potato burrito. Two consecutive bites later, my phone rang with Kalijero's name.

"I heard you got knocked around," Kalijero said.

I formulated the words "Hang on," then managed to swallow enough to say, "A little. Who told you?"

"Your mouth all swollen or something?"

"No, I'm eating. Who told you?"

"Brookstone called me. He wanted me to talk sense into you."

"So he called you? You're not dirty like him, why would he call you?"

"How the hell would you know if I was dirty or not? You don't know shit about me."

The bubble hissed loudly as it shrunk. I knew I held Kalijero in unrealistically high esteem, but hearing from his own mouth that, perhaps, he too could be bought, felt like another gut punch.

"So talk," I said.

"I know I can't talk sense into you, but you should know how much Brookstone hates public defenders. Especially the one you're working with."

"Did you tell him it's just a job? Jesus, can't a guy make a living?"

"Cops see public defenders as the criminal's associate. You know, the bleeding hearts blaming all crime on poverty; poor people can't help it; et cetera, et cetera."

"Innocent people going away for murder. How does he feel about that?"

"He doesn't give a shit. You know that. He's been working the Gold Coast murder from the start. He wants to look like a hero, the cop who put away the murderer of the beloved Chicagoan Jackie Whitney."

My call waiting chimed in with Linda's number. "I gotta go," I said and picked up the call. "Linda?"

"It's my meds," Linda said. "It affects my behavior sometimes. I didn't tell you everything about my conversation with Manny—the doorman."

"I'm all ears."

"Well, first, I think you should know that
Manny confided in me that Jackie talked down to
him. He said she ordered him up to her place to
hang pictures or help move furniture. And she
didn't tip him for the extra work! Other times she
told him he was ignorant and should go back to
school or get some training so that he could get a
real job. I told her she was being mean. She said it
was tough love and criticized me for wasting my
time with someone like Manny."

Perhaps it was her history of drug use that
prejudiced me to detect a phony manner in her
speech. Tears had brimmed forth from Manny's
eyes when I first spoke of Jackie Whitney's death.
"Manny had nothing bad to say about Jackie," I
said.

"He's too nice. And he was afraid of losing his
job if something he said got back to her. He won't
say anything bad about anybody."

"Back to your conversation with Manny. What
did you forget to tell me?"

"I forgot to tell you that he was upset about a
rumor that he had been hanging around Jackie's
apartment the night she came home."

"What does that mean? He was in Jackie's
private lobby? Actually in her apartment? How
would someone know unless they were there too?"

Linda's breathing was audible. "I—I don't
know. He didn't say any more. Maybe someone was
on the elevator and saw him get on or off."

"Did he say he knew the source of the rumor? Was he angry?"

"He didn't tell me who started it but he was worried sick someone might tell the police."

"People intentionally start rumors because they're scared to come forward. They don't want to explain how they knew what they knew."

"Are you going to tell the police about the rumor? I'm sure they'll believe you."

"Not unless someone comes forward as a witness."

"But as you said, the witness would be incriminating themselves."

That's not what I said, but Linda knew how to read between the lines.

I recalled Manny telling me he didn't know any of Jackie Whitney's friends. He apparently knew Linda Napier quite well. Maybe he thought I meant friends from the building. Regardless, I got the feeling Manny wasn't surprised to see me. "I saw you standing by the trees," he said.

"Thanks for not blowing my cover. You mind telling me what Linda was talking to you about?"

Manny seemed a touch bothered. "Gosh, is she in some kind of trouble?"

"I'm not sure. I hope not."

"Well, lately she's been coming up with foolish theories about Jackie. She likes to run them by me. I tell her she's letting her mind get away from her, then she starts flirting and I have to carefully ease her away.”

“What was Linda’s wild theory this time?”

“Actually,” he said, “today was a little different. She wanted to tell me about a silly rumor.” Manny’s demeanor had grown uncharacteristically solemn.

“She was telling you about a rumor?” I said. “Would you mind telling me about the rumor?”

Manny hesitated. “She said she’d heard that Dr. Kessler had a duplicate key to Jackie’s apartment and that he was in the area around the time the murder took place.”

“Did she tell you where she heard this?”

“I didn’t ask. I suggested she tell the police and excused myself.”

“She said you two were in a relationship.”

Manny groaned. “That poor girl. She wanted to be in a relationship. She was heartsick over Dr. Kessler breaking up with her. I gave her some encouraging words but she misinterpreted my intentions. I reminded her that I’m happily married with two children, Mr. Landau. I think Linda is very lonely.”

“She claims you crossed that line with her— once.”

Manny made a fist and pretended to bite it. “Oh, Lord! Please tell me you’re kidding. She doesn't think clearly. Drugs are involved, I'm afraid, and she's in denial that she has a problem."

"I suspected. What about Jackie?"

Manny looked confused. "You mean drugs? Oh, no, I don't believe that. It was Linda's continued drug use that pushed Jackie away from her."

"Jackie told you this?"

"Actually, Linda told me." My brain churned on all the complications drug addicts brought with them. Manny said, "I think I know what you're going to say, Mr. Landau. Go ahead."

"Jackie having money and her close friend having a drug problem—"

"I wondered too. Was Linda angry because Jackie cut her off financially? Maybe she came here to beg for money and lost her temper?"

"You never mentioned this before."

"Oh, I'm sorry. It was just a thought. Pure guesswork on my part. I had nothing concrete. Who am I to talk about others? But I see your point now. I should've said something."

"Forget it." I looked around the lobby and spotted a couple of CCTV cameras. "Do you know how the surveillance camera system works?"

"I know the server is in the IT room and that we have a couple of screens under the desktop, and each day is archived. That's it."

"Did the cops go to the IT room?"

"I don't know. Let me see if the security manager is home."

Manny walked to a small corridor behind his desk where the maintenance elevators and the utility rooms were located. He knocked on a door. Just as he started walking away, the door opened. He spoke to an unseen person for a while then waved me over and introduced Howard, a gray-haired, ponytailed man with a bushy mustache hanging over his lip. He had a naturally distrustful expression, which I guess was what one wanted in a security manager. We shook hands.

I said, "Did the police look at any of the CCTV footage from May sixteenth and seventeenth?"

"Nope," Howard said without hesitating.

"Did they even inquire about CCTV video?"

Howard glanced at Manny. "They mentioned it to Manny, but not to me."

"How long is each day kept archived?"

"Thirty days."

We were approaching the three-week point for May 16. "Would you let me look at the video from the sixteenth and seventeenth?"

"I'd have to ask my boss. What's this all about?"

"I'm investigating a murder that occurred in this building."

Howard glanced at Manny again. "It's true," Manny said. "I can vouch for him."

"You guys still throw money around when you want something done? Like in the movies?"

From my wallet I produced three fifties. "You mean like this?"

I tried handing the money over. He glanced at it then said, "Don't assume CCTV will get your man."

"Why?"

"The building uses wide angle lenses. They cover the whole lobby but the resolution may not be good enough for the courtroom. You still want it?"

Disappointing news. "Might as well."

Howard accepted the money then took out a small pad of paper and began writing. "I'm sure my boss wouldn't mind if you watched a little TV," he said.

"You have to burn the video on a DVD or something?" I said.

"Good God, son," he said, looking at me with utter disbelief. "You're still in the Dark Ages. Digital video security is all Internet protocol." He handed me a piece of paper. "As long as you have the proper ID and password—in this case mine— you'll have access to all the archives. After a week, I'm changing my password."

"A week? I doubt I'll need that long."

"No? Well, maybe you can stare all day at a television with nothing going on. My mind would start to wander. At some point I'd realize that I had no idea if I saw anything or not."

"Thanks for the warning," I said. "One more question. Do the service elevators give you access to an outside door?"

"'Course they do."

Chapter 17

Back home sitting on my couch, I leaned over the coffee table and typed Howard's web address into my laptop. The coroner's report estimated that Jackie Whitney may have been dead since May 16, so I began looking at video that morning, even though she didn't return from Palm Springs until the early evening. A split screen represented two cameras, one focusing on the front of the lobby toward the entranceway, the other directed toward the back that included the doorman's desk and elevators. I remembered Manny explaining how quickly doormen learned to remember faces, and assumed the people they simply tipped their hats to or nodded at were residents or their guests. Howard was correct on both the resolution issue and the lack of mental stimulation. Observations would have to be done in small allotments in order to ensure I knew what I didn't see. I gave it an hour, stopped, wrote down the time stamp, then started scratching Punim under the chin.

The public-defender-hating Detective Brookstone concerned me. I drove to Debbie's office without calling first. She was still in court, but I was invited to wait in her office. Stacks of books piled high on top of already full bookshelves. Numerous articles about prisoners exonerated from life sentences or death row filled bulletin boards. Amidst the clutter of her desk sat a glass triangle trophy, the Champion of Justice Award from the National Association of Criminal Defense Lawyers.

As I read through articles, Debbie walked in with an armful of files. She showed no surprise or curiosity at my presence.

"Detective Brookstone," I said.

"Asshole," Debbie said, piling the folders on the credenza before sitting down behind her desk.

"He's on the Kate McCall case. He's the guy that punched me in the nose."

Debbie eyed my nose. "He hates my guts," she said.

I moved some books off the guest chair and sat. "Brookstone was waiting for me outside Penguin House yesterday," I said. "They escorted me to meet DeWeldt in some West Belmont office. He offered to pay me off."

Debbie appeared deep in thought. I thought she nodded her head before saying, "Okay, so DeWeldt's paying Brookstone to keep tabs on you. Me, they know. They don't scare me. You, they want to intimidate. But just because DeWeldt's freaking out about something doesn't mean I'm going to drag him into Kate McCall's defense, unless there's some seriously compelling reason."

"There are rumors of other people hanging around Jackie Whitney's apartment during the time period she was killed and that someone had a duplicate key."

This irritated Debbie. "Rumors. I don't want to hear it."

"And you were right, the cops did not look at the surveillance video."

"See? You learned something."

"But what could DeWeldt possibly have to do with Jackie Whitney's murder? That's what I need to find out."

Debbie swore loudly under her breath. "Jules, you need to focus on Kate McCall's innocence. Otherwise, you're wasting my time."

"But if he's mixed up—"

"This isn't about DeWeldt. It's about whether Kate McCall picked up a hammer and bashed in Jackie Whitney's skull. That's it. That's all that matters. Got it? Once and for all?"

I rested my forehead in the palm of my hand knowing full well she'd be staring at me when I looked up. Humor me, I was about to say when an unknown caller interrupted.

"Landau Investigations."

"Come to Linda Napier's house for another visit," a male voice said.

"Who is this?"

"Just go to her house. She has more to tell you." The call dropped.

Debbie was leaning back in her chair, arms crossed against her chest. "Do we understand each other?" she said in that most condescending of tones.

I stood and said, "Understand this, Debbie," then stopped myself, stuffed the urge to say Go fuck yourself, and just walked away.

I returned home and spent more time reviewing the CCTV video. The substandard resolution prevented me from swearing under oath anyone was Kessler, but I did identify Jackie Whitney's return, unmistakable if only for the numerous suitcases Lenny hauled into the lobby. My phone rang again with the same unknown number.

"You're missing all the fun," the male voice said. "C'mon down to Linda's place. It's going to get crowded soon."

"Who the hell is this?" I said, but the caller hung up.

Two police cars, a police van, and an ambulance were parked outside Linda's townhouse. The door was slightly ajar. I pushed it open with the toe of my shoe and the grisly scene opened before me. On the couch, slumped on her side, Linda Napier lay with a gaping wound on the top of her head. Her hair was a dark, viscous mess contrasting the red liquid soaked into the white couch. The room crawled with uniformed police, forensic investigators, a photographer, and a couple of detectives, one of whom was Brookstone.

"Hello, private investigator," Brookstone said. "That was me on the phone disguising my voice. Not bad, huh? You want to explain your whereabouts the last couple of hours?"

"No."

"You may want to reconsider. I've got a pretty reliable source who tells me you was here not too long ago."

I noticed Linda Napier's cellphone on the coffee table. "The cellphone," I said. "You called the last numbers Linda had logged on her phone. One of them was George Mason. He told you that I was going to Linda Napier's house."

"Excellent work! You're a crackerjack PI, no doubt about it. Kalijero gave me your phone number, by the way, which is also in the victim's call log."

"Did you tell George Mason that Linda Napier was dead?"

"Of course."

The floor rolled on a nausea wave. Empathy did not serve a private investigator.

"What's the matter, Landau? You just figure out you're in an unpleasant business?"

His grin squeaked like Styrofoam. "I get it. As a joke, you're treating me like a suspect."

"A joke? I don't know. You got anything on that doctor you want to share?"

"I want to take a closer look at the victim."

"Sure. But mind the yellow tape. And I don't have to tell you I'm watching your every move."

Linda was slouched over on her side in the same position I imagined Jackie Whitney lay before her body was moved. No sign of struggle. I stepped around the couch to get a better view of Linda's head. That the bloody mess itself didn't affect me was testament to how callous I'd become. The wound resembled the description the coroner gave of Jackie Whitney's head. A forensic officer used tweezers to put bits of something into a plastic bag. I looked closer and saw what appeared to be dead skin shavings similar to the ones I saw in the photos from Jackie Whitney's apartment. Also in the bag were tiny tufts of black fur.

"DNA, Brookstone," I said. "Test the DNA on these skin shavings. They were documented at Whitney's murder scene too."

"Don't order me around, Landau. Tell the state's attorney."

"You find the weapon?"

"Nope."

"Looks a lot like Jackie Whitney's head."

Brookstone motioned for me to step over to him. I obeyed. "You're right. What do you know about that doctor?"

"Kate McCall hated him."

"Sure, now that she got caught, she hates him. They both knew the victim and both had access to the victim's apartment."

"Let me tell you about a lawyer named Henry DeWeldt. I think you're acquainted. He dated Jackie Whitney. She may have had damning information on him."

"Napier was a junkie. The doctor's number was on her phone. Maybe they was transacting drugs for sex."

"Did you hear what I said about DeWeldt?"

Brookstone laughed. "What were you doing here earlier today?"

"Can you prove I was here, Detective Brookstone?"

"Well, there is that surveillance camera on the telephone pole out front. So if you're lying, that's just going to make you look worse."

You should've looked for that! I heard Frownie moan. "I asked her a few questions, like a private investigator does."

"What time did you get here?"

"I drove here around nine or nine-fifteen then followed Linda to Jackie Whitney's building. I watched her talk to the doorman then followed her back here. It was probably around ten. We chatted for fifteen minutes then I left. That was the last I saw of her, although she called me one more time.

That was probably around ten-thirty, which you already know from her cellphone log.”

“Maybe you came back and killed her after she called you.”

“You’re full of shit.”

“The killer used the victim’s phone to dial 911 at 11:06.”

“Check your damn surveillance camera. You’ll see I came and left long before 11:06 and that I didn’t return. And why would the killer dial 911? Maybe it was the victim who dialed.”

“Don’t worry, we’ll be looking at the surveillance camera. You just pray someone else besides you shows up on it. Where did you go after you left her house?”

“To see the doorman and find out what they talked about.”

“And?”

“The doorman claims Linda Napier was in love with him, wouldn’t leave him alone, that kind of thing. He also made a call as soon as she left.”

Brookstone nodded. “The doorman,” he said to himself, staring at the ground. “Manny Alvarez. He may have been the last person to see Linda Napier alive. You say he made a call right after she left. Maybe he called someone to kill Linda Napier?”

“No, I ordered the hit on Linda Napier.”

“Maybe Alvarez called the doctor.”

"No, damn it. I killed her."

Brookstone was too impressed with his own genius to hear me. "Have you made any kind of connection between Alvarez and McCall?"

"Just a doorman/visitor thing. Anyway, you interviewed him, right?"

Brookstone stared at me thoughtfully. "You're right, Landau, I did. Yeah, I should've caught on that Alvarez could've been the last person to see Jackie Whitney alive. But you don't seem too hot on the doorman. Why not?"

"He's not my type."

"Asshole. You're so damn smart. Remind me when McCall found the body?"

"May nineteenth."

Brookstone started again with the nodding. "Oh, yeah, that's right. You know, we should get some probable cause on Alvarez to subpoena his phone records."

"Just make that shit up like you usually do."

"Fuck you! We know the doctor hated Jackie Whitney. Alvarez may have hated her too."

"Maybe."

"Do you believe it would've taken two people to move Jackie Whitney's body to the closet shelf?"

"Kate McCall didn't move anyone anywhere."

"And I say the person who killed Linda Napier is the same person who helped Kate McCall move Jackie Whitney's body."

"No, it's the same person who killed Whitney."

"Did you see all that cash from McCall's apartment? That's just the cash we found. We don't know how much was in that safe-deposit box to begin with."

"She's a thief. I'll give you that. What about your employer DeWeldt? What if I show you evidence?"

"Whatever you find isn't gonna convince anyone to do anything."

"You'll make sure of that."

"You flatter me, Landau. We can be friends, you know. Tell me what you and that public-defender bull dyke are doing. Lots of reasonable doubt?"

"You'll find out at the trial, won't you?"

"There's not going to be a trial—"

"Don't be so sure. You probably said the same thing when that bartender filed a lawsuit."

Brookstone didn't like that comment. "Kalijero tried telling me you weren't such a bad guy. But you're a prick, just like your old man." I turned to leave. "Where're you going?" I ignored him. Brookstone shouted, "I said where are you going?"

I shouted back, "You've got nothing to hold me on, Brookstone. So you'll have to excuse me while I go back to doing your job."

I walked away with my gut telling me Brookstone might be partially correct. Whoever killed Linda Napier also killed Jackie Whitney. Maybe two people were involved in both murders, but I was pretty damn sure neither person was Kate McCall. Once back in the alley, I examined every telephone pole within one hundred yards of Linda Napier's front door. I saw nothing resembling a surveillance camera. Eighty-five hundred bucks for DNA tests would be money well spent. Hopefully, Kate McCall felt the same way.

Chapter 18

There wasn't a private room available so Kate McCall and I were stuck talking to each other through Plexiglas. "You have eighty-five hundred bucks lying around?" I said. The question made her uncomfortable.

"You want more money?"

"For DNA testing. Flakes of skin were found in Jackie Whitney's apartment. Could they be yours?"

"I don't rightly know. I never thought nothin' of my skin flakin'."

"Dry skin does that."

"Lord, no. My skin is oily as hell."

"Okay, then. If someone else's DNA shows up, that means someone else was at the crime scene.

That means you got a good chance of walking free." McCall mulled over my words. Something was bugging her. "Kate," I said. "I don't care if you've got a pile of cash somewhere. But for God's sake, use it to get yourself out of a murder charge."

"Go'n talk to Mr. Chao at Youji Lu Grocer. Tell him how much."

"Mr. Chao's got your money?"

"Have friends you trust and spread your cash around. I learnt that as a child."

"I met Mr. Chao yesterday. Why would he trust me with your money?"

"He came to visit. I told him to trust you."

"Are you sure you trust Mr. Chao? He seemed wishy-washy on your innocence."

Kate nodded and frowned. "He's one of them Chinamen that's always talkin' in, uh, what's that word. Not jokes—"

"Riddles?"

"Yes! Riddles. Talkin' to him's like herdin' cats. You can't get no straight goddamn answer out of his mouth sometimes. But we get along good. He's used to hidin' valuables from Communists."

Mr. Chao stood at the entrance of his grocery offering free samples of an exotic white pulpy fruit. When he saw me he smiled broadly and bowed. The fruit had a sweet refreshing taste. "Good source for potassium and copper," Mr. Chao said.

I asked if we could speak privately. He gave his sample dish to an employee then motioned for me to follow him. We stopped at the back of the store in front of a beaded curtain I guessed was his office. "How I can help?"

"I need eighty-five hundred dollars for Kate McCall."

Mr. Chao stared at me, his eyes bouncing around my face. He nodded then said, "Wait here," before disappearing behind the curtain. He returned a few minutes later with a manila envelope. I couldn't resist asking him a few questions.

"Do you know where Kate got this money?"

"It is my money."

"What do you mean?"

"Kate give me money."

"You don't care where she got the money?"

"Money is energy. We call it qi. Kate attract qi energy flow and direct to me."

"What if the money was stolen qi? Isn't that bad energy?"

"Energy is not good or bad. Energy is energy. You help Kate with money?"

"DNA testing."

Mr. Chao gave me his broadest smile yet. "DNA is truth. Money was meant to be. Money help bring justice."

I thanked Mr. Chao then called Debbie. "I have the money for DNA testing," I said to her answering service. "Go ahead and file a motion for an order to allow testing by an expert." I assumed she knew the right expert.

That evening I stayed up late watching half-hour increments of figures entering and exiting Jackie Whitney's building. If I recognized Kessler, I could place him in the building during the window of time that Jackie Whitney was murdered. During my breaks, I thought about DeWeldt. What was he afraid of and how was this fear related to Jackie Whitney? Corruption and Chicago followed each other like conjoined twins. For the wealthy, laws could be changed, judges could be bought. Jackie Whitney had money and liked using it to control people. Kessler was also well off. I jumped to my conversation with Lucille, when she told me Jackie had suggested developing Kessler as a possible donor. Perhaps Jackie suggested the same cultivation for Henry DeWeldt?

Henry DeWeldt was Furry BFF's Francis of Assisi Champion, a designation that positioned his photo at the top of the list honoring the most generous benefactors. Next came Furry BFF's patron saint, Jackie Whitney. A treasure like Henry DeWeldt had to have a connection to Lucille Mackenzie, and she was only too happy to tell me about it.

"Oh, Henry's a doll!" Lucille said with a dreamy, reminiscent look. She rolled her chair back then crossed her legs. The plunging neckline of her blouse and tight knee-length skirt once again struck me for its sharp contrast to what everyone else wore. "I met him through Jackie. I told her she should get a finder's fee because he was such an easy sell. He's on the board and our single largest donor—and he's very handsome."

"What was your impression of their relationship?"

"Well, he was at least fifteen years older so I wasn't sure about it. But he's rich and still very attractive so Jackie probably found him hard to resist. And they seemed to get along so well just playing the role of Chicago royalty that I thought maybe they had a chance."

"But the relationship changed?"

Lucille shifted in her seat. "Well, things changed. They stayed friends, or at least that's how it looked to me."

"What happened?"

"Jackie didn't want to talk about it. Anyway, that's really none of our business, is it?"

"I'm investigating a murder. The victim's relationships are very much my business."

Lucille looked away then shifted in her chair again. "I understand what you're saying. It's just that I take privacy very seriously."

"What about you? Did you and Henry hit it off?"

"Oh, yes, we had a lot in common. As you know, my background is in estate planning and I combine this expertise with facilitating the shelter's long-term fundraising goals."

"You try to persuade people to leave something behind for the shelter after they die."

"Or while they're still alive. Since Henry is an estate-planning attorney and an animal lover, he recognizes how important it is for the shelter to secure sources of funding well into the future."

"Did Jackie and Henry both create their own future sources of funding for Furry BFF?"

A cold breeze blew. "Who told you that?"

"Nobody told me anything. Their names—"

"Nobody has the right to talk about someone's private financial agreements. Yes, we are a nonprofit charity, Mr. Landau. But that doesn't mean who gives what or how they give it is part of the public record. It isn't."

"Jackie Whitney's picture on the wall over the heading 'patron saint' isn't exactly a symbol of modesty."

Lucille looked at her watch. "Yes, well, many want the world to know how important they are and part of my job is to accommodate their wishes. But nobody has the right to discuss financial details."

"I see. Back to Henry and Jackie—"

"Wait just a second, please. Are you suggesting Henry DeWeldt had something to do with Jackie's death?"

"Are you aware of the complaints filed against his law firm for allegedly ripping off wealthy elderly folks?"

"I don't believe that."

"I've been threatened in DeWeldt's name to not find evidence exonerating Kate McCall."

"You don't think she did it?"

"I've been punched in the nose, thigh, and back. How do you feel about that?"

"That's terrible. But you have to understand that this shelter is my life. My raison d'être. I've explained how the future must be secured now with trusts and such. But these trusts are not irrevocable. They can be changed at any time."

"Do you think Jackie had information linking DeWeldt with illegal activity?"

"Oh, my God! I don't believe my ears. You're really saying Henry DeWeldt is the killer, aren't you?"

"Kate McCall may have been stealing from Jackie, but she didn't kill her."

"So you've decided Henry DeWeldt did it."

"I've decided he's a bad man, Lucille. He rips off old people and pays off others to hide it."

"And how do you really know this?"

"Eighty-three complaints filed with the disciplinary commission. Zero convictions. You can call it my working theory."

"A theory! You'd ruin a man's life over a theory?"

"If Jackie knew what he was up to, if she had information that could ruin Henry DeWeldt's life, don't you think that's a motivation to kill? Couldn't that be his motivation to see Kate McCall take the rap?"

"You don't know what you're talking about and I want you to leave my office." Lucille uncrossed her legs then rolled her chair up to her desk and began looking over some papers.

I waited, hoping she would hear the vitriol in her voice and feel guilty, but soon grasped that our meeting was indeed over.

Chapter 19

I stood on the sidewalk in front of Furry BFF writing down a few notes. Debbie's name appeared on my phone.

"How are you and Detective Brookstone getting along?" Debbie said over the phone.

"Linda Napier is dead," I said.

"I know. The cops are going to pick up Kessler for questioning."

"You almost sound happy."

"I can't control events, Jules. But it happened and it could help our case if we argue the same person killed Jackie Whitney." I had no response. Debbie said, "And don't tell me where you got the money for DNA testing. I don't want to know. Okay, I'll get the ball rolling on the motion to get those skin flakes—or whatever they are—tested."

"More of the same was found at Linda Napier's townhouse. Tufts of black fur too. It could link the two murders to the same person. I also got access to the surveillance video. Hopefully I can find out once and for all if Kessler returned to the building during the window of time Jackie Whitney was murdered."

"The state's attorney is going to offer Kate McCall a plea. Twenty years in exchange for naming her accomplice, and her cooperation in getting a conviction."

"McCall didn't kill anybody."

"Even if she did, that's a crappy deal. I'm countering with no prison time for full cooperation."

"You think Kate McCall is really protecting someone?"

"As long as she cooperates, who cares?"

"From the start, McCall insisted Kessler was the killer. But she doesn't really know anything. Somebody is holding information over DeWeldt's head. If it wasn't Jackie Whitney, who?"

"You're the investigator, Jules. You tell me. In the meantime, follow through to see if Kessler is on that CCTV video or not. And without solid proof on DeWeldt, I don't want to even hear his name."

I'm the investigator. After this job ended, I hoped I would never hear the name Debbie Lopez again.

Even with the help of caffeine, monitoring the CCTV video was excruciating. Now it only took twenty minutes until stupefaction set in. But I persevered, took lots of breaks, wrote down lots of time stamps. Little by little, I fast-forwarded through the evening of the sixteenth, stopping when people appeared, fairly confident I could pick out Dr. Joshua Kessler. As I moved into the wee hours, time moved along rapidly with little stopping since the average age of the building's tenants was well over fifty. Gradually, the building began waking up to the morning of the seventeenth. It occurred to me I had not spoken to Tamar since she kissed me goodbye the morning before last.

"Is this a bad time?" I said, knowing full well Tamar was dealing with the late breakfast–early lunch crowd.

"You know it is, goof."

"I'm sorry, I felt bad for not calling you since I saw you last."

"Well, you can redeem yourself by inviting me over tonight. I'm cooking. Make sure the door isn't attached. My arms will be full."

"Attached?" I said. "You mean locked?"

"Hey, be nice. I'm an immigrant, remember. English wasn't my first language. I gotta run."

Through the oval glass I saw Arthur sitting at the kitchen table, reading the newspaper. I knocked just hard enough to get his attention.

"Hey, how are you, Julie?" Arthur said after he opened the door.

"How's Dad?"

Arthur shook his head. "He's all over the place. He's not seeing the snakes anymore but he's convinced they were there—and don't even think about saying he's wrong. This morning he didn't recognize me. He said, 'Who the hell are you?' I said, 'It's me, Arthur, your caretaker.' He just stared at me then walked away."

Dad sat in his swivel-rocker-recliner watching a Rockford Files rerun. I couldn't remember the last time I hadn't seen him in that chair watching television. "Hi, Dad."

He peered at me, his eyebrows crimped tightly together. "You know that son of a bitch is telling me the snakes aren't real. He talks to me like I'm loony as a bin."

It took a moment but I realized what he meant. "You mean Arthur thinks you belong in the loony bin?"

Why did I say that? I thought, and wished I could push a rewind button. Then a smile crept over Dad's mouth. "Yeah, that's what I mean."

His grin came with a familiar twinkle in his eyes, followed by all the warm smile lines I had known for so many years. I said, "Did you really not recognize Arthur this morning?"

Dad considered my question. "He was wearing a wig! And a stupid-looking hat!"

I glanced out the door. Arthur sat at the kitchen table, shaking his head. I said, "I'll talk to him about messing with you like that."

"I wish you would. So what's new with you, Julie?"

His question sounded ridiculously natural. I couldn't help but respond in the way he would've expected.

"Remember I told you I'm helping the public defender assigned to the woman accused of killing Jackie Whitney?"

"You never told me that," he said. "So who did it, smart guy?"

"I'm not sure. Reasonable doubt is her lawyer's strategy."

"'Course it is. That's the defense's job. Who're you looking at?"

"Jackie Whitney rented out her place while she vacationed in Palm Springs. She got into a dispute with the renter over money. The renter insists he moved out before she returned. I'm checking surveillance video to see if he's lying about not returning to the building."

Dad nodded his approval. "Sounds right."

"Then there's the boyfriend. An older man who's a powerful corporate lawyer."

"Money's the motive, you know."

"Probably."

"Don't give me this probably shit. It's money. Rich old man, young broad. It's money."

"The young broad was rich. She didn't need this guy's money."

Dad glanced at the television a moment, then turned back to me. "Big-shot lawyers got big-shot egos. Losing reputation means losing power. No power, no money."

"Yeah, well, I think he's scared of information the victim had."

"Jules, what the hell was their relationship really about? You gotta ask that question. And after you do, then you go find the answer."

That Dad could still draw out a foggy kind of wisdom gave me hope. Then the door slammed shut. "But Jesus Christ, what're we going to do about those damn snakes?"

"I thought they were gone."

"What if they come back? They could come back, you know! Now get away from me and take that fat guy with you. I don't need this shit."

I let Dad get back to watching The Rockford Files.

I too saw snakes. They were all over the city wearing expensive suits. What was Jackie Whitney and Henry DeWeldt's relationship about? A damn good question.

From the parkway in front of Dad's building, I called Lucille Mackenzie expecting her to hang up on me, but I was wrong.

"Tell me again how Jackie and Henry DeWeldt met?"

"Uh, I introduced them."

"For some reason I thought Jackie introduced you to DeWeldt, as a potential big-money fish to catch."

Silence. "That's not what I said."

It is what she said. "Was it a blind date?"

"Oh, no, Jackie wanted information on her, um, financial planning, for her son. Phillip's all she has, after all, and she wanted peace of mind, should something happen to her."

"So they met to talk business and hit it off?"

"Exactly."

Debbie's name beeped on my call waiting. I thanked Lucille. "Jules Landau speaking."

"Kessler's been teaching all day," Debbie said. "They've got nothing to hold him on. How's the video surveillance coming?"

"I haven't seen anything suspicious yet."

"The plea deal fell through. Kate McCall still insists Kessler is Whitney's killer."

"Unless I can find him in a video going back to her apartment, I think he's clear."

"Let me know," she said then hung up.

The door hit the wall hard enough to bounce halfway back. "Oops, sorry," Tamar said. She walked to the kitchen holding two full bags of groceries. Food preparation was a serious business. In no time, the counter was covered with dough, vegetables, potatoes, walnuts, beans, and spices I'd never heard of.

"Watch and learn," Tamar said as she filled a pot of water. "First, I take these dumpling-like things and boil them. . . ."

It would've been a perfect setup for a cooking show, although I paid more attention to her backside moving under cropped terry cloth sweatpants than the secrets to making a great walnut paste.

"So what's new since I last saw you?" Tamar said while we waited for the food to cook. "Any more dead bodies?"

"Yes, actually."

When a gag line didn't follow she said, "You're serious?"

"One of Jackie Whitney's old friends was beaten to death in the same manner as Jackie."

Tamar stared at me. "We've got a serial killer in our midst?"

"Somebody wanted to shut her up. She knew more than she was letting on and she was unstable. At least that's my impression."

"But who? The same killer?"

"Or the same killer's accomplice if two people were in on Jackie Whitney's murder—although you're not supposed to know that."

Neither of us spoke. Then Tamar said, "So what else is new?"

I laughed at her unintentional irony. "Bad news first. My father's in the early stages of dementia."

"I'm so sorry."

"The good news. Soon he'll be a perfect match for your aunt."

The joke might've been a mistake. Then I noticed Tamar struggling to keep a smile from creeping over her face. I laughed, Tamar giggled, game over. Our mirth grew into hysterical crescendos of glee. Images of Dad's reaction after being introduced to Tamar's aunt sustained my laughter for a good five minutes which only fed Tamar's hilarity. That is, until she remembered food was cooking and rushed to the kitchen.

After dinner we drank tea in the living room where my laptop was still opened to the website that stored the surveillance video. I explained that I was trying to establish whether a suspect had returned to the victim's building.

"What're you writing down?" Tamar asked.

"Those are the start and stop time stamps—for when I take breaks from watching."

Tamar studied the piece of paper as if there was something interesting about it. "Wow, you really watched for eight hours straight? I didn't realize you had such a strong work ethic," she said with a teasing smile.

"What?"

"According to what you wrote . . . or else you have an eight-hour gap."

"That's insane. At most, I watch an hour then quit for a while." I took the piece of paper and she pointed to the start time of 23:15:41 on Saturday evening with an end time of 07:51:26 Sunday morning. "Holy shit," I said. "Someone shut off the surveillance system then turned it back on again. Kessler could've snuck in and out without being recorded."

"Who's Kessler?"

"The guy who was renting from Jackie Whitney. He paid in cash and they got into a dispute over allegedly unpaid rent. He said he moved out of the apartment by the time Jackie Whitney came back from Palm Springs, and never returned."

"Who has access to the surveillance system?"

"I don't know. I wonder if the guy working the graveyard shift turned it off by accident. He's in his eighties."

"You know, the city has video cameras all over. Check out the lampposts and trees and telephone poles. Cameras are everywhere."

I stared at Tamar. "There could be footage somewhere of Kessler entering and leaving the building."

We talked awhile longer until her repeated yawns and heavy eyelids once again demanded the baker's timetable be honored.

Chapter 20

As expected, I woke up with only the memory of a beautiful woman having shared my bed.

"What can you tell me about the city's video surveillance program?" I asked Kalijero over the phone.

"Just look around. They're watching. It's called Operation Virtual Shield. Everything's computerized and politicized. Not just high crime areas. If you're rich enough, you can get cameras on your street so you'll feel safer."

"That's what I wanted to hear. How can I look at footage?"

"It's controlled by the Office of Emergency Management and Communications. I wouldn't bother. They don't respond quickly to inquiries.

And they're sure as hell not going to trust a private eye."

"But this has to do with a murder case."

"Then get the state's attorney to request the video."

I couldn't help but sigh loudly. The thought of talking the state into obtaining video they could easily say wasn't relevant hurt my brain. The ACLU had been on the city's case about not tracking individuals unless the evidence was compelling. I was just looking for probable cause, after all.

"I got another dead body," I said.

"I heard the chatter on the police radio. That's your stiff?"

"Old friend of Jackie Whitney's. On your police radio? Is that what retired cops do? Sit around listening to the police radio?"

"Shut up. It's background noise. Keeps me company."

"Well, since you're keeping score at home, how about some insight? The dead woman, Linda Napier, was killed the same way as Jackie Whitney. And she was dating the renter, a Dr. Kessler, the guy I'm trying to find on surveillance video. The police already questioned Kessler and let him go. But Brookstone still has a hard-on for him."

"Have you questioned Kessler about the new corpse?"

"I want to see the surveillance video first."

"Why? Just tell him you saw him in it. See if he'll call your bluff. You'll know right away if the guy is full of shit or not."

I knew there was a good reason to keep a guy like Kalijero interested in police work. He couldn't help but school a guy like me when I needed to learn something that, in retrospect, was ridiculously simple.

The door to Dr. Kessler's office was partly open. I knocked and stepped inside. He sat at his desk leaning on his elbows, head cradled in his hands.

"Sorry to bother you—"

Kessler looked up. "I already spoke to the cops! What do you want from me?"

"The truth."

"I gave them the truth. I don't know anything about what happened to Linda."

"What about Jackie?"

"I told you what I know about Jackie. Oh, my God. I can't believe this." The doctor returned his head to his hands. I watched him stew in his own misery juice for a solid minute before he looked up again and said, "You're still here. I thought maybe this was all a bad dream."

"Did you know Chicago is the most camera-surveilled city in the country? Everywhere you go there are cameras."

"Why are you telling me this?"

"All those rich folks on East Lake Shore Drive? They like being watched. It makes them feel safe. It didn't help Jackie, but it might help us catch her killer."

Kessler looked sick. "Just say what you mean already."

"I'm going to ask you a question and I want you to think very carefully about how you're going to answer it. Did you go to Jackie Whitney's apartment between eleven p.m. on Saturday, May sixteenth and five-thirty a.m. Sunday, May seventeenth?"

He licked his lips, swallowed hard. "You mean a camera saw someone who looked like me in the lobby?" he said.

I leaned forward. "I'm saying there are cameras outside the building, trained on the entrance."

His dread was palpable. "Close the door, please," he said.

I did as told. When I turned around Kessler was standing in front of his desk. "I swear to you I didn't kill her," he said, hands clasped at his chest, forehead shiny with sweat.

"Did you go back to her building?"

"Yes. Around two a.m. Sunday morning, the seventeenth. But just to get a few things I forgot to pack."

"How did you get past the doorman?"

"He escorted me up to the apartment. He was with me the whole time."

"That's nuts. A doorman would never do that."

"It's true! I was desperate. I told him I had a key and that one way or another, I was going up there."

"I thought you gave the key back when you moved out."

"I made a duplicate."

I let his words simmer awhile before I said, "Why the hell would you do that?"

"The fact Jackie didn't believe me when I said Kate was stealing my rent pissed me off. And I was afraid she might get a lawyer and come after me for the six months of rent she'd say I owed since our agreement was that I'd stay through September. Then I'd have to pay for a lawyer and deal with all that crap. I saw having a key as leverage, just in case Jackie tried to do something like that."

"You planned to steal something valuable as leverage? Do you keep an appraiser on retainer?"

"There was a statue. Lalique. I know this name."

"And then you slinked in to get things you forgot to pack."

Kessler looked away then back to me. "Drinking makes me stupid," he said. "I had a key. I imagined Jackie sound asleep. I knew exactly where my stuff was. All I had to do was sneak in and sneak out. It would've been easy."

"Was it easy?"

"Yes. Her bedroom door was closed. I tiptoed into the guest room, found my stuff, tiptoed out. That was it. That doorman witnessed my every move."

It was hard for me to picture an old guy like Marv going along with this, but I let it go. "Did you notice anything strange about the place?"

"What could I notice? I walked from the door to the guest room. All I saw was the hallway and the kitchen. And it was dark."

"Why didn't you speak up earlier?"

"And give the cops a reason to suspect me? I told them I was out for good on the fifteenth. If I said I had gone back, my God, you could've placed me in the apartment around the time of the murder! But I didn't touch her! I swear to you, Detective Landau, you've got to believe me." Kessler dropped to his knees, sobbed. I didn't feel sorry for him.

"C'mon," I said. "Keep it together. What did you go back for? What was so important that it couldn't wait until people are typically awake?"

Kessler slowly climbed back to his feet. "Personal items. Very personal."

"Dude! You're gonna need to do better than that. Convince me, damn it! You don't seem like the murdering type, but prove your case a little stronger, please."

Kessler stared at the floor. "I had left some things that men use—some men use."

"Use for what?"

"You know what I'm talking about."

"I don't know anything. Use for what?"

"For pleasure! You know what I mean!"

"Things some men use for pleasure. What the fuck are you talking about? Dirty magazines?"

Kessler lowered his voice. "Prostate massaging devices."

I knew where the prostate gland was located, and I knew of only one route to get there. "Things you stick up your ass?"

"Fuck you."

"You went back to fetch some kind of vibrating devices and such. You and Jackie were not on friendly terms, so you wanted to sneak them out without Jackie knowing because of the potential embarrassment if she found them. I don't blame you. I would've done the same thing."

"I can't tell if you're serious or not."

"Listen to me. You're exactly what Kate McCall's lawyer was looking for. Expect to get subpoenaed. Hopefully, you won't have to talk about prostate massaging devices on the stand, but I can't promise. Anything else I should know?"

Kessler pretended to think about it. Then he said, "I wasn't alone that night."

"Someone else besides the doorman?"

"Linda Napier."

"Why was she there?"

"I asked her to come, in case Jackie confronted me. She was doing me a favor."

"So Marv the doorman, you, and Linda went to Jackie's apartment together. You think Linda snuck into Jackie's bedroom and killed her while you were retrieving your toys?"

"What? No! Linda met me in the lobby that night. She said there was no doorman or any security present when she got there. Then the elevator door opens and out walks the doorman. He looked troubled, she said. And his posture was kind of weird, like he was trying to hide something under his jacket."

Kessler's words sobered me. He had no reason to make this up. "Finish my sentence. You're suggesting Marv—"

"He's as much a potential suspect as I am."

"He'll say he works for the building."

"Where was he coming from when Linda saw him get off the elevator?"

Kessler had a point. Debbie wanted reasonable doubt, now she had two people for a jury to buy.

Chapter 21

I returned to West Lincoln Park and strolled the blocks adjacent to Furry BFF hoping to see Phillip by himself or leading a patrol of dog walkers. After a while, it occurred to me that his duties probably included sitting in an office being an administrator. Ignoring the woman at reception, I walked up the flight of stairs to the second floor offices and was met by the same young man I had met on my first visit.

"Looking for Lucille?" he said.

"Phillip."

He pointed to his office. I walked to the doorway and saw Phillip standing in front of a large shepherd mix sitting attentively, transfixed by Phillip's closed hand that undoubtedly held treats. A female volunteer in a green smock watched.

"Skipper, twirl," Phillip said. Skipper bolted to his feet then turned a tight three hundred and sixty degrees. After giving Skipper a treat Phillip said, "Skipper, where's your nose?" Skipper lifted his right paw high enough to graze his muzzle and was promptly treated. Then Phillip said, "Skipper, take a bow," and the dog lowered its chest and head almost to the ground while keeping its rear end up. Treats, praise, and laughter from all three of us ensued. Phillip seemed not to mind my unannounced presence. After the volunteer took Skipper out of the room, Phillip sat down behind his desk. "What's up?" he said, as if he had not a care in the world.

"I'm sorry about Linda Napier," I said. "I know she was an old friend."

"Didn't really know her. She was around when I was a little kid, but it was only recently that I met her as an adult. Was this related to my mom?"

"I'm not sure. Did your mom ever talk about Linda using drugs?"

"Never. She would not have wanted me to know that about Linda. You still think Kate McCall is innocent?"

"I do. But listen, do you remember your mom dating a guy named Henry DeWeldt?"

"Dating? I don't know if they were dating. I told you she wouldn't admit to being in that kind of a relationship. I mean, she liked the company of guys like Henry DeWeldt. Rich. Smart. But just as companions to go to some fancy event."

"Okay, but whether friend or lover, he was in the picture for an extended period of time, right?"

"True."

"Was there anything that occurred between them recently? Something that made her angry or changed the way she felt about being associated with him?"

Phillip thought about it. "Well, before she left for Palm Springs, I remember asking how Henry was and she said she hadn't seen him in a while. When I asked her why, she just shrugged and said it didn't matter."

"DeWeldt told me he was in charge of her estate. Was that true?"

"Is this man bothering you, Phillip?" Lucille said, walking into the room, trying to sound only half-serious.

I said, "How long have you been sniffing around out there, Lucille?"

"We're just talking," Phillip said.

Lucille stood over Phillip. "You really shouldn't discuss your family's personal financial information, Phillip. It's nobody's business."

I locked eyes with Lucille and then turned back to Phillip. "You've heard of people taking advantage of the elderly and their money? I have reason to believe Henry DeWeldt is one of those scumbags. I'm wondering if your mom found this out too."

"Confidentiality is very important, Phillip. If you have personal information on a donor, you need to keep that to yourself. Henry DeWeldt is a very important philanthropist. If someone found out Furry BFF is saying bad things about him, we could lose a lot of money."

"What if the rumors are true and involve murder?" I said.

"Oh, my God, will you stop?" Lucille said. "He thinks Henry had something to do with your mother's death."

"Think about it, Phillip," I said. "What if your mom knew something about Henry that was so vile it could ruin him?"

"Don't listen to him," Lucille said. She closed the door then said, "The woman the police arrested is guilty! That's why they arrested her. They have evidence. That's when they arrest people!"

Phillip sat quietly under Lucille's glare. She reminded me of an irate mother berating her son.

Lucille stepped toward me. "And you said yourself that Henry had complaints filed against his firm. So there's no news here."

"That information is hidden away," I said. "I had to look for it. Maybe Jackie was going to make something public. She had a lot of connections."

"Phillip, you're not listening to this nonsense, I hope. Remember what I said about confidentiality."

"Relax, Lucille," Phillip said. "I'm old enough to know what nonsense looks like."

Phillip held his gaze on Lucille long enough to suggest there was something between the lines that required reading. I dropped another card on his desk and left. Another chat with Manny needed to occur, but first I wanted to consult the "eyes and ears" of Jackie Whitney's building.

Chapter 22

While I was on my way to the Senior Tricks bridge club, Phillip called. "I need to talk to you privately," he said but wouldn't elaborate. We arranged to meet at my office in two hours. Lois Goldman, the director of the bridge club, recognized me from two days earlier.

"How are you, Mr. Landau? How goes the investigation?"

"Slowly but surely."

"And how's your father?"

"He stopped seeing snakes but still insists they're real." Lois nodded knowingly. "We were having a nice conversation, which pleasantly surprised me, then boom. He was in another world."

"Yes, unfortunately that's the pattern. What can I do for you today?"

"I'd like to speak to Gloria when she's available."

Lois led me into the bridge room. Gloria stood at a table where three others sat. "I think you're in luck," Lois said. "Gloria is the dummy. Her cards are all on the table to be played by her partner."

Lois walked to Gloria and whispered in her ear. Gloria turned to me and waved as if we were old friends. She started to walk over when her partner said, "Don't go too far!"

"Oh, you'll do fine," Gloria said and continued toward me. "You're that friend of Manny's, aren't you?" Gloria said. "The one who loves cats."

"Yes, that's me. I was wondering if I could ask you a few questions about Jackie Whitney?"

Gloria's smile vanished. She kind of shivered and said, "Ooh, I don't know if you want my opinion. I hated that woman. The way she treated Manny was disgraceful."

The bitterness from that sweet, elderly face slammed into me. Linda Napier's depiction of Manny's maltreatment was no longer dubious.

"Jackie was mean to Manny?"

"Heavens, yes! She ordered him around as if he was her personal slave. Right out in the open, in front of anyone who happened to be there. 'Manny, get me my cab; Manny, carry in my groceries; Manny, don't slouch; Manny, you don't look respectful around people; Manny, you don't act appreciative enough; Manny, you want to be a schlep your whole life?'"

"She demeaned him."

"Exactly! I once told her to shut up and she called me an old bitch."

"Manny doesn't seem bitter."

"He's the sweetest soul who ever lived. Secretly, he's probably not sorry she's dead and I don't blame him."

Hearing someone Gloria's age unafraid to speak with such conviction captivated me, as did her clear blue eyes. "What about the person at the concierge desk?" I said. "Did you notice how Jackie Whitney spoke to him?"

"Uh, no. Not really. The only time I saw them together was when she sat practically on his lap behind the desk, whispering back and forth."

"Did Jackie have any friends living in the building?"

"I don't know. Maybe some of those rich old guys liked having her around."

"Do you remember one of those visiting guys as being Henry DeWeldt?"

Gloria shuddered. "That man took advantage of us. He convinced a judge to put my husband in a nursing home even though I was going to pay for home healthcare. He dared to claim that I was not a competent caretaker."

Gloria choked up on the word "caretaker." I said, "How in the world did DeWeldt get involved in your estate?"

"I went to see that idiot woman at the animal shelter, Lucille. I knew who she was from when she visited Jackie."

"She met Jackie in the lobby or did you see her go up?"

"I only saw her in the lobby. They acted like spoiled little girls. Sometimes that DeWeldt crook would join them. I don't like to even think about those people. And the way Lucille flirted with Manny! It made me sick."

"Lucille flirted with Manny?"

Gloria leaned into me and said quietly, "I pray it never went beyond flirting. I told Manny to think about his family and stop acting like a jackass. He swears he was just having fun, going along with the act, nothing more. But I wasn't born yesterday. Manny's a good, decent person, but he has the same weakness all men have."

I filed the info then said, "You went to see Lucille about gifting the shelter, right?"

"Yes. I wanted to include a financial support legacy in my estate planning. Manny accompanied me and asked a lot of questions on my behalf and helped me with the paperwork. My husband, Sy, was not well and also wanted his estate put in order. Lucille recommended Henry DeWeldt. When Sy's health deteriorated, that bastard DeWeldt convinced a judge that I wasn't competent to act as his caretaker. While my children fought over control of the finances, DeWeldt had Sy placed in one of those expensive Contentment nursing homes. All this without even talking to me. We wanted to take care of him at home."

"I'm sure Manny didn't know anything about this."

"Of course he didn't, but he still blames himself just because he introduced me to Lucille, who recommended DeWeldt. I'll never forget the tears running down Manny's cheeks when he begged for my forgiveness. The poor man. It's been well over two years and he still tortures himself."

"But what was in it for DeWeldt? I mean, what did he care if your husband was in a nursing home or not?"

"I can only guess. I started a lawsuit but it dragged on and on. I didn't want to waste my money on lawyers, so I gave in. Sy was being taken care of but it cost a chunk of our personal wealth. Money we never planned to spend on a fancy nursing home."

"What about your estate?"

"It's safe. I have a nice gift for the shelter, but I'm not working with that Lucille woman. Manny wondered if we should give Lucille the benefit of the doubt because she was just trying to help. That's the way Manny is. He has this childlike faith in people."

"Do you think Jackie Whitney was aware of Henry DeWeldt's devious ways?"

"I wouldn't put it past her. But who knows?"

Gloria's bridge partner beckoned. "One more thing," I said. "What kind of dog is Louie?"

"He's called a bichon frise." Gloria spelled it out for me. "Why do you ask?"

"Just curious. A good dog for apartment life?"

"Oh, yes. He's perfect for an old broad like me. Easy to care for and oh so loving."

Manny stood with his hands behind his back staring through the lobby. I sensed a spark missing from his demeanor. "Hello, Mr. Landau," Manny said.

"Hello, my friend."

"I guess you want to talk about Linda."

"Yes, but first I have a question about Gloria."

"Oh, God, did something happen to her?"

"No, no, she's great. But think back to when you helped Gloria include Furry BFF in her estate planning. Was that when you first met Lucille?"

"No, Lucille and I had chatted many times while she waited for Jackie to come down. She's very friendly."

"And that's how you learned about Lucille's role at the shelter?"

"Yes."

"Did Henry DeWeldt chat with you too?"

Manny flinched. "No."

"Gloria told me—"

"I'd rather not talk about it."

"DeWeldt's a suspect, you know."

This interested Manny. "Really? Can you place him here when . . . ?"

"Nope. Unless you can?"

Manny shook his head.

I said, "Let's go back to the tragic news of Linda."

"Drugs?"

"I assume the cops stopped by to talk to you?"

"Yes, but why do you assume that?"

"Because I told them Linda had spoken with you a short time before she was found dead."

The implication struck Manny hard. He staggered backward a few steps then leaned on the doorman's desk. "Oh, my God. You're not accusing me of murder, are you?"

"Nobody's accusing you of anything."

"But what are you thinking? You don't think I'm a murderer, do you, Mr. Landau?"

"Relax, Manny. I'm not thinking anything. My job is to prove someone besides Kate McCall could have killed Jackie Whitney. But you have to tell the cops everything, otherwise they might think you're hiding something. Are you sure no hanky-panky happened between you and Linda?"

Manny blinked several times, then began pacing, running his fingers through his hair. "I'm sorry, Mr. Landau. I should've admitted it before. Yes, we were together—just once. That's the absolute truth. I felt so ashamed and told her. She took it very hard."

I patted his shoulder. "Water under the bridge," I said. "You mentioned that the old guy, Marv, is still clear-thinking."

"Yes. That's always been my impression."

"His showing up a few times a week in that royal getup, then manning the front door like it's Buckingham Palace—isn't that kind of weird behavior?"

Manny thought about it. "Well, he's always been kind of a character, so I don't think so."

"Has he ever done anything out of character? Something considered unbecoming of a doorman?"

"How unbecoming?"

"Entering an apartment uninvited?"

Manny gave me a strange look. "I highly doubt it. Unless the police were present, a doorman would never do that. What brings this up?"

"I'm a little embarrassed to say, but I have to look at every angle, every possibility."

"I get it."

"I should probably just interview Marv."

Manny ran his fingers down his jawline a few times. "It might be kind of hard on him," he said. "Marv had known Jackie since she was a little girl. It's tough to see a man his age cry."

I nodded. Even the imagery was tough to take. "Did Jackie Whitney ever make you cry?"

"You're making a joke?"

"I've heard she could be very mean, demeaning."

"I never took anything she said to me that way."

"Sorry. It wasn't a serious question."

East Rogers Park was an eclectic lakefront neighborhood of students, working class folks, immigrants, old hippies, and professionals. Where Kate McCall fit in was hard to say. She lived on the third floor of a vintage six-flat, the middle building of three identical six-flats. Typically, apartments in these buildings were large and spacious with built-in bookshelves and crown molding—luxury by McCall's Appalachian standards.

The manager for the three buildings lived in one of the garden-level apartments of McCall's building. I pushed the buzzer for M. Spatafora, waited a minute, then shook hands with Marie, a sixty-something woman with shoulder-length gray hair.

I introduced myself and handed her my ID. "I assume the police questioned you already about Kate McCall in 3W?"

Marie handed my ID back, nodding her head. "I told them what little I knew."

"What kind of things did you tell them?"

Marie pondered a bit. "Well, she paid her rent in cash—which was odd. But she always paid on time and never complained about anything. I once loaned her a socket wrench. That's about it."

"Did she have visitors very often?"

"Hard to say. I don't really pay attention to the tenants' guests. It's none of my business as long as they're quiet. It just so happens the woman she's accused of killing came over several times. She was easy to remember because of the loud, rude way she spoke to Kate, and I'm just talking about as they walked through the hallway and lobby. That Whitney woman treated Kate like a forsaken stepchild who could do no right."

"Did you ever have a conversation with Kate?"

"Not really." Marie laughed. "She'd just smile and say, 'Hidee.'."

"What did Jackie Whitney criticize Kate about?"

"Oh, some errand she was supposed to run or some other favor she owed her. She criticized the way she talked and always corrected her and made her repeat the offending word over and over. The clothes she wore were never good enough. It was like Kate's job was to listen to and obey Jackie Whitney. I understand why she killed her."

I paused to see if she was kidding. "You really believe she would kill someone for being verbally abusive?"

Marie sighed. "When you put it that way, it's kind of presumptuous of me, I guess. I know I wouldn't put up with it."

"Would you kill someone over it?"

"No. I can't imagine killing anyone except in self-defense. Maybe I'm being prejudiced because Kate's from Appalachia. But then again, who knows what people are capable of?"

What people are capable of. When does killing become a feasible, practical option? Can the urge to kill overtake anyone at any time given the right circumstances? With Marie's permission, I knocked on the door across the hallway from Kate's apartment. A young man named Jake wearing a Loyola T-shirt answered. I introduced myself and went through the identification routine.

"A real private eye? You're the first I've met."

"Yes, it's not a popular major at universities. How well did you know Kate McCall, who lived across the hall?"

"I didn't know her. I just heard her come and go and I heard the shouting when some woman came over."

"That woman was Jackie Whitney, the murder victim you may have heard about in the news."

"No shit? The rich socialite?"

"What did they shout about?"

"It wasn't they, it was the Whitney woman. All you really heard was her voice, 'Why didn't you do what I asked?' or 'That's not what I wanted!' Man, she sounded like a real bitch. I felt sorry for the other woman. I only occasionally heard a whimper in reply."

"You never had a conversation with Kate?"

"I barely saw her. Once in a while we would both be coming or going at the same time. She just looked at the floor when she passed you."

I handed Jake a card, thanked him for his time, then headed back to my office.

Chapter 23

Sitting at my desk, eating a bean burrito, I stared out the open door. I never went to her apartment, Lucille said at our first meeting. We'd meet at a restaurant and waste the afternoon with drinks and gossip. According to Gloria, they also met in the lobby of Jackie Whitney's building. The outside door groaned open then slammed shut. Footsteps ascended the stairs until Phillip appeared in my doorway.

"Have a seat," I said pointing to the club chair in front of my desk.

He sat and got down to it. "You asked if my mom used Henry DeWeldt for estate planning. That's how they first met. Henry helped Mom set up a trust to make sure the shelter got money every year. She and Henry were in the process of changing the trust when she died."

Phillip held on to the punchline. "You stressed the changing part," I said.

"She wanted to stop Furry BFF from getting money."

His words had a prophetic quality, although the reason was unclear. "Why cut out Furry BFF?"

"Something pissed her off."

"Yeah, I assumed that much. But what was the something?"

"I don't know for sure, but I think it had to do with how money was being used."

"Did she tell you anything to draw this conclusion?"

"Several weeks ago she flew me out to Palm Springs and sat me down to talk about family money and my responsibility. Mom wanted me to get a monthly allowance to help supplement my income. Animal shelters don't exactly pay great, but that's not why I work there. Anyway, she made me promise I wouldn't buy drugs like my father or wouldn't waste money on fancy cars, et cetera. To demonstrate how serious she was, she told me about changing the trust to exclude Furry BFF, but she wouldn't elaborate."

"Was the trust changed?"

"No."

I put my feet up on the desk, leaned back in my reclining chair, and began thinking out loud. "I wonder if Lucille knows about this? Would DeWeldt have told Lucille that Jackie was changing the trust? Why would Henry give a damn either way? He probably didn't. But if your mom was really holding incriminating information over DeWeldt's head, why would they be working together professionally to change her trust? Goddamn it, Phillip, you just weakened my theory for DeWeldt being the killer."

"One less bastard to think about."

"Hang on, I'm not acquitting him just yet. Maybe DeWeldt didn't know Jackie had taken incriminating information until after she died. I still think he's got his tentacles wrapped around some aspect of this case."

"And you're still convinced Kate McCall had no motive?"

"She had nothing to gain and everything to lose." I picked my feet up off the desk and sat upright. "Hey, Phillip, Lucille and your mom were great pals, right?"

He considered my question. "Meaning what?"

"Their personalities and lifestyles fit together nicely, so they enjoyed hanging out like girlfriends."

"Yeah, that sounds right."

"But your mom was someone who couldn't help but give advice. That's just the way she was. And she expected her friends to listen, especially if she gave them money—"

"Lucille didn't need Mom's money. That's not what their blowout was about."

"What blowout?"

"They got into a big fight about something and that was the end of their friendship."

"When?"

"Uh, late last year, before she left for Palm Springs."

"Around the same time your mom and Henry DeWeldt stopped talking?"

"Yeah, I guess that's right."

"And once again your mom didn't tell you what the something was they fought about?"

Phillip shook his head. I stood and began walking around the office. Lucille said she last spoke to Jackie Whitney in May, shortly before she returned from Palm Springs. Why would Jackie call her if they were no longer friends?

"Lucille said you're way overqualified for your job. She doesn't expect you to stay long."

"I got an MBA in finance to make Mom happy. Lucille's too shallow to understand why I would want to work in an animal shelter."

"I don't think you like her very much."

"She's a phony, pandering drama queen. But a rock-star fundraiser."

"Next time, don't hold back. After Lucille and your mom stopped talking, did Lucille treat you any differently?"

Phillip frowned. "I hoped she'd ignore me. Instead, I got the big sister–mom attitude. Or a lecture on confidentiality, as you witnessed. Then I'd suddenly become her gal-pal and she'd jabber about her love life—as if I gave a shit about her Latin lover."

I remembered Lucille on the phone all lovey-dovey in a little girl's voice, not the least bit uneasy a stranger stood in her doorway.

"Cha-cha-cha," I said.

Phillip's riotous laugh startled me. "Lucille-speak for dancing!"

"Yeah, I picked up on that."

Like everyone else who came to my office, Phillip walked to the room's only window. "You know that husky bald guy standing on the sidewalk across the street? I saw him at the shelter too."

I didn't have to look out the window to know who it was but I walked to Phillip's side. "His name's Brookstone. DeWeldt hired him to intimidate me."

"No shit? DeWeldt hired muscle to threaten you? Like a mob boss?"

"No, like an asshole. DeWeldt is scared, Phillip. But why? If he wasn't involved in your mom's death, why does he want Kate McCall to take the rap? C'mon, let's go meet Brookie."

Chapter 24

Phillip and I stood on the sidewalk in front of my building watching Brookstone trot toward us from across the street. He moved rather nimbly for a fireplug of a man. "Hello, detective shit for brains," Brookstone said. "How lucky for me to have you both in the same place. A true coincidence."

"This is Detective Brookstone, Phillip," I said. "He's the cop who beat up a defenseless woman bartender who refused to serve his drunken ass."

Phillip shrunk back a step. "Hey, Landau," Brookstone said. "You know I've been pretty tolerant so far. But that can change real fast. That little pop in the nose I gave you could be the side of your face caved in next time."

"Why're you following Phillip around, Brookie? Let's get it all out in the open."

"To see if he's in touch with you, genius."

"And now you can tell DeWeldt that I am in touch with Jackie Whitney's son."

Brookstone glared at Phillip. "Let's hope he's not telling you a lot of BS he can't prove."

"If DeWeldt wants to know what I know, have him call me. Here's another business card for him." I tossed a card at Brookstone's feet. "Something else you can tell him is that we know all about his little retirement home scam."

Brookstone stepped away, paced around a bit, then came back. "Listen, kid," he said to Phillip. "I'm just trying to make sure your mom gets justice. That woman they arrested, she's guilty, I know it. Landau and that public defender want to get her off, for chrissake!"

I laughed. "Come off it, Brookie. If you just tell me what he's scared of, then maybe we can do things your way and I'll leave DeWeldt alone. But as long as you keep harassing me, I'm gonna assume he's hiding something."

"How about you just do what I tell you so you don't get hurt, huh? Isn't that the easiest way to do things?"

"Your dedication to that scumbag is admirable. You getting a better health insurance policy than what the city gives you?"

Brookie shook his head with that annoying grin. "Are you too stupid to see I'm doing you a favor? DeWeldt can crush you. He's got a lot of powerful friends in this town."

"They sit behind raised benches. They're called judges."

"And you'll just take 'em all on all by yourself. What do you think you've got on DeWeldt?"

"Tell me, Brookie. If I presented you with a solid case implicating DeWeldt or anyone else in Jackie Whitney's murder, would you pursue it?"

"DeWeldt isn't a killer."

"He ripped off his niece's estate just to pay his taxes! Someone like that would stoop to murder to save his own ass."

Brookstone went through a few facial contortions. "I'm tellin' you—"

"DeWeldt and Jackie Whitney spent a lot of time together. She gained his confidence enough to find out DeWeldt had a whole scam going with elderly citizens and his private rubber-stamping team at the Attorney Registration & Disciplinary Commission. All those complaints slithering off his back like Lake Michigan slime. Nothing sticks to this scumbag."

"Old goddamn news. He's a businessman—"

"Who's scared of something—"

Brookstone shouted, "That don't mean he'd kill someone!"

"It's a long fall for guys like DeWeldt. They get scared of heights easy when someone gets a little information. Panic sets in. Just permanently close someone's mouth and the problem's solved."

Brookstone rubbed his bald head. "I'll be honest with you. Whether the rich broad knew more than she was supposed to know or not, I don't care. Honest! I really don't care."

"And that's why he hired you to muscle me, because he knew a guy who beats up women wouldn't care. You'd be happy to take his money to make sure nobody gets in the way of Kate McCall going to prison."

Brookstone struggled to keep cool. Phillip moved to the grass, just a few steps from the lobby window, and started fiddling with his phone. "The thing is, I really want to see justice. Sure, I want to make a buck too. But I really think Kate McCall is guilty and Kessler or Alvarez are in on it. Maybe both."

"Sure you do, because everyone knows Kate McCall could not have moved the body by herself. So you gotta find an accomplice to help your story."

"She fingered the doctor on the 911 call. Otherwise she was gonna take all the blame."

"She was framed. Jackie Whitney's keys, car registration, and prescriptions thrown away in the dumpster that McCall knew her boss would check at work?"

"She knew, huh? Did she tell you she saw her boss checking the garbage? She's lying about that too. She may have thrown it away thinking it was as safe as any place."

Brookstone's premise burned in my stomach. "You and your boys interviewed Kessler. You know as much as I do."

"You better hope so."

I glanced at Phillip and saw he held his phone down near his waist, facing us. "Or you'll beat me up? Meanwhile, instead of digging around like a good detective would do, you sit on your ass waiting for Kate McCall to break down and tell you everything."

Brookstone let his chin fall against his chest, mumbled something, then looked up. "Tell me something," he said. "Surveillance cameras show McCall entering Jackie Whitney's building on the eighteenth and then again on the nineteenth, the day she called the cops. What's your excuse for that?"

"The eighteenth?" I said. "But how would you know? You guys didn't bother checking the CCTV."

Brookstone smiled. "Oh, didn't we? Who told you that?"

"Howard, the security—" I said, then remembered I had only inquired about the sixteenth and seventeenth. Since Jackie Whitney had been dead for at least thirty-six hours, I hadn't considered the eighteenth as a possibility. I also remembered Howard looking at Manny two different times before answering two different questions.

"Your good pal, Manny Alvarez," Brookstone said, "slips Mr. Security a few bucks to give out only so much info should a private investigator come snooping around. Manny Alvarez, the doorman who may have been the last person to see Linda Napier alive."

"Oh, were back to Manny calling in a hit on Linda."

Brookstone swore. "How did I know about McCall coming back on the eighteenth, Landau? Manny Alvarez told me she was there. Alvarez only tells the cops about the eighteenth because he wants McCall to go down alone for the murder. He knows if she fingers him, they could go down together for both murders."

"But the coroner said Jackie Whitney had been dead at least thirty-six hours."

"Well, it's not an exact science, is it?"

No, I guess I should've known that. "I'll have another talk with my client," I said. "But I'm not done with DeWeldt."

"Goddamn it, Landau! DeWeldt didn't kill anyone. But if you're collecting info on that doctor, you better tell me or I swear to God I'll—"

My smile was involuntary. "Beating up civilians. You just can't help it. Is that what they teach you at the police academy? Give it a try, tough guy."

Brookstone moved toward me. I slipped my hand under my jacket. He stopped then laughed. "What? You're gonna shoot me? I think you caught some of your old man's brain crud."

"Your reputation as a maniac is known far and wide, Brookie. I'd enjoy blowing you away. And I have a witness."

He looked around for Phillip who had since positioned himself on our periphery, holding his phone at eye height, as if making a video. Brookstone's petrified block of a head turned crimson.

"You know who I hate as much as bleeding-heart-dyke public defenders?" Brookstone yelled. "You cocky private investigators! Do you hear me, you son of a bitch?"

We watched the angry man trudge off in his ill-fitting sport coat.

Phillip walked over. "Would you have really shot him?"

"Probably not."

"Then what?"

"Then I'd get beaten to a bloody pulp."

Phillip studied me. "You were antagonistic with that guy."

I found his sincerity disarming. I almost felt ashamed. "Hostile, repugnant people incite me to act that way. It's a personality flaw, I guess."

"A fatal flaw. Why aren't you afraid Brookstone will lose it and beat the crap out of you?"

"I never said I wasn't afraid."

"Then why act like that?"

I stared at Phillip, feeling a bit unmasked. "Because I can't help it."

Chapter 25

It had been at least twenty-four hours since Linda Napier's death. In the window of Verkakte Fashions, Hannah fitted a cobalt blue outfit over a mannequin. She probably recognized me from the previous week and guessed I wasn't in the market for a dress.

"He's in his office," she said.

"How's he—?"

She shook her head.

I walked to the back. The office door was open. George sat in a steno chair hunched over his desk. I knocked lightly. He looked up at me with red, puffy eyes.

"May I come in?"

He rotated his chair around and pointed to a small couch where I sat. "My two oldest friends are dead."

"I'm sorry. I know that's not much solace—"

"Am I next? Is someone going to kill me now?"

"Of course not."

"Of course not? You say that as if you really know. Did you think Linda was going to get murdered?"

"Hang on. Linda had many years of risky behavior under her belt. Who knows what kind of people she had lurking in her past? Maybe it caught up to her."

Neither of us spoke, then George said, "Jules, what are you doing here?"

I knew what he meant. "You and Linda aided my investigation and shared your personal lives with me. I can't help but identify with your loss."

"I would've thought a private investigator needed to be more callous about such matters."

"I probably should be."

George surrendered a small smile. "That detective who called, he thought Linda's death was related to Jackie's murder."

"There are similarities."

"Meaning what? Linda had some connection to Jackie's death?"

"I don't know what to think. Do you have any reason to believe Linda was using again?"

"You mean maybe this was a drug deal gone bad? Hard to believe. I could always tell when she was stoned. Did the cops find any drug paraphernalia?"

"No. But if the same person did kill Jackie and Linda, there had to be a reason. What the hell was that reason?"

"What about the renter? Linda was dating the doctor guy, right? She knew something incriminating about the doctor and he had to shut her mouth."

"Linda said they broke up a while ago and were still friends. Besides, why would Linda have covered for him all this time?"

George massaged his temples. "Maybe she was obsessed with him. Linda used to glom on to men. A doctor would've been hard for her to resist. Every week a new guy was going to change her life. Jackie and I would tell her to chill out but she wouldn't listen. The holidays were the worst. Every time Linda went to a party she would meet the perfect man. These were always short relationships, sometimes ending with threats of restraining orders."

The word "holidays" tripped a switch. Holiday had been a recurring theme. "Think back to our first meeting," I said. "You told me Jackie's fight with her lawyer-boyfriend happened around the holidays. Probably a Christmas party, right?"

"Probably."

Kate McCall told me it was the day after a Christmas party that Jackie Whitney went on her tirade about DeWeldt. Phillip said his mother stopped talking to DeWeldt and Lucille during the holidays. Another breaker tripped, this time with a spark. Henry was a doll, Lucille had said. A Francis of Assisi Champion whose privacy and reputation Lucille would stop at nothing to protect. And he was handsome.

"Something wrong?" George said.

"Do you know who Lucille Mackenzie is?"

"Of course. She's the whore that Jackie's lawyer-boyfriend was screwing."

It was one of those moments when intense satisfaction descended over me and every impulse of my investigation made perfect sense.

"That's what I thought," I said, then stood up. "Thank you, George, and take care of yourself. I'll let you know of any new developments."

"I'm sorry I can't be of more help."

"Believe me, George, you've been a great help. And that's no BS." I turned to leave then stopped. "Hey, George, real quick. Uh, the transman concierge. He would be attracted to women, right? I mean that's the whole point?"

George looked at me with his head slightly askew, perhaps mildly amused. "And because I'm gay you assume I would know all about this?"

"Oh, I'm sorry. I didn't mean—"

"It's fine, it's fine. I'm just messing with you. There are no rules designating gender with sexuality. The combination can be anything."

I thanked George again for pointing something out that suddenly seemed glaringly obvious. Once outside the shop, I strolled the neighborhood wanting to assimilate what I thought was a clearer picture of the investigation's dynamic. Jackie Whitney's final holiday season had been a festival of treachery. Who knew what betrayals the party revealed? I pictured a teeming, raucous affair with uninterrupted streams of Dom Perignon. As inhibitions deferred to the wine and season, so did the secrets and innuendo readily flow. Who knew what intimate details leaked out? Poor George. He might have been the only one who legitimately loved Jackie Whitney.

The phone rang with Debbie's name. "I need the money for the DNA test," she said. "We should have the results in a couple of days."

I drove home, grabbed the eighty-five hundred dollars, but decided to watch a little television before heading to Twenty-Sixth and Cal. Punim sat in my lap as I fast forwarded the CCTV video to the eighteenth. Kate McCall appeared at about four-thirty. For some reason Manny was still on duty. The two chatted a bit then Manny made a call from his desk phone. After he hung up, they chatted a while longer before McCall signed the guest book and walked to the elevators.

Debbie locked the money in the top drawer of her desk, announced she was hungry, motioned for me to follow her out of the room, then locked the door to her office. From one of the many neighborhood Mexican restaurants, she ordered a huge chimichanga. I got a couple of vegetarian tacos.

"How will the evidence get to the lab?" I said.

"I'll check it out from police evidence and take it myself. That way I can discuss the case with the lab's forensics team. So what's up, Jules?"

I told her about Detective Brookstone waiting for me in the loading zone. "McCall went to Jackie Whitney's apartment on the eighteenth. It's on the CCTV video."

Debbie took a moment to absorb the implication. "Hmmm. The day before she reported finding the body, she conceivably could've been in the apartment. Not good. Why didn't she tell us?"

"It doesn't make sense. A murderer wouldn't return to the scene and sign the guest book."

"Maybe she had a reason for not telling us. It's probably a shitty reason, but let's give her a chance. Meet me on the courthouse steps at nine tomorrow and we'll go talk to her."

"By the way, how hard is it to subpoena somebody's phone records?"

"If the somebody is not part of the cops' investigation, we would need a damn good reason for a judge to allow it. Why?"

"Just curious. Anyway, Kessler admitted to going back to the building during the murder time frame."

Debbie straightened up. "No shit? You got him on the video?"

"I bluffed him. I told him a surveillance camera on the street caught him entering the building. He collapsed like a house of cards."

"So what's his story?"

"He came back with Linda Napier around two a.m. to get some stuff he forgot to pack."

"Then he's on the CCTV."

"He would be, except there's an eight-hour gap in the time stamp."

Debbie's eyes widened. "Interesting. And what was so important to come back at two in the morning?"

"He had to collect some very personal items."

"Are you going to tell me what they were?"

"Prostate massaging devices."

Debbie choked on a laugh then spit her food in a napkin. "That's fucking brilliant!" she said. "Tell me more."

"Kessler said the doorman escorted him and Linda Napier to Jackie's apartment. He was running interference in case Jackie woke up. I told Kessler to expect a subpoena. I'm going to have to check in with Marv, the overnight doorman. So now you'll have two living, breathing specimens of reasonable doubt to offer the jury."

"Three, assuming they both admit Linda Napier was there too. And I can argue the real killer is also the person who killed Linda Napier."

"Kessler also said Linda saw Marv stepping out of the elevator before she or Kessler had arrived. He could've been up there alone."

"Why didn't Linda tell you this?"

"That's an excellent question that will never be answered."

"Look," Debbie said. "Marv was in the apartment, that's what matters. Alone or otherwise, I don't care."

"Just so you know, Marv is an old man. And he looks the part."

Debbie stared into her plate while chewing. Without looking up she said, "He was in Jackie Whitney's apartment. What else?"

Only halfway through my first taco, Debbie's tone ruined my appetite. "Jackie Whitney was not the kind, benevolent soul I thought she was. Two of McCall's neighbors said she mercilessly criticized McCall for all to hear. Linda Napier and one of Jackie's neighbors said she treated Manny Alvarez the same way."

"It doesn't help McCall if the jury knows she was getting pissed on by Jackie Whitney, does it? What else?"

"Jackie Whitney had a trust that paid out to the animal shelter. Phillip said she was in the process of cutting the shelter out of the trust when she died."

Debbie scooted her chair forward then returned to staring at her plate while chewing. "Why do I care?"

I wondered if I should've brought up Lucille Mackenzie stealing Jackie Whitney's boyfriend, but realized I had never mentioned Lucille to Debbie before, and thought she would just chalk up another detail to wild conspiracy theories.

"C'mon, Jules, here's your chance," Debbie said. "Convince me why I should care about the shelter getting cut out of the trust."

"I don't know yet, but it's a strange coincidence that Henry DeWeldt was Jackie Whitney's estate lawyer and DeWeldt is determined to see McCall convicted."

"You can't just bring up a person's name in the courtroom and say, 'Hey! There might be a conspiracy theory here!' Defaming a private citizen could get us into a lot of trouble. How the hell can I make you understand that our job is not to solve this murder, but just to show that someone else besides Kate McCall might be guilty?"

"If there's a chance to solve this murder, I'm not ignoring it. But I'll do my best not to include you."

Debbie chewed her chimichanga. I offered her my tacos then walked out.

Chapter 26

The next morning we walked in silence from the courthouse to the jail. Kate McCall entered the room with a deer-in-the-headlights look mixed into her usual mournful expression.

Debbie wasted no time. "Did you go to Jackie Whitney's apartment on the eighteenth, the day before you found her body?"

McCall nodded.

"Why didn't you tell us?" I said.

She looked at me then back to Debbie. Barely above a whisper she said, "You'ns asked me to account for my whereabouts on Saturday the sixteenth and Sunday the seventeenth. And that's what I told you'ns."

"The medical examiner thinks the murder most likely occurred on the sixteenth or seventeenth," I said, "but I 've since learned it's not an exact science. Don't you think your defense team would've wanted to know you were in the victim's home so close to the murder window?"

"The police had done told me I was on the television goin' in on the eighteenth. I figured you knowed already or you would've said somethin'."

I looked at Debbie for an answer. "The prosecutor hasn't given me all their discovery yet," she said. "The assholes delay information so the defense has less time to figure out a plausible explanation. They may even hold info until the trial and claim all the defense had to do was look at the CCTV, like they did."

"I stopped watching when I noticed the time stamp gap," I said, "which was late Saturday night through Sunday morning. Okay, Kate, what were you doing at Jackie Whitney's apartment on the eighteenth?"

"To see if she was home is all."

"What did the doorman think about you going up?"

"First he called up to her place. When she didn't answer, he didn't like the idea of lettin' me go on up. But he knowed Jackie gave me a key. I told him I was worried and just wanted to take a look. Him and me talked a bit longer and he become more friendly to the idea and let me go."

"Had you gotten to be friendly over time with the doorman Manny Alvarez?"

McCall shrugged. "He was always a nice enough fella."

"How did Jackie treat Alvarez?"

"Jules, what're you doing?" Debbie said.

"Well," Kate said, "Jackie can be all forceful like in her talkin' sometimes. But she's only tryin' to help. Tryin' to make you better."

"She talked down to Alvarez," I said. "Like she talked down to you."

"Jules!" Debbie said. "Don't badger her."

"Sorry. So you went in. What did you see?"

"The door to her bedroom was closed. I opened it. She wasn't in bed. Somethin' smelled bad and I got real scared. I knowed how dead animals smell. I panicked and ran out of there."

"You came back the next morning at two-thirty and called 911."

Kate nodded.

"Again, the doorman didn't mind you going up?" I said.

"I told him about goin' up earlier, and the smell, and that I had a bad feelin'. He let me on up."

"Kate, did you kill Jackie?" I said.

"She already told us she didn't!" Debbie shouted

"I didn't kill nobody!" Kate said, tears falling down her cheek. "I swear to Christ Almighty, I didn't kill nobody." She started sobbing into her hands.

Debbie whacked me hard on the shoulder. "What's the matter with you?" she said.

"I just wanted to hear the truth again, from her mouth."

"You and your truth. Maybe you should get off the defense team and go find truth on your own."

"No," Kate said. "Mr. Landau, I've done bad things. I've taken stuff not belongin' to me, but I ain't got no reason to kill nobody. Please believe me and stay and help."

Debbie's jaw muscles strained. She wanted to lecture me again, or beat the crap out of me.

"Okay, Kate," I said, standing up to leave. "From now on, no matter what, you're innocent of murder, if only because it's my job not to think otherwise."

Tamar sat at a table in the Kutaisi Georgian Bakery, reading the paper.

"What's this?" I said. "Sitting down on the job? What kind of example are you setting for your staff?"

"I'm the boss, remember?"

"May I join you?"

"It's a free country."

I sat. Tamar smiled and put the paper down. "What?" she said. "Say it out loud, maybe I can help you figure it out."

"I'm that transparent?"

"Of course. A bloodhound's behavior is ruled by the scent it's following. You're no different."

"Calling me a son of a bitch is nothing new."

"Shut up. There's no better tracking dog than the bloodhound."

"I keep following the scent back to Jackie Whitney having some damning information on the dirtbag lawyer, which would've been his motivation to kill her."

"So what's bothering you?"

"My training tells me anybody can be a murderer. But this guy's so easy to hate. It's almost too easy. I don't trust it."

Neither of us spoke. Then Tamar said, "You said the dirtbag lawyer likes to take money from old folks?"

"He also likes to put them in expensive nursing homes. He convinces a judge that the spouse is not equipped to take care of their mate."

"I looked into putting Deida into a nursing home if she got too difficult to take care of. We either warehouse the old in dreary state supported facilities or put them into expensive resort-like places owned by a corporation."

The word "corporation" washed over me, inspired DeWeldt's face to flash through my brain as the embodiment of aloof, corporate arrogance. It was only natural DeWeldt should turn the "prosperous elderly" into a commodity waiting to be exploited.

"Did you look at a place called Contentment?"

"Yeah. They're popping up like Starbucks and cost around ten thousand a month. More if you need skilled nursing."

DeWeldt must have a stake in these nursing homes. Each new arrival was another one hundred and twenty thousand dollars of annual revenue. He probably paid bonuses to his associates based on how many clients ended up living at a Contentment facility—or how much they managed to embezzle from bank accounts, estates, or trust funds. Having the Attorney Registration & Disciplinary Commission covering his ass ensured a good night's sleep. The stress of losing a loved one plus collecting the deceased's financial information was probably enough to discourage lawsuits.

"Jules! Where'd you go?"

"Can I borrow your laptop?"

"Now?"

"If it's not a hassle."

Tamar walked through the kitchen and into the prep room. A door on the far wall opened to a cluttered office. She reappeared a minute later carrying her open laptop, then put it down next to me. "I have to get back to work," she said. "Bring this to the counter when you're done."

"What time are you coming over?"

"Just leave the door ajar."

She turned to leave. I tugged her arm. "Wait. You mean leave the door unattached, don't you?"

"Why are you making fun—" I handed her a key. She smiled, kissed me.

"Now it won't matter if the door is attached or unattached."

Tamar held the key up to eye level. "You may regret this," she said then walked away.

I searched for Contentment Corporation at the Securities and Exchange Commission website. It took a while, but I was able to find the documents stating the percentage of stock owned by the company's executives. It was no surprise that one of the majority stockholders was Henry DeWeldt, a fact that seemed even more fortuitous after I answered my phone to hear DeWeldt's voice.

"I want you to come to my downtown office," DeWeldt said. "Let's clear the air."

"My nose feels better and the bruises on my thigh and back are almost healed," I said. "Do you mind leaving Brookstone in the lobby?"

"Just come to my office. We'll talk like two reasonable adults. That's all."

That's all. Henry and I would sit and chat. Maybe after one resided too long in an unscrupulous legal system, corruption no longer blipped on one's ethical radar. How else to explain a debased corporatist like Henry DeWeldt thinking himself "reasonable"?

The receptionist expected me. "Corner office to the right," she said as I walked in.

I knocked twice. The door opened magically, then closed just as magically after I entered. Behind me stood a bouncer in an Armani suit. I smiled, extended my hand. He ignored me. DeWeldt offered me a view of his back while he took in the sweeping lakefront spectacle. I sat in the chair in front of his desk.

"Here I am, Henry. The meter's running."

"I know what you think," DeWeldt said, still with his back to me. "Regardless, that doesn't make me a murderer." He swiveled around. "Why do you insist I'm a murderer?"

"Remember our last meeting? The one where you had me kidnapped and taken to your West Belmont office? You asked if I had some documents, then you accused me of wanting to blackmail you. Remember? And do you remember your thugs punching me in the back?"

DeWeldt readjusted himself in the chair. "My apologies."

"But let me answer your question. Jackie Whitney had damning information and you couldn't take a chance on what she'd do with it. Sound like a motive?"

"She stole from me. But I didn't kill her! Don't you think I would've retrieved the stolen item if I had gone to the trouble of killing someone?"

"Tell me what you were fighting about."

"What fight? When?"

"The argument at the Christmas party."

"Who the hell told you about that?"

"Doesn't matter."

DeWeldt loosened his tie, unfastened the top button. "Jackie had set up a trust for the animal shelter. She wanted to change it so the shelter no longer received money."

"What pissed her off?"

DeWeldt cleared his throat. "It was about the development director, Lucille Mackenzie. Jackie was upset about her salary."

I waited. "What about it?"

DeWeldt looked away, folded his arms. "She thought it was too high."

"How much too high?"

The question irritated him. "Do you have any idea how much money it took to build that place? Furry BFF hired a seasoned, proven, professional fundraiser in Lucille Mackenzie. Without Lucille, there would be no building."

"Okay, so who decided how much she got paid?"

"The board of directors approves employee compensation."

"So a board member must've told Jackie how much Lucille made?"

"That wouldn't have been necessary. Nonprofit finances are part of the public record."

"But considering Lucille's prestige, the board must've deliberated over how much she would be paid."

DeWeldt chose his words carefully. "The board studied the issue in an executive session, meaning it was discussed confidentially among the officers."

Confidentially among the officers. "Lucille's salary was so flagrantly high, Jackie wanted to cut the shelter out of her estate? I need to know how much if you expect me to believe that."

"Don't tell me what I need to do, Landau. Lucille's salary is irrelevant. I didn't kill anybody, that's why you're here."

"Okay, Henry. Did Jackie end up changing the trust?"

"No. I reminded her how dedicated Lucille was and how much money she had raised for the shelter. She agreed to think about it."

"Did it anger Jackie that you defended Lucille?"

DeWeldt stood then walked to that same corner window. "I know Jackie could be very insulting at times," DeWeldt said. "But deep down she was a well-meaning, intelligent woman." He turned to face me. "I warned her about it. Specifically the way she spoke to Kate McCall. And that doorman. She thought she could make people better by being tough. Sometimes she spoke to me that way. It made sense that Kate McCall snapped. She's from a different—uh, civilization, with different codes."

DeWeldt recognizing verbal abuse of Manny and McCall impressed me. I said, "You didn't answer my question. Did it anger Jackie that you defended Lucille?"

"I suppose."

"What about your affair with Lucille? That probably pissed her off too."

"She heard something at that damn party and overreacted."

"Are you still seeing her?"

"I was never seeing her. We had a couple of meaningless encounters."

"What's your relationship with Lucille like now?"

"Purely professional."

"Professional in the context of a large donor and the chief fundraiser. Tell me about the stolen information."

DeWeldt sat back down. "Doesn't matter."

"It must really threaten your standing in society."

"That doesn't mean I would kill to get it back."

Murders are committed for much less, I wanted to say. "Kate McCall has no link to your stolen information."

"One has nothing to do with the other. The evidence against McCall is undeniable."

"But the killer must've taken the info from a dead Jackie Whitney. McCall doesn't know anything about it. How did you discover someone else had the information?"

"I was sent a copy of a page, with a note."

"How much do they want?"

"They want only that I ensure Kate McCall is convicted of Jackie's murder."

"Which is why you hired Brookstone to harass me."

"Many people will suffer if this information is made public—"

"The pressure must be very unsettling. All those distinguished fellows facing disbarment and extended stays at Club Fed."

DeWeldt didn't appreciate my candor. "The alleged motive you're suggesting will destroy me. The world will assume a man of my means wouldn't hesitate to stoop to murder. I'd be guilty regardless of what a jury said."

"And all the publicity might bring unwanted attention to how Contentment rapes and pillages the elderly."

"Contentment provides top-of-the-line care!"

"You agree Jackie took something from your home. Can we call it a record of transactions?"

DeWeldt responded by not responding.

"When did she take it? And how the hell did she know where it was?"

DeWeldt swore under his breath. "Before going to California, she asked to see me. To make amends, I thought. We talked in my home office, which I also use as a den. I was called away for an hour or so to attend other business. Jackie being alone in my home was not unusual. She must've searched through my desk drawers. She left for Palm Springs a few days later."

"You don't lock up incriminating evidence?"

DeWeldt's hand closed into a fist then relaxed. "I do, damn it. But in this case I just didn't take this kind of possibility seriously enough. And now it's come back to bite me."

"She stole the information before she left town in early January. However, you agreed to perform legal work on her trust when she returned four months later?"

DeWeldt pursed his lips. "Jackie called and very calmly admitted taking the information. She said she wanted to hang on to it for a while—to think about what to do, or something like that. I tried to reason with her. I offered to pay, but she wouldn't listen. We spoke several more times over the next few months. I apologized repeatedly for my behavior. I hadn't realized how strong her feelings were for me. The last time we spoke she told me about coming back to deal with the renter. She promised to return what she stole. She asked only that I amend the trust to exclude the animal shelter."

The odor of bullshit drifted past. I walked behind his desk, took my turn soaking in the view. I said, "How much did she know about your assisted living business and how you operated?"

DeWeldt walked to an antique-looking bar cart and poured a drink. He didn't offer me one. "Our relationship got stormy at times. We drank too much. We argued politics. She used her big mouth to get at me. It was a kind of game she played." He sat back down behind his desk. "Let's just say I talk too much when I drink, and Jackie knew it."

DeWeldt withheld details, but I felt confident enough to draw some conclusions. "Jackie betrayed you for defending and screwing Lucille Mackenzie. Your bragging about power and influence also helped erode her opinion of you. There was an ad in a magazine on Jackie's table for the Senior Tricks bridge club. Maybe discovering that you used the club to fish for dupes pushed her over the edge."

"I told you I did nothing illegal!" He opened the top drawer to his desk and took out a checkbook. "Let's get down to what matters. I'll write you a check for fifty grand if you drop your investigation. It's that easy."

"Are you sure there's not more to the story behind Jackie's betrayal?"

"You know everything you need to know."

I returned to the guest chair. "Even if I did walk away, Kate McCall's public defender has plenty of potential evidence to sway a jury."

"Tell me what it is. We can get to people—"

"I'm not going to help you, Henry."

We both stood. He walked out from behind his desk. "I'll double whatever they're paying you, on top of the fifty thousand."

"Kate McCall is innocent. You can afford a good lawyer if it should come to that."

I turned to leave. Henry grabbed my arm with both hands. "Goddamn you!" he yelled and shoved me as a frustrated little boy might do. Had there not been an obstacle behind me, the incident would've been laughable, but I stumbled over the chair, onto the floor, where DeWeldt's bouncer felt the need to place his foot over my throat. DeWeldt stared at me a moment then said, "Let him up."

I sat up, felt my throat. "Thank you for being so reasonable," I said then walked out.

Sitting on the grass near Lurie Garden, I held the phone to my ear while massaging my neck with the other hand. A pleasant female voice answered at the National Council of Nonprofits.

"I have a question about salaries," I said.

"How much is too much?"

"I get the feeling someone asked this question once before."

The woman laughed. "What position?"

"CEO of animal shelter."

"Around here, 80K to low 100s."

"What if the development director was getting paid more than the CEO?"

"Too much. Way too much."

I thanked her, closed my eyes, let the ugliness of my job dissipate into the warm breeze of a June afternoon. The world couldn't possibly be as miserable a place as it seemed. Then my phone rang.

"I'm at the Taverna with Brookstone," Kalijero said. "He asked me to set up a meeting."

"Why're you going out of your way for that guy?"

"Because that's what cops do."

"That badge never comes off, does it?"

"I don't expect you to understand loyalty, brotherhood, that kind of stuff."

"That kind of stuff should be earned, not just pinned to your shirt. Anyway, I'll be there. In the meantime, ask Brookstone about yesterday's rendezvous and how I was ready to draw down on his psychotic ass."

"Do me the smallest favor, Landau. I'll even say please. Try not to be a prick."

Chapter 27

Through no fault of its own, Anagnostou's Taverna had transcended the "sleazy saloon" identity to reach the revered rank of anti-renovation establishment, complete with a "cool" nuance. Protocol dictated that barstools belonged to old-timers while hipsters, emos, and post rockers bellied up to the bar only long enough to get their Schlitz, Pabst, or Old Style, before decamping to a table of chipped Formica and cigarette burns.

Ordinarily, the bar was Kalijero's home, but today he and Brookstone occupied a vinyl booth accented with duct tape. I slid in next to Kalijero.

"Happy to see me, Brookie?"

"I'm happy to rub that smile off your face."

"All right, all right," Kalijero said. "You're on the same goddamn team."

"DeWeldt's paying Brookstone to ensure an innocent person goes to prison in his place. That ain't my team."

"You're a sucker," Brookstone said. "You think that McCall broad is just some dumb hick? She's making a fool out of you, Landau. I've been over to the jail, I've seen her tears. All bullshit."

"How about we find some common ground?" Kalijero said. "You both think there's a second person involved, right?"

"And don't say DeWeldt," Brookstone said.

"What about the doctor?" Kalijero said. "Give us what you got on the doctor."

Kalijero's presumption irked me. "I should just readily hand over my hard work to Brookstone?"

"What difference does it make?" Kalijero said.

"I got a lot more experience than you, Landau," Brookstone said.

"Oh, I see. I owe it to you, as a public service—"

Kalijero banged his fist on the table hard enough for all patrons to take a look. "Landau, you asked me to help you, remember? That's what I'm doing. You've got nothing to lose by sharing info with Brookstone."

I enjoyed seeing Kalijero fired up. I said, "I need to see a little effort before I start giving up info."

The two venerable lions sized up a crippled gazelle. Kalijero said, "Brookstone says you been spending lots of time talking with that doorman."

I laughed. "Manny Alvarez. Brookstone thinks he ordered a hit on Linda Napier as he stood manning his doorman post."

Brookstone said, "You said yourself Alvarez called someone as soon as Linda Napier left and that Alvarez may have been the last person to see Linda Napier alive—besides you, that is. Manny Alvarez got a connection with Jackie Whitney you don't want us to know?"

"Get his cellphone records if you're so hot for him," I said. "Maybe he called Kessler, who moonlights as a hit man."

"Answer the question!" Brookstone said. "You got a connection?"

"He works as a doorman in the building where Jackie Whitney lived."

Kalijero kicked me hard in the shin. "You got anything or not?" he said.

"Brookie, what if I found solid, undisputable proof that DeWeldt was at least involved in the murder? Would you take a closer look or does he have too much money for you to see straight?"

"If it's DNA-solid, Brookstone wouldn't ignore it," Kalijero said.

"I want to hear Brookstone say it. And, Jimmy, are you sure you're helping me and not working for this shithead?"

"Shithead?" Brookstone said. "That hurts my feelings."

Kalijero closed his eyes, rubbed the bridge of his nose, swore in Greek.

"It's not Jimmy's fault," Brookstone said. "When I found out you was helping that public defender, I called in a favor because I knew you'd be the pain in the ass you are."

Kalijero had no comment. He should've told me about owing a debt to this ass-clown. "I'll make a deal with you, Detective Brookstone," I said. "If I show you DNA-solid proof of a DeWeldt murder-for-hire scheme, you'll promise to sniff out every square inch of him, expose all his crimes, and present everything to the DA or the FBI. That includes his corrupt network at the Attorney Registration & Disciplinary Commission. In exchange, I'll tell you right now about Kessler's fat, juicy lie."

Brookstone squirmed a bit, looked around, exchanged glances with Kalijero. "Just agree," Kalijero said. "If Landau really gets the proof, it'll help people forget that bartender business."

"Fine," Brookstone said. "But it's gonna have to be damn good evidence for me to go after DeWeldt."

"Okay," I said. "Kessler returned to Jackie Whitney's building after he said he had moved out for good."

"This better not be bullshit," Brookstone said.

"He came back at two or three in the morning of the seventeenth, to collect things he forgot to pack. He was inside Jackie Whitney's apartment. Scout's honor."

"He was there!" Brookstone said, banging his fist on the table. "That lying piece a shit! Gone on the fifteenth, my ass."

"How do you know he came back?" Kalijero said.

"I said I had a video showing him entering the building and he was glad to tell me. Two others accompanied him to her apartment."

"Who are they?" Brookstone said.

"One's already dead." I waited for a lightbulb.

"That Linda Napier junkie!" Brookstone said, his face aglow. "That's why she's dead. You can't trust a junkie to keep her mouth shut. She tried to blackmail money out of Kessler, so he had someone shut her mouth for good.”

“Who’s the other witness?” Kalijero said.

“Really, Brookie? Now it’s an orthopedic surgeon hiring a hit man? Maybe Kate McCall broke out of jail, killed Linda Napier, then snuck back to her cell. And when she gets acquitted, she and Kessler are gonna run away together!”

“Landau!” Kalijero said. “Who’s the other witness?”

“I get it,” Brookstone said, leaning over the table. “You kind of like saying Kessler might be the accomplice because that’s reasonable fucking doubt. You and that lawyer-bitch are just drooling over getting another murderer out of prison.”

“Isn’t that ironic?” I said. “The woman-beating cop helping the bleeding-heart public defender spring McCall from jail.”

Brookstone grabbed my arm, tried twisting it off my shoulder. Kalijero passively watched our struggle until Brookstone let go and swore.

“Who’s the other witness?” Kalijero said.

“Marv, the graveyard doorman. You want me to explain what irony is, Brookie?”

“Shut the fuck up,” Kalijero said, kicking me again.

Brookstone said, “Maybe Alvarez and Kessler are working together. That’s why Alvarez made sure I knew McCall came in on the eighteenth, but he didn't tell Landau." Brookstone looked at me. "How do you know for sure that doorman went inside Jackie Whitney's apartment?"

"His name's Marv," I said. "And who knows anything for sure?"

"Here's what I think," Brookstone said. "Marv got paid off to allegedly witness Kessler grab the stuff he forgot to pack, and then leave. Nothing more."

Kalijero said, "But how do you place McCall with Kessler or Alvarez at the crime scene?"

"We'll bring all three in, then play them off each other. Someone's going to crack, and when they do, McCall will cut a deal. Either way, Landau, your client is going bye-bye."

"Impressive how you deductively reasoned DeWeldt's money into your pocket. Remember our deal."

Kalijero turned to me. "And you remember the evidence against McCall. The victim's jewelry in McCall's home. McCall's fingerprint on the weapon. The victim's car registration, keys, and prescription in the trash at McCall's job. McCall had the victim's apartment key. McCall had signature privileges on the victim's safe- deposit box. McCall didn't tell you about going to the victim's building on the eighteenth. The victim treated McCall like a stupid cracker. The bottom line is that McCall had plenty of motive and plenty of access to the victim."

"And don't forget the cops' talent for beating false statements out of people."

Brookstone leaned over the table. "You better hope you don't got Daddy's brain-rot going on," he said, "because I want you to understand I don't give a shit you're working for the defense. If McCall doesn't get convicted and I find out you've been holding back anything, you're going to wish you was locked away with Daddy in some nuthouse—"

"I'm curious. So after you're done ripping off old ladies, does DeWeldt pay you extra to suck his cock, or do you do that for free?"

Once again, the stubby Brookstone impressed me with his agility, first jumping to his seat then diving across the table. For the second time in two hours, somebody had hold of my neck.

"You think you're so special?" Brookstone snarled. "You want murderers going free?"

"Let him go, Tommy!" Kalijero shouted as he tried to pry Brookstone's hands off my neck. I focused on easing the pressure of his thumbs against my trachea. Panic began creeping in as my ability to breathe weakened. I moved my hand under my jacket, un-holstered my .40 caliber, then pushed the barrel against Brookstone's forehead.

Kalijero took his turn climbing up to the seat before launching his body across our outstretched arms, pinning my gun hand and one of Brookstone's arms underneath him, but my neck remained in the grip of Brookstone's other hand. Somehow, Kalijero found the leverage to bring his arm back far enough to deliver his fist square into Brookstone's face, stunning him long enough for Kalijero to freely repeat the action until my assailant fell over, semiconscious.

I sat on the floor, catching my breath. Patrons walked over. A bartender holding a billy club asked Kalijero if everything was okay.

"We're good, Dino," Kalijero said, panting.

I got to my feet. Kalijero looked at me, then turned away. I left without saying goodbye.

A phantom compression around my throat accompanied the drive home and stayed all the way back to my couch. Sipping ginger tea helped loosen the grip, although it hurt to swallow. Images of Brookstone's maniacal eyes and gritted teeth had been stamped into my consciousness during the struggle. I wanted to declare that Brookstone tried to kill me, but was it true? Then I thought how convenient it was to blame murder on an uneducated woman from Appalachia. Who knows anything for sure? I had rhetorically asked Brookstone and Kalijero, unconsciously waxing on the human condition. I sure as hell didn't.

Neck bruising and hoarseness greeted me the next morning. From the Internet, I learned of fatal outcomes associated with collapsing windpipes. I called Kalijero. No answer. I waited a few minutes then called again. Still no answer. On the third attempt, I told his answering machine I was on my way over.

Chapter 28

Kalijero lived in a one-story brick worker's cottage about five miles west of downtown. The outer bands of Hurricane Gentrify first brushed the neighborhood last year, raining permit applications over empty lots. Now, "Coming Soon!" signs on former dollar stores and bodegas warned of vintage clothing boutiques, cafés, and yoga studios. I parked in front of his house and slammed the car door. By the time I crossed the weed-infested strip of dirt between the street and the sidewalk, Kalijero was stepping out the front door. He hobbled toward two metal chairs looking like a retired linebacker after a career on painkillers.

"Have you checked the value of your house lately?" I said while climbing the short flight of concrete steps leading to the porch. I sat next to him. Together we stared across the street at a boarded up warehouse waiting to become loft condominiums.

"You sound terrible," Kalijero said. "If your voice doesn't get better soon, get it checked out by a doctor."

"You may have saved my life yesterday," I said. "You also saved me from manslaughter charges."

"No way you were pulling that trigger."

"Ever had someone choking off your oxygen? I guarantee I would've pulled that trigger."

"Fine. What are you doing here?"

"You were in a galaxy of pain walking out of your house."

"I paid a price for saving your miserable life."

I flashed back to the Taverna. Kalijero sprawled across the table, his torso dangerously torqued while punching Brookstone's face. "I'd say your debt to Brookstone is paid up."

"I doubt he'd see it that way."

"Let me guess. When you guys were both cops, you did something stupid. Meaning, you got accused of something, Brookstone took credit for saving your ass even though his contribution was dubious at best."

"What do you want, Landau?"

"Just to say thanks and also fill in a few blanks from yesterday."

A group of kids on skateboards and bicycles rolled past. "What're they so damn happy about?" Kalijero said.

"It's weird," I said. "Every spring, unvaccinated kids fall victim to joy and optimism."

Kalijero took out a stick of gum. He didn't offer me one. "All right," he said, "tell me about these blanks you want to fill in."

"It's about when Kessler and Linda Napier came back to Jackie Whitney's building. They didn't arrive together. She got there first and said there was no one around. So while she's waiting for

Kessler to get there, the elevator door opens and out comes the graveyard-shift doorman."

"What do you know about this guy?"

"Only that he was at Outpost Harry during the Korean War."

"He's gotta be in his eighties."

"You know anything about Outpost Harry?"

Kalijero journeyed beyond the bounds of space and time awhile, then said, "My uncle Kostas was part of the Greek Expeditionary Force. Sparta Battalion. For eight days Greek and American troops held the hill against artillery, mortar fire, and thousands of Chinese swarming over their position. Eight straight days of hand-to-hand combat in the trenches. He called it a slaughterhouse."

I got the feeling Uncle Kostas had shared some other gory details with his nephew. I said, "Imagine carrying that around the rest of your life from age eighteen or nineteen."

Kalijero turned toward me, grimacing as if his back was on fire. "Are you saying an old man killed Jackie Whitney?"

"I don't know what I'm saying. But if he was really coming out of the elevator like Linda Napier said, he would've been up there alone."

Kalijero righted himself. "Alone anywhere in the building. And the motive was what? PTSD?"

"More reasonable doubt to throw at a jury."

"You're starting to sound desperate, you know that?"

I knew it and I didn't like it. "DeWeldt had motive, damn it. He probably used a contract killer. Flies in, does the job, flies out."

Kalijero's glare filled my periphery. "Why would a hit man hang around to put a one-hundred-and-thirty-pound body inside a bag, then deadlift it over his head to put it on a shelf?"

"Maybe that was part of the deal. Hide the body. Maybe Kate McCall helped lift it."

"Whoa! Where'd that come from?"

"I don't know. Maybe Brookstone's right. She's not a dumb hick. In fact, she's crafty as hell."

Silence, then Kalijero said, "But how do you connect DeWeldt and McCall?"

I turned my chair to face Kalijero. "If I could connect them, do you think Brookstone would really honor our agreement? Despite what happened yesterday?"

Kalijero didn't need to think long. "Brookstone's been dreaming about DeWeldt's money, that's for sure. But a high profile murder case that he gets all the glory for cracking? If you can really deliver on the evidence, he'd forget what happened yesterday and he'd forget DeWeldt's money."

Silence again until Kalijero said, "Where's this coming from all of a sudden? You been hiding something?"

"Let's say I ask you to bring Brookstone to meet me somewhere. You think you can you do it?"

"What do I tell him?"

"Tell him I'm going to lay out the whole story and that he was right about McCall. Tell him I'm ready to prove who her accomplice was. Tell him he'll get all the credit because if I turn on my employer, my name would be dirt in this town. Tell him you don't owe him anything and describe his grip on my throat. Then remind him what second degree murder is."

Kalijero did not look optimistic.

"As a last resort," I said, "tell Brookstone you'll let him beat the shit out of me if I don't deliver. That should get him to show up."

A black-haired woman tongue lashed the swing-shift doorman. She had long red nails, smudged lipstick, and a windswept face of barbed features. A pink handbag swung erratically from her leathery arm while she gesticulated wildly, as if performing an incantation. I maneuvered behind her then closed the space.

". . . This is a luxury building. Do you understand what that means? We expect to get our packages delivered promptly. . . ."

Lenny explained that the building was not staffed to guarantee same-day package delivery, which was why he had called her when the package arrived. But the woman was in no mood for excuses and suggested his age played a role in his inability to understand what the affluent expected from the help. I was impressed how Lenny remained calm under her venomous glare. She walked away, convinced the barbarians had indeed arrived at the gate.

"Ouch," I said. Lenny scribbled in a notepad. "You need a hug?"

He looked up, smiled. I sensed an appreciation for empathy. "Sore throat?"

"Just a little strained. Was that woman as painful as she appeared?"

"Nah." Lenny dropped the notepad into his jacket pocket. "Just part of the job."

"I hope your good attitude is making you prosperous."

"Oh, I'm definitely prosperous."

"Good tips?"

Lenny waved me off. "Manny's the tip whore. For me, it's more about material. I'm a writer."

"What do you mean, 'tip whore'?"

"He's always selling himself. You think there's a resident who doesn't know about Manny's sick kid? 'Poor Manny has a sick kid, we better give him a good tip. He's such a nice man and he supports his wife who has to stay home and take care of their sick child.' He plays it up for every penny."

I took a moment to walk a mile in Manny's shoes. "You know what? I don't blame him. You have any idea how hard it is for a working man to support a family? The cost of healthcare alone beats you into despair. Anyway, does his wife ever come in with the kids?"

"I've seen her, but not with kids. She should bring 'em in, though. Manny could probably seal the deal on a lot of fat Christmas bonuses with a kid wearing an oxygen mask."

"Is she as nice as Manny?"

"She's nice to look at, that's for sure. I assumed you knew her by now since she was friends with Jackie Whitney."

I took a moment to process what Lenny just said. "Manny's wife was friends with Jackie Whitney?"

"Yeah. She used to stop by during my shift, sit on the couch, and wait for Jackie to come down."

"What makes you think the woman who stopped by was Manny's wife?"

"I just assumed because I saw them so often driving away or getting into a cab after Manny's shift."

"Interesting. Anyway, what do you write?"

"Short stories. This place is a gold mine for tragic characters."

I smiled. "I can totally see it. Probably helps you tolerate the job."

"Stephen King was a janitor before he got published. The more the residents talk to me, the more material I get."

"You told the cops Jackie Whitney arrived at the building between four and five on the day she returned from Palm Springs, right?"

"I did."

"Did you interact with her on that day?"

"No choice. She had a ton of luggage."

"Did she give you her usual witchiness?"

"Of course. But her shitty mood was well worth a twenty-buck tip."

"Twenty bucks just for bringing up her luggage?"

"And unloading it in her bedroom."

"By any chance, did you leave the luggage cart in her apartment?"

Lenny gave me his are you really that stupid? look. "Why would I do that?"

"I don't know. Maybe you were in a hurry and forgot to take it?"

"That didn't happen."

"Does it ever happen? To any of the doormen?"

"It's hard to picture ever happening."

A short, plump man wearing a black suit and chauffeur's cap approached Lenny and asked him where he could get a good hot dog. Lenny directed him to a Rush Street location a few blocks away.

"The old guy who works overnight, Marv. Have you gotten to know him at all?"

"A little bit. Sometimes I stay late and chat. He's known some of these families for fifty years. Jackie Whitney's death made him real sad. He likes to talk about his army days in the Korean War. He showed me his medals. A lot of his buddies died at a place called Outpost Harry. I'm surprised he's still got the will to live considering how much death he's seen."

"Did he ever talk about the police questioning him?"

Lenny looked confused. "Oh, you mean about Jackie Whitney's murder? Marv was in the hospital for all that." Lenny's words buzzed around my head, grazed my face and hair, tempted my reflex to swat at them. "What's the matter?" Lenny said.

"Okay, bear with me. What happens when someone's sick or takes vacation? You work overtime?"

"We're offered the overtime and if nobody wants it, an agency covers for us."

"Do you know the name of the agency?"

Lenny wrote down some information off a business card taped to the desk. "These idiots," he said handing me a piece of paper. "I think they just grab guys off the street and send them here."

"The night Jackie Whitney returned from Palm Springs, the agency covered the graveyard shift?"

"Yeah, I assumed that's what happened."

"What do you mean assume?"

"Because the dumbass showed up late and I wasn't going to hang around waiting on a Saturday night."

"You're sure it was Saturday night, May sixteenth?"

"I'm sure, unless bringing up all that luggage and the twenty-buck tip was a hallucination. Oh, and I hallucinated Manny's wife too."

"Manny's wife? Manny came in with his wife?"

"No. She came in alone, a few hours after Jackie got back."

Chapter 29

Sharp hunger pangs reminded me I had skipped breakfast. I drove to Penguin House and ordered their special of the day, a dish of baked fries covered in a "cheesy, beefy," allegedly vegan sauce. Whatever it was, my body welcomed it. Debbie called as I was getting ready to leave.

"The DNA results are in," Debbie said. "The lab is southwest of the city. Where are you?"

I told Debbie I'd meet her at the courthouse. Fifteen minutes later, I parked in the sprawling lot and dialed Debbie's number. Before the second ring, I heard several honks. A late nineties Ford F-150 with an extended cab roared toward me.

"Nice ride," I said as I climbed in to the sounds of Melissa Etheridge's raspy vocals coming through six-inch speakers and a powered subwoofer.

Debbie looked at my bruised neck, said nothing, then hit the gas. After we merged onto the interstate I asked if something was bothering her.

"Battle fatigue," she said. "Sexual predators and mothers beating their babies take their toll."

"Maybe you'll get some good news for a change and get Kate out of prison."

Debbie had no opinion on my optimism, but said, "Did you get strangled recently?"

"Twice yesterday."

Untroubled by my disclosure, Debbie retreated back to her dark world. We rode in silence the rest of the way, stopping at a two-story modernist cinder-block structure with floor-to-ceiling glass and a cantilevered roof. The receptionist checked our IDs then picked up the phone. A minute later a skinny man smiling broadly and wearing a white lab coat appeared.

At five minutes before three, I double parked on East Lake Shore Drive near the entrance to Jackie Whitney's building and watched seven or eight guys in red vests park and retrieve vehicles. They ranged from teenagers to mature adults and moved in a synchronized rhythm of commerce, climbing in and out of cars, eagerly anticipating the first gesture of an approaching gratuity. Manny showed up exactly at three, his doorman's jacket draped over his arm. The valets surrounded him, smiling and laughing as if just hanging out on a street corner. They must've joked around for a good ten minutes before the youngest looking valet ran off. His return was preceded by ten seconds of deep, throaty rumbling followed by a screeching halt in a fire-engine-red Mustang GT. Howls of laughter ensued as the kid revved the four-hundred horsepower a couple of times before surrendering the car to the doorman.

Manny eased the car into the street then peeled out to the stoplight, the squealing tires providing great joy to the valets. I pulled up behind him, confident he was unaware of being followed. As I observed him through the Mustang's rear windshield, his fingers and palms struck the steering wheel in rhythm to the loud bass thumping through open windows. When the light changed, Manny turned right on Michigan then merged onto northbound Lake Shore Drive. He exited at Montrose, headed east to a side street near Damen, then stopped in front of a tiny clapboard house. It looked like one of those "relief cottages" slapped together after the Great Chicago Fire of 1871. I doubted the house was more than four hundred square feet.

I parked about thirty yards down the other side of the street, and watched from my car. Twenty minutes later, Manny reappeared in a black jacket, shirt, and slacks. He jumped into his car, pulled a tight U-turn, and roared away. I waited for him to turn back onto Montrose, then gunned my four-cylinder Civic to catch up. The red Mustang was easy to spot. Manny retraced his route back to southbound Lake Shore Drive, exited at North Avenue, then turned left on Clark, where I was disheartened to see him pull into the underground garage of a high-rise apartment building.

I thought it too risky to follow him in my car, so I circled the adjacent blocks until I found a place to park then walked back. The building would be considered luxury by some standards, but not Gold Coast caliber. The residents I observed appeared younger than forty, well groomed, and may or may not have been receiving monthly allowances from their parents.

What else could I do except scan the names on the building's directory? I did so reluctantly, as one who followed through on any useless exercise, although Frownie's voice scolded me for dismissing the yet-to-be-discovered payoff that mundane tasks often generated. Several times, a resident held the door open, waiting for me to enter. The fact I carried a gun offered a great learning opportunity regarding why buildings had security doors, but I chose to say, "That's okay."

Maybe Manny was divorced and his wife and kids lived in the building. Manny's last name, Alvarez, did not appear in the directory but she may have remarried. Certainly, she didn't live there on a doorman's income. Manny's Rolex watch could've been a cheap knockoff and the gold chain around his neck could've been just stainless steel with gold plating. But it was hard to reconcile Manny driving his fancy muscle car while supporting a wife and two kids, unless he had something going on the side. And just as staring at the lobby on a computer screen had numbed my brain, so did the letters on the directory pass mindlessly through my vision, until a name stopped me cold, not only a name I recognized, but a name that proved Frownie's praise of tedious chores to be self-evident.

Over the phone, the concierge transferred me to the doorman's desk. "Lenny, it's Jules Landau."

"What's up, Mr. Landau?"

"Do me a favor. Tell me what Manny's wife looks like."

Frownie tried to make me in his image, a PI with old-school gumshoe sensibility. If bad guys played by rules excluding the Fourth Amendment, then that's how the game was played. From my knees, I examined the pin-and-tumbler lock on Manny's back door, the same type of lock Frownie had forced me to spend a billion hours practicing on. Ten minutes earlier, I'd been sitting in my car, fiddling with a roll of masking tape, pondering why the thought of breaking into someone's house induced such a distasteful feeling. The best investigators do what they have to do, would've been Frownie's answer, followed by an unsympathetic suggestion to re-evaluate my career choice. On the way over I had prayed for an unlocked window. Climbing through an open window sounded—for some reason—less unsavory.

Manny's minuscule house was really a glorified dorm room with a kitchenette. Spices, cologne, and body odor battled for olfactory domination. A pork chop shared a frying pan with a pile of rice. A neat row of satin and velvet dress shirts hung in a metal-framed portable closet. Manny's taste showed a bias for black collarless shirts with mesh panels, or white stand-up collared shirts with tuxedo ruffles. At the end of the row, a coat of arms with a red lion rampant caught my eye. I tore off a piece of masking tape, pushed it against the gray jacket's vented backside, then pulled it off.

Chapter 30

Debbie leaned back in her chair, feet on desk, one leg crossed over the other. In front of her face she clutched a thick document held together with a giant binder clip. I took the guest chair and read a newspaper clipping about a man exonerated after serving thirty-five years of a life sentence. Halfway through the article, an airborne stack of papers landed on the desk. Debbie stared at me from her reclined posture, fingers interlaced behind her head, an ambiguously calm expression on her face. "What's up?" she said. I put a plastic bag in front of her.

"The particles attached to this piece of tape came off Manny the doorman's jacket. It looks like the stuff we had tested."

Her eyes bounced between the bag and me. She cleared her throat. "Who collected this stuff using this piece of tape?"

"I did."

"And where was the jacket at the time you applied the tape?"

"In his house, on a chair."

Debbie was not pleased. I knew why. "And under what circumstances did you enter the house?"

"Okay, I know—"

"Are you familiar with the first ten amendments to the Constitution?"

"Don't kill, don't steal, don't covet your neighbor's wife. . . ." Debbie was not amused. I said, "Let's just get it tested with the other items and see if it matches the fur at Linda Napier's house or something found at Jackie Whitney's apartment."

"The evidence was illegally obtained."

"But at least we'll know—"

"It doesn't matter what we know! Not only did you illegally enter someone's house, DNA evidence has to be collected by a forensic investigator, someone who's trained to follow the guidelines. That piece of tape is the most worthless fucking evidence I've ever seen!"

Debbie stared somewhere over my head. I said, "What if we can get a warrant to search his house? I'm sure we can find more particles."

"What's your probable cause? The evidence you obtained illegally?"

"I know a retired police detective. If I show him that the particles on Manny's coat match the particles at both murder scenes, then I'm sure he can convince Brookstone to find probable cause to get a warrant."

Debbie laughed. "Sure. Brookstone drives by the doorman's house, says he smells a meth lab, then kicks in the guy's door. You'd stoop that low, Jules?"

"You got me, Debbie. I'm desecrating the memory of everyone who fought, died, and suffered so the Constitution could live."

"I'm getting pretty sick of your smartass comments."

"You're testing the particles from Linda Napier's home next, right? Just include this in a separate bag, give me the results, and I'll take it from there. You won't know anything about it."

Debbie straightened up in her chair, leaned forward over her desk, then rested her face in her hands. Defending the Fourth Amendment deserved respect, but her sanctimonious delivery challenged my sympathy. She uncovered her face, reached for the plastic bag, then said, "Get the hell away from me."

Tamar sat on the couch, Punim stretched across her lap. I stood in the doorway re-living the memory of handing Tamar a key, then her words, You may regret this.

"You look so serious," Tamar said as she caressed Punim's back. "You want your key back?"

I looked at my watch. "Not just yet." Tamar kicked my shoe. I sat down next to her and started scratching Punim behind the ears.

"I know," Tamar said. "You're not allowed to talk about it."

Two days ago, Tamar noticed the time stamp discrepancy on the CCTV video. Yesterday, she inspired me to discover DeWeldt's corporate-greed motivation for his nursing-home scheme.

"Imagine if there was a genetic database of every dog and cat somebody owned."

Tamar didn't say anything, just ran Punim's tail through her partially closed fist. She looked at me. "Is that the whole setup?"

"What do you mean?"

"The first part of a joke is called the 'setup.'"

We locked eyes a moment. I struggled not to laugh. "No, really," I said. "This guy was convicted of murder because he stepped in a pile of dog poop that was traced to the scene of the crime."

Tamar contemplated my remark. "In other words, the police matched the poop with the perp?"

Tamar kept a straight face when she spoke those words, which made my laugh impossible to suppress. "That's true."

"Does this have something to do with your investigation?"

"It does, but I collected evidence illegally."

"Without the dog's permission?"

This time we both laughed, startling Punim. She leaped off Tamar's lap then streaked down the hall. "I entered someone's property illegally. The evidence is no longer admissible in court."

"Well, go back to the house and collect it legally this time."

"Wow, you're sassy tonight! We'd need a court order, sweetheart."

"How hard is that?"

"Unless you got a compelling reason, pretty hard. In this case, there are a lot of little details that need to be laid out in the proper order for others to see the same big picture I see. If I had a chance to present my case that way, maybe I could get the cops to go into the house and do their job."

"You have to convince the cop who warned you to stop trying to help Kate McCall?"

"Yep. Good memory."

"You'll find a way to convince him."

"He hates my guts. I'm going to need Kalijero's help. Kalijero tolerates me."

"In the meantime, it's not like whoever the suspect is can gather up all the animal DNA in their house and bury it in the backyard."

Tamar's words tripped a breaker just as George's words had done at Verkakte Fashions, although the significance wasn't quite clear yet. "No backyard, just an alley," I said.

"Are you okay?" Tamar said. "You look kind of zombie-like."

"It's not like he can throw the cat DNA into the dumpster," I said, "and watch the garbage truck haul it to the landfill."

"Jules," Tamar said. "I hate being around spaced out people."

I focused on Tamar. "The murder wasn't premeditated," I said.

"Lay out all the details to Kalijero," Tamar said. "See if he'll convince that cop to listen to you."

"DNA is too small to hide. Hiding a body would take planning."

"I'm not sure what you're getting at," Tamar said, "but it's good to see you smile, so I don't care."

Chapter 31

Punim stared at me from the foot of the bed. Another morning, another blurry recollection of Tamar spending the night. I remembered coming home yesterday to find my cat lying across Tamar's lap. The display of divided loyalty hurt.

I showered, ate, drove to Jackie Whitney's building, then pulled up to the parking attendant's station. A stocky, older Hispanic man with a happy round face walked out of the office. Two teens followed, one Hispanic, one white. I had expected little enthusiasm for my shabby 1983 Civic, but the three valets appeared delighted to see me.

"Do you have short-term parking?" I said.

"Are you here to visit a resident?" the older man said.

"Does Manny qualify? He practically lives here."

The man smiled. "You're here to visit Manny?"

"I wanted to surprise him."

"I'm Ray." He motioned to the white kid who ran up to me and took my key. "We'll just put it over there." Ray pointed to an area marked with slanted yellow lines.

I thanked him, walked into the building, then stood behind the stand of trees in the middle of the lobby. Manny was leaning against the counter talking with two men wearing suits. They chatted a few minutes, started laughing, said their goodbyes. Manny took his seat behind the doorman's desk. From my location, he was visible from the forehead up. His cap turned back and forth. Probably reading the paper. I hung around five more minutes then returned to the valet station.

"He's too busy," I said to Ray. "I'll stop by again some other time."

"That Manny," Ray said shaking his head, laughing, "always busy talking to somebody. I'll get your car." He turned to leave.

"Hey, you know my nephew needs a job while he goes to school. What's it like working here?"

"Those other two kids you saw, they're still in school."

"You guys get tipped pretty good?"

Ray shrugged. "Sometimes. Depends."

"What about when you take in the dry cleaning or do the grocery shopping? The residents must tip you for that too."

Ray chuckled. "Nah. They think it's just part of our job."

"Get outta here! All these Mercedes and Porsches and Cadillacs, and they can't tip you for delivering their fifty-dollar mustard?"

"The car doesn't mean nothing. Guys in old cars tip better than rich guys."

"Man, if I had to put up with that shit, I'd look for some unofficial tips. Like running personal errands in the company van while still on the clock."

Ray grinned, shuffled his feet. "Yeah, well, that probably happens sometimes. I'm not saying I do it, but maybe others."

I smiled, nodded. "Okay, now I get it." I laughed. "That's how Manny does it."

Ray joined in with the smiling and nodding. "Manny's been working here a long time."

"What's the system? Sneak in and sneak out when nobody's looking?"

Ray gave me a dismissive wave. "No sneaking. He tells me when he needs a van, I mark it in the book."

"You keep track of these things."

"Oh, yeah, you gotta make sure a van is available when someone needs it."

"You know what? Good for him. Good for all of you. I mean, you work hard. Why not take advantage once in a while? As long as you're careful and don't smash up the van, nobody cares."

"That's right. All jobs have little secrets."

"Hey, would you mind if I looked at that book you mentioned?"

Ray's friendly demeanor faded. "What for?"

I reached for my wallet, took out a fifty, then stuffed it in Ray's shirt pocket. "That's for parking my car. There will be another fifty to let me look at the book."

Ray barely thought about it. He returned with a spiral-bound daily planner book and handed it to me without a word. I gave him another fifty then paged back to May 18. My first impulse was to tear out the page. Instead I said, "You got another datebook in case this one gets suddenly lost?"

Ray stared a hole through my forehead. "I'm not sure."

I handed over two more fifties. "Think about it."

He stuffed the money in his pocket. "Oh, hell, I'm sure I'll find one somewhere."

I pulled out of the garage then backed up to the last legally parked car along the curb. From what was technically the right-turn lane, I stared through the windshield, vaguely aware of vehicles whizzing past on Michigan Avenue. Henry DeWeldt's affair and Lucille Mackenzie's salary still nagged me as thin motivators for Jackie Whitney's actions. And I wasn't buying DeWeldt's suggestion that an epiphany allowed Jackie to recognize the uselessness of dragging poor Henry down. I closed my eyes, let my head fall back. Perhaps Jackie had always assumed family money enabled Lucille to live so grandly, I thought. Then Jackie discovered Lucille's salary and the shock was such that she couldn't help wondering why the board allowed it.

"It's Jules Landau," I said to Phillip over the phone. "Can you talk?"

"Lucille's not looming over me."

"Good. I want to look at the board meeting minutes when Lucille's salary was approved."

"I don't know anything about minutes."

"I was hoping you'd do a little investigating and get back—"

"Hang on."

If board meetings were not part of the public record, I'd ask DeWeldt to show me the minutes approving Lucille's salary. Despite his invoking "executive session," I suspected confidentiality didn't command the veto he implied.

Phillip picked up the phone. "They're posted on the website."

"Wow. That was easy."

"Case closed."

I put the phone down then noticed the cop who had pulled up next to me. He pointed at the no parking sign. I smiled, waved, then followed the right turn lane onto Lake Shore Drive.

Punim crouched on my thigh, front claws holding fast to my jeans. An awkward movement meant ten pinpricks becoming ten tiny scabs. Laptop over knees, I scanned Furry BFF's archive for agenda items and found a three-year-old meeting that included the incoming development director's compensation.

The meeting began by approving the previous month's minutes and followed with the treasurer's report. Next came an update of the year's adoptions and intakes, including a reference to how beautifully Bunny and Peanut were blossoming in foster care. Then the chairman called for old business. Henry DeWeldt moved that the board approve an augmentation of the development director's sixty-thousand-dollar annual salary with a six percent commission on donations. After the motion was seconded, the chairman opened the floor to discussion. Henry DeWeldt stated that human nature required a percentage-based incentive to realize maximum gains for fundraising. DeWeldt also stated that incentive programs conducted efficiently at for-profit businesses functioned equally as well in nonprofits, regardless if one sold Porsches or solicited subsidies for animal shelters. No other opinions were offered. The chairman then put the motion to a vote. The motion failed with five opposed and only Henry in favor. Although the issue fell under the old business category, I found no mention of adjournment into executive session in previous or future meeting minutes.

"Sorry to pester you," I said to Phillip over the phone. "Did your mom ever mention Lucille's pay structure?"

"No. But I told her there was a rumor she earned commission on donations."

"How did you hear about that?"

"This is how it went: some volunteers were always kidding Lucille about her BMW and how she must be raking in the bucks. After a while, she got defensive and said her salary wasn't so great but she got a percentage of the donations she brought in. Some thought she was joking, others weren't sure."

"Did you look into it?"

"Why would I?"

"What did you think—if it's true?"

"Maybe that's how rock-star fundraisers are paid. What do I know?"

"You asked your mom?"

"Later. It came up in a conversation, somehow. She thought the idea of paying commissions on donations sounded nuts. She wanted to know why I asked. So I told her."

"What was her reaction?"

"Something like, 'That's interesting.'"

A suspicious female voice repeated in my head "that's interesting," several times. Even if Jackie Whitney hadn't set up a charitable trust that possibly contributed to Lucille's earnings, she would've pursued the truth. "Hey, Phillip," I said. "You and the treasurer are friendly, right? How would you like to do some more investigating?"

Chapter 32

Lucille and I needed a heart-to-heart about her doll of a man, Henry DeWeldt. I suggested meeting at Penguin House where the Francis of Assisi Champion's bad habits wouldn't sully Phillip's ears—or those of anyone else with a conscience. As expected, my invitation received an icy response. Thawing required hints of DeWeldt's finances having caught the attention of "certain people," and included questions surrounding his nonprofit tax deduction claims. My intentions were in the best interests of Furry BFF, I assured her. I doubted she believed me. Nevertheless, Lucille strolled into Penguin House looking tres stylish with her red wallet on a chain over the shoulder of a sleeveless floral print midi dress.

"Thank you for meeting me here," I said.

Lucille smoothed her dress down as she sat. "I don't have much time, Mr. Landau."

"Please understand that this is all very preliminary. It's because I admire your hard work on behalf of Furry BFF, and because I understand that developing relationships with wealthy donors is crucial for the shelter's success, that I wanted to give you this heads-up. Can I trust you to keep this conversation confidential?"

"I give you my word, Mr. Landau. Now who's making these accusations against Henry?"

"I have a police contact, but he won't acknowledge whether it's FBI, IRS, or BCI."

"What is Henry accused of?"

"He hasn't been officially accused of anything, but they're looking into alleged use of Furry BFF for money laundering and tax evasion."

Lucille covered her mouth a moment then fell back in her chair. "But how do they know? What have they seen?"

"I don't know what tipped them off, but I'm sure they just followed the money."

"How will this affect the shelter?"

"That's why I wanted this meeting, to give you plenty of time to prepare for the possible loss of donations."

Lucille sat up. "Does this mean someone at the shelter was also involved?"

"I don't know."

"What does this have to do with Jackie Whitney's murder?"

"If Jackie knew what DeWeldt was up to . . ."

"Oh, yes, she had all sorts of terrible information about Henry, therefore Henry killed her."

I let the moment linger. "Information can ruin people's lives. And Jackie may have been angry about something else that had transpired between her and DeWeldt. Something having to do with relationships, maybe?"

Lucille tried not to look uncomfortable. "I cannot picture Henry DeWeldt killing another human being."

"In my experience, rich and powerful men fearful of losing their fortunes will do anything to protect what they have. And that includes hiring someone to kill."

"You have someone in mind?" Unmistakable sarcasm.

"I'm sure a man like DeWeldt knows how to make an arrangement for a contract killer. Or he knows local folks who'll do the job for the right price."

Lucille blinked several times. "You can't be serious."

"Lots of facts added up before I decided DeWeldt should at least be a suspect."

"Facts? As in evidence?"

"Yes. Mostly circumstantial, but there's too much of it to ignore. This might sound far-fetched, but could DeWeldt be linked somehow to Kate McCall?"

Lucille laughed. "That's ridiculous."

"Well, DeWeldt spoke of Jackie Whitney's interactions with Kate McCall. So she resided somewhere in his consciousness."

"Yes, but that doesn't mean he knows her, as if he had conversations with her."

"McCall and DeWeldt were both important people in Jackie's life. They both spent a lot of time with her. It's not completely nuts to assume their time with Jackie overlapped now and then."

Lucille appeared to consider my logic then took out a compact and freshened up her lipstick. "What if Henry did know Kate McCall in a limited capacity?" Lucille said. "What difference would it make?"

I held my gaze upon Lucille longer than she would've preferred. At least, that was my intention. "Then McCall could, somehow, be a component of my theory about DeWeldt's guilt."

Lucille smiled, shook her head. "A conspiracy involving Henry and Kate McCall? You're really starting to sound silly, Mr. Landau, and I think it's intentional, as if you're playing a game."

I shrugged and returned her smile. "I assure you it's not intentional."

"But aren't you working for Kate McCall? Aren't you trying to prove her innocence?"

"My job is to help find reasonable doubt so McCall's lawyer can get her out of jail. I've held up my end of the bargain and did a damn good job. The guilt or innocence thing is a side gig. I guess you could say finding the truth is a hobby of mine."

"I'd imagine that hobby could be dangerous at times. Maybe you should try something safer, like skydiving."

Lucille's ironic humor caught me off guard. My boisterous laugh startled the both of us. "Maybe I should," I said. "Anyway, you probably want to inform the treasurer what's going on with your single largest donor—for budget forecasting considerations."

Lucille stood, then looked down at me. "Yes, I'll talk to her first thing," she said then walked out.

"Detective Tommy Brookstone cracks Gold Coast murder!" I said to Kailjero when he answered the phone.

"What're you talking about?"

"That should work, don't you think?"

"Is this about that meeting you want to set up?"

"I got a story to tell, Jimmy. Tell Brookstone he gets McCall but he's gonna have to take DeWeldt down too, because I've got them connected. Tell him it's DNA-solid-proof connected."

"You wanna tell me how you did it?"

"No, it's too long a story and I don't want to have to tell it more than once."

"Just give me a summary for fuck's sake."

"A Reader's Digest version isn't going to help my cause. I have to tell it my way or it's not going to make sense. C'mon, Jimmy, tell Brookstone he was right about McCall. Don't even mention DeWeldt if you don't want to, just tell him I got McCall's accomplice and Brookstone will be the hero of the day."

"Does your public defender boss know what you're up to?"

"Not really."

"You're going to piss off a lot of people turning on your employer like that."

"I know, Jimmy. Relax. I'll give all the money back."

"That's not the point, idiot."

"Let me worry about that stuff. A woman was murdered. Those responsible need to be held accountable. Don't you want justice to be served? That's the only issue I see."

I imagined Kalijero shaking his head while staring off into never-never land. "Frownie's turning in his grave. But fine, I'll talk to Brookstone. Where and when are you telling your story?"

Chapter 33

I stood in the threshold of Lucille's office door, facing the back of her head. She sat staring out the window holding a cellphone to her ear with one hand, drumming her fingernails on the desk with the other. Phillip peeked out of his office. I flashed a thumbs-up sign. He responded in kind. Lucille disconnected the call and swung her chair around.

"Oh," she said, startled. "How long have you been standing there?"

I stepped into her office, stood at the side of her desk. "I need your help," I said.

Lucille glanced at the accordion file in my hand. "Help with what?"

"A couple of detectives are on the way. They want to hear what you and I have to say about DeWeldt."

"Oh, my God, you're really going through with this?"

"It's the police, Lucille. They're going through with it. All that circumstantial evidence has caught up with him."

"But why are you bringing them here?"

I looked at my watch. "Manny Alvarez, the doorman, just got off work and he's coming too. I told him the cops wanted to talk to you about DeWeldt and he insisted on being here."

Speechless for a moment, then Lucille said, "This is absolutely crazy. Why would you say that to him? He's not going to just rush over here because of me. We only know each other in passing."

"That's just how Manny is. He gets easily attached to people."

Movement outside the door caught my eye. Kalijero and Brookstone had reached the top of the stairs.

"Okay, the detectives are here. Try to relax."

Lucille sat back down, still incredulous. I stepped through the doorway and waved. Brookstone had bruises over the bridge of his nose. He looked pouty, as if Daddy was dragging him to his little sister's piano recital. I made the introductions then offered the two detectives the sofa under the window.

"Gentlemen," Lucille said. "I have a purely professional relationship with Henry DeWeldt. I really don't know what you're expecting of me."

"That's fine, ma'am," Kalijero said. "Mr. Landau is going to present some concerns. Feel free to challenge him. And we appreciate you letting us use your office."

My attention was again drawn out the door where I saw a determined Manny fast-walking across the common area. "Here's Manny Alvarez," I said.

Kalijero and Brookstone sat directly in line with the doorway. Manny slowed down then cautiously entered. "What's going on, Lucille?" Manny said. Lucille motioned toward me with her head. Manny turned around. "I didn't know you were coming too, Mr. Landau."

"There's no reason for you to be here, Manny," Lucille said.

Manny looked at the two detectives then turned back to Lucille. "What's DeWeldt trying to do?"

"I think you've met Detective Brookstone," I said then closed the door. "This is Detective Kalijero. Why don't you take a seat, Manny." I gently put my hand on Manny's back and directed him to the guest chair in front of Lucille's desk.

"Okay, Landau," Brookstone said, "we're ready for your little show."

I was about to tell Kalijero to control his pet chimp, when Kalijero whispered something in Brookstone's ear. "I'm sorry, everybody," Brookstone said with obvious sarcasm. "I promise to behave and let Landau lead story time."

I took a few pieces of paper from the accordion file and held them up. "Just for you, Brookie," I said. "DNA tested lab results of evidence collected at the crime scene." I held up a copy of the police photo showing a plastic bag. "Inside are some kind of tiny shavings. At the time, I thought it was dead skin. The report says they're made of keratin, which is what fingernails are made of. It turns out these are sheaths from a cat's claw. Cats shed these sheaths naturally when they scratch."

"Did Jackie Whitney own a cat?" Kalijero said.

"Not that I know of," Manny said.

"I've never been in Jackie's apartment," Lucille said. "And Henry DeWeldt doesn't own a cat either."

"How would you know whose cat the nail shavings belonged to?" Kalijero said.

"Tiny, almost invisible strands of fur were attached to these sheaths," I said. "Because cats are such meticulous groomers, the lab was able to extract DNA from the cat's saliva on the fur."

"The cat's DNA?" Brookstone said.

"Exactly," I said. "Believe it or not, a database of cat-fur DNA has already been established for use as forensic evidence. The database looks at specific markers that have been identified in the cat genome. Cat fur has solved several murders already."

"That's your DNA-solid proof?" Brookstone said. "A cat?"

"There's more," I said. "Also embedded in the cat sheaths were particles of skin, human skin. And from this human skin, the lab was able to extract DNA that doesn't belong to Jackie Whitney or Kate McCall."

More silence, then Brookstone said, "That's great for your reasonable doubt, but unless the cat's the killer, so what? The human DNA could be McCall's accomplice."

"At Linda Napier's crime scene," I said, "more sheaths and fur were found. According to the lab, the human and cat DNA are identical to the human and cat DNA found at Jackie Whitney's crime scene."

"Proof the same person was at both murder scenes," Kalijero said.

"Exactly," I said.

"We already assumed that," Brookstone said. "Did you think everything through before calling this meeting, Landau? Or were you too excited over cat DNA?"

"Manny," I said. "The other day I saw you vigorously using a lint brush on your doorman's jacket."

"We talked about that," Manny said. "My jacket is a magnet for any loose fuzz and fluff. And Gloria's dog, remember? I was taking care of Louie. His fur gets all over the place."

"That reminds me. I found out what kind of dog Louie is. He's called a bichon frise. Ever heard of it?"

Manny shook his head.

"It's a non-shedding breed," I said.

Manny stared at me. "Then I guess the stuff on my coat isn't dog fur. And I don't have a cat, if you're wondering."

"Jackie Whitney and Linda Napier didn't have a cat either," I said.

Manny looked at the two detectives then back to me. "I don't understand what you're getting at."

"Yeah, Landau," Brookstone said. "What the hell are you saying?"

"What did Manny Alvarez and Kate McCall have in common?" I said. "The obvious answer is Jackie Whitney. The better answer is the derisive, insulting, humiliating manner in which Jackie Whitney spoke to Manny Alvarez and Kate McCall."

"That never bothered me," Manny said. "Ask anyone in the building."

"Outwardly it didn't," I said. "You called her your friend. I even saw you wipe tears from your eyes the first time we talked about her."

"Manny doesn't have a violent bone in his body," Lucille said. "Many people will gladly testify to this."

"Jackie Whitney's treatment of Manny Alvarez and Kate McCall was no secret," I said. "She never considered who was standing nearby before she fired off a belittling remark. In fact, Henry DeWeldt told me himself that he was well aware of the abusive way in which Jackie Whitney spoke to Manny Alvarez and Kate McCall. And we're all aware that Henry DeWeldt knows how to recognize and exploit an opportunity when he sees one. And we also know he's the type of man not disposed to getting his hands bloody—I mean dirty."

I stopped to allow some dead air to enhance my words. Brookstone said, "I think you're saying DeWeldt hired McCall and Alvarez to kill Jackie Whitney."

"You're out of your mind," Lucille said. "Don't listen to anything he says, Manny. I'll make sure you have a great lawyer in case these detectives decide to believe this nonsense."

"I would never kill anyone," Manny said, staring into the floor.

"This is all just part of Mr. Landau's fantasy," Lucille said. "He's convinced that Jackie acquired some damaging information about Henry, which prompted Henry to have Jackie murdered."

"You got anything to back up your theory?" Kalijero said. "Or are you just talking out of your ass?"

I leaned back against the office door. "Jackie Whitney comes home from Palm Springs between four and five p.m., on Saturday, May sixteenth. Lenny, the swing shift doorman, is on duty. He has the good fortune of loading Jackie's suitcases on to a luggage cart in order to bring them up to her residence. Lenny leaves her apartment with the empty luggage cart and twenty extra dollars in his pocket. When Lenny's shift ends at eleven o'clock, Marv, the graveyard shift doorman, comes on duty."

"Bring McCall into your story," Brookstone said.

I said to Manny, "When I suggested to you that DeWeldt might be up to something regarding Lucille, you were concerned because you remembered the way DeWeldt tried to bilk Gloria's estate out of tens of thousands of dollars. That's why you wanted to be here."

Manny looked at Lucille. "I'm sorry, Lucille," he said. "It must seem strange that I'm here."

"Not so strange," I said. "You care about your friends—or people you consider your friends. That's just the way you are, Manny, which is why you have no reason to hide anything."

Manny looked at me with sad, imploring eyes. "Why're you doing this to me, Mr. Landau?" he said. "I'm not hiding anything. What would I be hiding?"

"Jackie Whitney's building has three doormen," I said. "When there's an uncovered shift, the extra hours are first offered to one of the other doormen. If nobody wants the overtime, an agency covers the shift. Is that correct?"

"That's what usually happens."

"On the evening of May sixteenth, Marv is in the hospital recovering from pneumonia. Lenny is expecting an agency doorman to arrive at eleven, but he's late. Being a Saturday night and Lenny being a young guy, he isn't going to wait around. So he goes home unaware that the substitute doorman never shows up the night Jackie Whitney is murdered."

"You don't know for sure when she was murdered," Brookstone said. "The coroner didn't rule out the seventeenth or eighteenth."

"You're right," I said. "I could be wrong about when Jackie died just as I could be wrong about the graveyard shift going uncovered Saturday night, May sixteenth. In fact, I know I'm wrong because I called the agency and they told me the order was canceled—by Manny Alvarez."

"That's right!" Manny said. "I remember now. I decided I wouldn't mind getting some overtime."

"When did you call the agency to cancel?"

Manny's eyes darted around. "In the morning sometime, I think."

"You're sure it was the morning?"

"Stop treating him like a criminal!" Lucille said. "Manny, you should go—"

"I wouldn't leave just yet," Brookstone said, surprising the hell out of me. "All I need is reasonable suspicion to detain someone."

"But you're free to go if you'd like, Lucille," I said.

She looked at Manny then at the two detectives. "I'm staying. For Manny's sake. If I know anything, it's that the police can't be trusted."

"Maybe I called the agency later in the day," Manny said. "I can't be sure."

"Maybe you called the agency much later in the day," I said.

Manny stood up. "Y-you can't really think I killed her, right?"

"If these detectives think you're not being truthful, they're going to wonder why."

Manny stepped toward Brookstone and Kalijero. "Maybe it was much later in the day. I might've called the agency that evening."

"Why didn't you tell me this when I first questioned you?" Brookstone said.

"I don't know," Manny said quietly. He walked back to his chair. "I guess I didn't think it was important."

"Don't say another word," Lucille said. She walked to Manny's side, knelt down, whispered in his ear. Brookstone and Kalijero started mumbling angrily at each other. I walked over to them.

"What?" I said.

"I'm handling this, Landau," Kalijero said.

"Get Alvarez to talk about McCall," Brookstone said, "or I'm gonna take him in right now."

"You agreed to let me tell—"

"That son of a bitch was in the victim's apartment with Kessler—"

"Arrest him now and he lawyers up, dumbass!"

Kalijero shoved me hard in the chest, knocking me backward into a display table. Stacks of Furry BFF brochures fell to the floor. Lucille glanced my way then walked back to her chair.

I approached Manny. "Since I'm the cynical type," I said, "I'm going to wonder if overtime was the true reason that Manny decided to work the graveyard shift." I put my hand on Manny's shoulder. "What do you think, Manny?"

"I don't know what you mean."

I said, "Around two o'clock Sunday morning, May seventeenth, Dr. Kessler returned to retrieve some personal items from Jackie Whitney's apartment. He asked Linda Napier to meet him in the lobby. Since you were working the graveyard shift that night, Manny, you ended up accompanying both of them to Jackie Whitney's apartment. Did that escape your memory?"

Manny stood, shoved his hands into his pockets, stepped away then turned back to me. "Dr. Kessler showed up in a panic," Manny said. "He had this frightening look in his eyes. He said he had a key and was going up to Jackie's apartment. He wasn't asking me, he was telling me. He seemed really desperate and scary. His breath reeked of alcohol. I thought it better to just go along with him than call the police. And Linda was there. With all of us present, I thought maybe Jackie wouldn't be too upset if she discovered us."

"The three of you entered the apartment," I said. "Then what?"

"Linda and I stood in the hallway outside of Jackie's bedroom while Dr. Kessler retrieved his belongings from the guest bedroom. A few minutes later, we were gone."

"That's risky behavior, isn't it?" I said. "I mean, you could be fired for entering a resident's home uninvited, no less bringing in a couple of other people. You must've been pretty confident you wouldn't be caught."

Manny looked down, slid his foot back and forth across the floor. "I shouldn't have done it. It was foolish." He looked at me. "But Dr. Kessler had a key to her apartment! I didn't want to take a chance—"

"Did he show you the key?"

"Of course."

"You were protecting Jackie Whitney," I said. "You didn't want to take the chance of Dr. Kessler coming back on his own. Who knew what he was capable of?"

Manny sat back down. "Dr. Kessler was acting very, very scary."

"Although there's one detail you left out," I said. "Linda Napier walked into the building first. She told Dr. Kessler she saw you coming out of the residents' elevator shortly after she arrived."

"What? Why? For what? I had no reason! I never did that."

"Were you in Jackie Whitney's apartment before Dr. Kessler or Linda Napier got there?"

Manny jumped out of his chair, approached the two detectives holding his hands palms up. "I didn't kill anyone. They're trying to make me look bad. I swear to God Almighty! I swear on the lives of my children! I didn't kill anyone!"

Lucille walked out from behind her desk, stood about a foot from Manny. "They can't touch you with this," she said to Manny, making sure everyone heard. "It's all hearsay because—"

"Because Linda Napier is dead," I said, "and Dr. Kessler is just repeating what Linda allegedly told him. But we can check the CCTV video and see if—oh, wait a minute. There's a gap in the time stamp from eleven-fifteen Saturday night to about eight o'clock the next morning." I looked at Lucille and said, "Detectives Brookstone and Kalijero, I want you to ignore everything I said about Manny coming out of the elevator. Hearsay is inadmissible in court and the CCTV had unfortunately malfunctioned."

Chapter 34

"Manny," Brookstone said, "tell us about McCall. What's McCall's connection to DeWeldt?"

"Henry has no connection to that woman," Lucille said.

"DeWeldt is evil and greedy," Alvarez said. He had returned to staring at the floor.

"You're right!" I said. "He even sucked Lucille into his slimy trap."

Lucille gave me a savage look then said, "You don't know what you're talking about."

"Let's talk about money, that greatest of motivators," I said then removed several papers from the accordion file. "An associate of mine did a little detective work for me. He got the treasurer of Furry BFF to check the pledged donation amounts against the money actually deposited into the Furry BFF account."

"The shelter has an independent auditor," Lucille said. "They keep track of these things and have never found anything out of the ordinary."

"No doubt that's been the case since you've worked here, Lucille. But just for fun, I'm gonna wonder out loud how truly independent the auditor was? I mean, what if the auditor had some kind of association with a scumbag like Henry DeWeldt?"

"Henry provided the seed money to build this place!" Lucille said. "Over a million dollars."

"What's your point?" Kalijero said.

"Nonprofits try to maintain the smallest paid staff possible," I said, "so employees often end up wearing more than one hat. For example, Development Director Lucille Mackenzie is the chief fundraiser, but she also assists the treasurer with administrative tasks—like depositing checks."

"What are you suggesting?" Lucille said.

Brookstone sighed loudly and said, "What do you got on DeWeldt? And don't tell me cat fur."

"Here you go, Brookie. DeWeldt is such a sneaky bastard that Lucille didn't even realize she was depositing donation checks into an account under the name of—wait for it—Henry DeWeldt!"

The detectives cast their eyeballs upon Lucille. She leaned back in her chair. "Oh, stop looking at me like that!" she said. "I'm sure there's a logical reason. He's on the board of directors, after all."

"The real issue," I said, "is the ten-percent discrepancy between what ended up in Furry BFF's operating account and the original donations Lucille deposited."

"I endorsed and deposited every donation check exactly how it was received!" Lucille said.

"What does the treasurer say about it?" Kalijero said.

"She wanted to call the police, but my associate suggested he be allowed to get all the facts first." I looked at Lucille. "So we don't jump to conclusions."

"How much money are we talking about?" Brookstone said.

"Almost eight million over two years," I said.

"Whoa!" Kalijero said. "At ten percent? Somebody skimmed eight hundred grand?"

Lucille said, "Mr. Landau is ignoring the possibility that Henry was utilizing his knowledge of financial loopholes or other arrangements to save the shelter from hidden fees and such. Henry's most likely putting money aside to cover future accounting costs or payroll taxes, or for the rainy-day fund."

"Well, then," I said, "when the attorney general's office gets their warrant to examine the comings and goings of the donations from DeWeldt's account, they'll see there's nothing illegal going on."

"That's right," Lucille said. "But in the meantime, we will have insulted our most important benefactor and lost our biggest source of funding, thanks to your nonsense."

I took another page out of the accordion file. "Lucille, did you know that DeWeldt tried to get you a raise before you even started working here?"

"I have no idea what you're talking about," Lucille said.

"Make your point!" Kalijero said.

"At a board meeting about three years ago," I said. "DeWeldt motioned that the incoming development director's compensation include a six percent commission on donations. When put to a vote, however, the motion failed. Maybe DeWeldt's original plan was to skim your six percent after you deposited donations into his account. But then he thought, 'Hey, if the board won't let me steal six percent, they might as well not let me steal ten percent.'"

Brookstone stood. "This is an embezzlement issue."

"Money motive, Detective Brookstone," I said. "Money motive makes a murder issue." Brookstone looked at his watch, sat back down, folded his arms.

"Maybe DeWeldt's not as greedy as I thought," I said. "Maybe he kept, like, four percent, and transferred six percent to someone else's account." I looked at Lucille. "Do you still consult privately on estate planning?"

"On occasion," Lucille said.

"In fact, didn't you help Jackie Whitney set up a charitable trust to benefit Furry BFF?"

"I did."

"Did you do any consulting for DeWeldt's law firm?" Lucille didn't respond, just stared a hole through me. I said, "I wonder if DeWeldt paid you consulting fees with money he skimmed off donations."

"I don't believe that. Henry will explain everything, I have no doubt."

I walked to the side of Lucille's desk. "Lucille," I said. "Was there anything you didn't think was important enough to tell Detective Brookstone?"

"Of course not," Lucille said.

"Did you tell Detective Brookstone that you and Jackie were close gal-pals and that Jackie's boyfriend was Henry DeWeldt?"

"No, you didn't," Brookstone said.

I said, "Imagine Jackie's anger after discovering Henry and Lucille's affair."

Once again the two detectives looked at Lucille. "The situation wasn't nearly as dramatic as Mr. Landau is portraying," Lucille said.

"According to DeWeldt," I said, "just a couple of meaningless encounters. But that didn't diminish Jackie's anger or her urge to lash out. Like all good mobsters, DeWeldt kept a record of transactions to maintain the corruption equilibrium should one of his judges or aldermen betray him. Electronic surveillance being what it is today, DeWeldt probably handwrote the incriminating activity in a spiral notebook."

"Oh, my God, what nonsense!" Lucille said. "Jackie stole the notebook, therefore, Henry had her killed. Absolutely absurd."

"The notebook included records of DeWeldt's scam with Lucille's donation deposits. Jackie was a very important donor. Because of her charitable trust, Furry BFF bestowed on Jackie the title patron saint. Isn't that right, Lucille?"

"You know it is," Lucille said. "So what?"

"Now imagine Jackie's anger upon discovering that ten percent of her quarterly trust distribution was split between Henry DeWeldt and someone owed a 'consulting fee.'"

"There you go again with the consulting fee," Lucille shouted. "You're making an assumption. You have absolutely no proof!"

"It was bad enough DeWeldt had an affair with Jackie's gal-pal, but to steal from Jackie's charitable trust as well? Would anyone blame Jackie for wanting to strike back by changing the trust to exclude Furry BFF?"

Chapter 35

"Manny," I said. "Anything else you thought wasn't important enough to tell Detective Brookstone?"

Kalijero said, "Just make your—"

"Point," I said. "Okay, let's talk about Manny's wife."

Manny looked up. "My wife?"

"What's your wife's name?"

"What does she have to do with anything?"

"Lenny said your wife visited Jackie a few hours after Jackie returned from Palm Springs."

Manny gave me a bizarre look. "What? That's impossible. Lenny's mistaken. He doesn't know her."

"Wouldn't he recognize her?"

"No. He's never met her."

His sincerity sounded authentic. "My bad," I said. "I shouldn't assume people know what they're talking about. But a woman who Lenny thought was your wife did visit Jackie."

"I wouldn't know about that," Manny said. "Check the guest sign-in book."

"Well, if Lenny thought this woman was your wife, I'm sure he would've waved her through."

"You didn't check the guest sign-in?" Brookstone said.

"Did you, Detective Brookstone? Did you, the policeman, check the guest sign-in?"

"Okay! Forget it!" Kalijero said.

"Manny," I said, "you say Lenny has never seen your wife."

"He hasn't. He's never met her."

"Is it possible the woman Lenny thinks is your wife is really your girlfriend?"

Manny ran his hands through his hair. "I don't know what you're talking about."

"Is it possible you don't have a wife—or children? Could your girlfriend and the woman Lenny called your wife be the same person?"

"Stop it!" Lucille shouted. "Stop with your wild accusations! Manny doesn't deserve to be treated this way."

Brookstone stood up. "Is it true, Alvarez? Because if it is, I need to know who she is and why she was visiting Jackie Whitney."

"Lucille," I said, "you and Manny only know each other in passing. That's what you told me. Yet here you stay, at his side, apparently very invested in what he has to say."

"You're a son of a bitch, Mr. Landau," Lucille said. "You make your accusations without giving a damn how they affect people's lives."

"Okay, okay," I said. "Enough with the accusations. I'll try some rumors instead. Lucille has a boyfriend who likes to go dancing. Anyone we know?"

"That's none of your business."

"Kalijero," Brookstone said, "I'm losing my fucking mind with your boy."

I looked at Manny. "Manny, you silly boy! Are you the one wearing white or black shirts with mesh panels and tuxedo ruffles?"

The two detectives looked back and forth between Manny and Lucille.

"Landau!" Kalijero said. "Whatever the hell you're saying, just say—"

"I'm going to talk about you for a while, Lucille," I said. "You too, Manny. Feel free to interject if you don't like my accusations. Or you can leave if you're not interested."

Lucille pretended to think about it. I knew neither of them were going anywhere. "Just let him talk, Manny," Lucille said. "Telling a story and proving anything are completely different."

"Saturday, May sixteenth," I said. "At precisely 7:42p.m., Lucille Mackenzie enters the lobby of Jackie Whitney's building. Whether Jackie called Lucille or Lucille called Jackie, we won't know until the cellphone records are checked. But what I'm fairly certain of is that Lucille wants to talk about the charitable trust Jackie had set up. The trust Jackie planned on changing to exclude Furry BFF."

"DeWeldt told her about Jackie changing the trust?" Kalijero said.

Lucille laughed.

"Exactly," I said. "Furry BFF losing the trust money along with the possible consequences should Jackie inform the board that ten percent of donations are missing must've caused Lucille much anxiety. How could she explain the checks deposited in DeWeldt's account and then six percent transferring to another account in Lucille's name? Maybe Lucille could reason with her old friend and they could reach some kind of agreement."

"What about DeWeldt?" Kalijero said. "Does he know what Lucille's up to?"

I looked at Lucille. "I don't think so," I said. "The evening started off nice enough. Jackie opened the first bottle of wine and the two friends chatted about how nice it was in Palm Springs and how great things were going at the shelter. Jackie knew their discourse was all an act and probably felt empowered watching Lucille tiptoe around the giant squid sprawled out in the living room. But she was content to follow Lucille's lead all the way through the second bottle of wine, when Lucille decided to bring up the trust."

"What about McCall?" Brookstone said.

"Lucille," I said. "What kind of drunk are you? A silly drunk? A sleepy drunk? An angry drunk?"

Lucille had no comment.

"Jackie's blood alcohol level was 0.139 percent. And since there were only two of you at this party, I'm thinking Lucille was also pretty drunk after the second bottle. When the subject turns to the trust, it's not hard to imagine how the conversation might've become heated. Jackie may have cut loose on Lucille, letting her pent-up anger spill out. Having an affair with her boyfriend? What kind of friend does that? Then she starts talking about the notebook she stole and how it revealed what a crook DeWeldt is, and, by default, what a crook Lucille is too."

Manny looked up. "DeWeldt is the evil one," he said. "He used Lucille for his own gain."

"Pay no attention, Manny," Lucille said. "Let Mr. Landau have his fun playing the sleuth. Who are you, Hercule Poirot? Or maybe Miss Marple?"

I couldn't deny I was enjoying myself. Knowing how a puzzle fit together was tremendously empowering.

"Did Jackie make you beg her not to change the trust?" I said. "Did she make you get down on your hands and knees? Maybe that was it. You gladly humiliated your drunken self, thinking if you just let Jackie have her way that night, she'd get the anger out of her system and let the problem be solved without changing trusts or instigating inquiries into financial misconduct. But you were wrong. And when you realized Jackie was enjoying every moment of your humiliation, you hit your breaking point. A hammer lying on the end table caught your eye. The same hammer Kate McCall had used many times to help Jackie hang pictures. In a flash, you grabbed it then brought it down on the crown of Jackie's head. The anger behind the blow rendered Jackie unconscious and forever unaware that her life was about to end with two more strikes that would follow."

"You're a very good storyteller, Mr. Landau," Lucille said. "Even the two detectives seem taken in."

"Manny," Brookstone said. "You got anything to say?"

"Lucille's a good person," Manny practically whispered. "DeWeldt's the evil one."

"After Lucille realizes what she has done," I said, "she calls her boyfriend, the person she knew wouldn't allow her to deal with this mess alone. A check of Lucille's phone records will tell us she called Manny between nine thirty and ten thirty. A check of Manny's phone records will indicate he called the agency during that same time period. You can have those records checked, can't you, Detective Brookstone?"

Brookstone said nothing, just stared at me. "Yes," Kalijero said. "Keep talking."

"The CCTV was turned off at eleven fifteen, about the time Manny showed up to cover the graveyard shift. Sometime before two the next morning, Manny meets Lucille in Jackie's apartment. Lucille is frantic. She swears she didn't mean to kill Jackie, and also tells him about a notebook full of information that will ruin her. Manny sends her home. His thinking is nearsighted. Hide the body. Move it somewhere else. He puts Jackie in a garment bag. He fetches a luggage cart from the lobby and brings it up to the apartment. He uses the cart to move the body to Jackie's closet. He's strong enough to maneuver Jackie over his shoulder. Then he carries her up the ladder to the top shelf, where she'll remain until Manny figures out a way to take the body out of the building."

"More fiction," Lucille said.

Kalijero said, "When Linda Napier sees Manny exiting the elevator, he had just put the body in the closet."

"Yes," I said. "Kessler shows up shortly after Linda. Since Kessler has a key, Manny can't risk him sneaking up on his own and possibly seeing the bloody mess on the couch or peeking into Jackie Whitney's bedroom. So he escorts them. The excursion works out nicely since Kessler wants only to get the hell out of there as quickly as possible and Manny knows he doesn't have to worry about Jackie waking up."

"You're looking at accessory after the fact, Manny," Brookstone said.

"In the late afternoon of Monday, May eighteenth," I said, "Kate McCall stops by to check on her friend Jackie Whitney. Manny is on duty because he switched with Lenny in order to work the swing and graveyard shifts back-to-back. Manny calls up to the apartment, no answer. McCall says she's worried and wants to see if Jackie's okay. At first, Manny doesn't want to let her up, but he realizes McCall will be setting herself up as a suspect, so off she goes."

"How about it, Manny?" Brookstone said. "Accessory after the fact to murder doesn't bother you?"

"Not a word, Manny," Lucille said. "From now on, his lawyer will speak for him."

"McCall notices the odor of death," I said. "She gets the hell out of there but doesn't know what to do. She comes back in the wee hours the next morning, sees Manny again, and tells him about the smell. McCall finding Jackie's body will ruin Manny's special plans for his graveyard shift. But he's smart enough to know that if McCall tells the police he wouldn't let her up, despite the 'odor of death,' it wouldn't look good. So Manny lets McCall go back up, she sniffs out the body, calls 911."

"Manny was going to move the body," Kalijero said. "That's why he took the graveyard shift."

"You got proof he was going to move the body, Landau?" Brookstone said.

From the accordion file I took out the valet's daily planner, opened it up to May 18, then held it in front of the two detectives.

I said, "You'll notice that one of the valets had written, 'Econoline #586, Manny,' and then drew an arrow from Monday evening through Tuesday morning. Manny reserved a van."

"Manny," Lucille said, "you'll also notice they've got nothing to prove you were even in Jackie's apartment other than Dr. Kessler's claim."

I took a small strip of masking tape from my pocket. "After you walked in, Manny, I put my hand lightly on your backside. I directed you to the seat you're sitting in while sliding my hand down your jacket. In my hand was this piece of tape. If you look closely, you can see some strands of what looks like fur. If it is fur, we've already established it can't be Louie's fur, because Gloria's dog doesn't shed. But could it be cat fur?"

"Don't let him scare you," Lucille said.

I said, "If I had this fur analyzed, is it possible I might find the same DNA that was found at the two crime scenes?"

"Manny," Brookstone said, "I'll be getting a court order to test the fur. And look for more fur at your house."

"Dr. Kessler or Linda Napier or Kate McCall could've easily killed Jackie," Lucille said.

"Or you," I said.

"Oh?" Lucille said. "I'm still waiting for something besides your storytelling imagination that suggests I killed somebody—or actually puts me in the building at the time you say."

"The CCTV hadn't been turned off yet when Manny's girlfriend-wife arrived," I said.

"And?" Lucille said. "That video alone isn't proof of anything."

"Then there's the guest sign-in book the police neglected to examine," I said. "Early in my investigation I looked for Dr. Kessler's name. A couple of days ago I spoke to Lenny over the phone. He told me the page for the evening of May sixteenth had been torn out. This was disappointing news, but then Lenny surprised me. It seems the book is two-part carbonless paper and the second page was still intact." I took a folded piece of paper from my pocket. "Not great quality, but I think the signature is identifiable." I handed the page to Brookstone. He stared at it then handed it to Kalijero.

"Accessory after the fact, Manny," Brookstone said. "Class X felony. You could get six years or thirty years. Or you could get probation. A clean record helps. So would cooperation."

"He's trying to turn you against me, Manny," Lucille said. "These gentlemen think a killer is dumb enough to sign their name while a camera watched."

"No, Lucille," I said. "Manny's girlfriend-wife signed in because she never intended to kill Jackie." I took a few steps toward Brookstone. "Which is why the charge will be second degree murder, don't you think, Detective Brookstone?"

The room stayed silent until Brookstone said, "Anything you want to say, Manny?"

"By the way, Manny," I said. "Shortly before Linda Napier was found murdered, she was talking to you in Jackie's lobby. As soon as she walked away, you called someone. Once that court order is approved, Detective Brookstone will be able to find out." I looked at Lucille. "That would probably be a first degree murder charge."

Kalijero stared at Lucille. Her eyes fixed on an unknown point, her lower lip quivered slightly. "Anything, Lucille?" Kalijero said.

"Phone calls, hearsay, alleged video and signature," Lucille said. "I'm not impressed."

"One last factor to consider, Lucille," I said. "You have a cat, don't you?"

Chapter 36

As expected, the press conference announcing two new arrests in the Jacqueline Whitney murder caused an uptick of excitement throughout the Chicago area and propelled Detective Thomas "Tommy" Brookstone into the limelight as the face of breaking news. When reports identified the suspects as a doorman romantically linked with an affluent fundraising professional, ratings across the board surged. But it was the disclosure of cat DNA playing a key role in securing their arrests that sparked a full-scale media frenzy. All broadcast and publication outlets, blogs, and webzines competed to outdo each other with headlines such as, "Fundraiser Forsaken by Faithless Feline," "Pussycat Payback," "Tabby Treason," and "Mouser Mendacity." Inevitably, Manny's and Lucille's passion for salsa dancing also found its way into the rhetoric and led to scandal-sheet scrutiny with suggestions of hedonistic lifestyles financed by Furry BFF's unsuspecting donors. Sadly, Manny's make-believe family too was exposed and thoroughly criticized as a lowly tactic to extract pity money.

As Brookstone had predicted, Manny was charged with accessory after the fact, which in Illinois meant he faced the same sentencing guidelines as the perpetrator of the actual killing. The judge set bail at one hundred thousand dollars, ordinarily an insurmountable sum. But Manny's twenty-plus years of exemplary service to the forgiving residents of Kenilworth Manor,was enough to overcome the court's hardship and even procure Manny the services of Gloria's son-in-law, an experienced criminal defense attorney.

Thanks to advances in technology that enabled DNA extraction from fingerprint skin cells, lab tests on the hammer found at Jackie Whitney's murder scene confirmed the presence of Lucille's DNA. In addition, tests performed on the items found in the Youji Lu Grocery dumpster found Lucille's DNA on Jackie Whitney's prescription pill bottles, vehicle registration, and keys, while Manny's DNA was identified on the plastic bag. Thus far, the purported book of financial and judicial misdeeds. allegedly taken from DeWeldt's home, had not been recovered, although the book's hypothetical existence had been widely speculated upon in the press. Manny denied possession or knowledge of such book. When the book found its way into the hands of Post reporter Ellis Knight, the story of Jacqueline Whitney's murder took on a new dimension, and even provoked some pundits to call upon the memories of legendary bribery sting operations with names like Greylord, Gambit, and Silver Shovel.

Angry that he had been unable to keep his name out of the press, Henry DeWeldt publicly accused me of expediting the book's placement into the hands of the Post reporter and then claimed I slanderously exposed him as the owner of an otherwise anonymous spiral notebook. Just as publicly, I labeled DeWeldt's acknowledgment of the book's existence as an arrogant display of invulnerability to the law.

Although one could argue that Kessler's testimony and Manny's DNA on a plastic bag were all the state had to allege Manny's presence in Jackie Whitney's apartment, his chances of acquittal still looked bleak. Ultimately, Manny's jacket and home were found to be full of Lucille's and her cat's DNA, his graveyard-shift attendance, CCTV time-stamp gap, van reservation, and well-timed phone calls with Lucille comprised a heap of dangerously incriminating evidence. What Manny did have going for him was a highly skilled lawyer who deftly argued Manny's absolution based on his having no prior criminal record, playing no part in the commission of the murder, and not following through on moving the body out of the building. The defense's characterization of Manny as a working-class immigrant's son who had fallen under the spell of Lucille's sex appeal and money may have also helped convince the district attorney to respond with a plea deal. In exchange for no prison time, Manny would plead guilty and cooperate fully with the prosecution of Lucille Mackenzie for the murders of Jackie Whitney and Linda Napier.

At bond court, Lucille's lawyer acknowledged the tragic loss of life, but argued that the defendant did not pose a physical danger to the public, had no previous criminal record, and had strong ties to the community through her work at a humane animal shelter. The prosecution disputed the claim that Lucille posed no threat, then relented somewhat, contending that if bail was to be granted, the defendant should be placed on home confinement and wear a GPS monitoring bracelet. The judge agreed with the prosecution and set bail at one million dollars. When Lucille's bail was posted by a man later identified as employed with DeWeldt's law firm, speculation grew that DeWeldt was afraid Lucille might get some kind of break in exchange for testifying against him, should charges be brought at a later date.

Because of the identical DNA evidence at both crime scenes and the similar manner in which the victims died, the prosecution successfully argued for a single trial to cover both murders. Doing his best to avoid eye contact with his former lover, Manny testified to receiving a frantic phone call from a drunken Lucille Mackenzie hysterically describing something terrible having happened to Jackie Whitney. Manny then admitted to canceling the order for a substitute doorman so that he could attend to Lucille's predicament. Upon arrival at Jackie Whitney's apartment, Manny said he found Lucille sitting on the floor, head in her hands, mumbling incoherently. He needed only a look to know Jackie Whitney was dead.

After Manny coaxed Lucille into again telling him what had happened, Lucille described a semi-coherent patchwork of scenes suggesting the scenario I had depicted, of former friends chatting nicely at first, but slowly succumbing to the wine's influence, until diminished inhibitions culminated in tragedy. Manny's initial thoughts were to first get Lucille home, and then try to make sense of the situation. He ushered her to the freight elevator, made sure she had money for a cab, then explained that she was to exit through the alley.

About an hour after returning to his post in the lobby, and for reasons he couldn't explain, an intense need to remove Jackie Whitney's body from the living room prompted Manny to take a luggage cart and return to her apartment. From the victim's closet, he then took a garment bag and brought it to the living room. Before packing Jackie Whitney's body into the garment bag, Manny removed his own clothes to avoid bloodstains. Once he had positioned the bag onto the cart, he wheeled the body to the bedroom closet, maneuvered it over his shoulder, then climbed the ladder to the top shelf.

With the body now out of sight, Manny returned to the lobby just in time for Linda Napier to see him exiting the elevator. What, if anything, transpired between them, he didn't say. When Kessler showed up, the subsequent events regarding Kessler's retrieval of personal items occurred as both Kessler and Manny had previously described. Despite reserving a van, Manny claimed he never would've gone through with the alleged plan to move Jackie Whitney's body to another location outside of the building. Manny also testified that he called Lucille on the day Linda Napier was killed and told her that their conversation included innuendos of where Manny had been when she saw him exiting the elevator. It was during this phone call that Manny revealed to Lucille that he and Linda Napier had engaged in a brief affair. Manny said he never thought Lucille would go to Linda's house and kill her, and that all along, Lucille denied having anything to do with Linda Napier's death.

Despite a robust defense from her lawyers, Lucille was found guilty of murder in the first degree of Linda Napier, and murder in the second degree of Jackie Whitney. She received a life sentence plus twenty years.

Chapter 37

I would tell my story one more time with Tamar while celebrating at a Persian restaurant in Andersonville. It was still a few days before the arraignments and all the details had not yet been validated, but Tamar's curiosity gave me no choice but to answer her questions.

"It seems kind of weird that Lucille would just sit there the whole time listening to you unravel the truth," Tamar said. "I mean, you said it wasn't until the end of your speech that you started implicating Lucille."

"She thought I was going to present my case for DeWeldt murdering Jackie Whitney," I said. "Lucille didn't realize she was a murder suspect until the end, although I was a little concerned she would run out of there before I had a chance to spin my web around her." The waiter came to the table and put a glass of red wine in front of Tamar and a root beer in front of me. I said, "And when I made Manny the initial focus of my statement, Lucille realized that she absolutely had to know what Manny was going to say."

"How did you bring in Lucille's financial scheming with DeWeldt?" Tamar said.

"I tried to suggest Lucille was an unwitting victim of DeWeldt's sneaky banking tricks," I said. "But I'm sure everyone knew Lucille's culpability would be easily discovered if the police looked into it."

"Having someone as powerful as DeWeldt on her side probably made her feel confident," Tamar said.

"No doubt," I said. "If this whole meeting was just about stealing the shelter's donations, Lucille probably would've walked out as soon as the detectives walked in. But she knew I was there to talk about murder. And people with her background know running away is like an admission of guilt. They'd rather stay and use their money and influence to fight the accusations. I also think she legitimately cared about Manny and didn't want to abandon him."

"I guess Manny wasn't the man everyone thought he was," Tamar said.

"Yes and no," I said. "His house was absurdly small for a family of four, and there was nothing about the interior that conveyed a sense of family or homemaking. No games or toys or photos of the kids, et cetera. However, I do think Manny's personality was authentic. That is, he was a genuinely nice person who figured out a way to manipulate his clientele."

"What do you mean, 'clientele'?"

"By definition, doormen are supposed to be friendly and courteous. I would think a doorman who embraced this role without giving off the slightest air of self-consciousness or bitterness, and was also married with small children, endeared him to many of the people he served. And his charade agreed with him financially, of course."

"How did you come to realize Manny and Lucille were a couple?" Tamar said.

I laughed. "'Cha-cha-cha,' was the first clue," I said, then described my initial encounter with Lucille, waiting for her to get off the phone. "Other clues included Lucille supposedly referring to a 'Latin lover,' and Lenny referring to Manny as a 'salsa athlete hoofin' on the dance floor.' Then one afternoon I followed Manny to the building where Lucille lived, and that sealed the deal."

Tamar nodded enthusiastically, smiled. "The note to DeWeldt demanding McCall be convicted," Tamar said. "That was Lucille's idea."

"Nope. Manny."

"Really?"

"Kessler stated that when Linda Napier saw Manny coming out of the elevator, she told him he acted like he was hiding something under his jacket. I'm sure it was DeWeldt's book of crooked financial deals. Manny's smart enough to know what the book represented. He knew McCall showed up on the eighteenth, he knew she had a key to Jackie's apartment. But putting Jackie Whitney's personal items in the trash where McCall worked, that was probably a collaboration."

"How could either of them have possibly known that the grocery store owner checked his trash for illegal dumping?"

I gave Tamar a sly smile. "Ah," I said, "that required my brilliant observational skills and more than a little luck. I knew Lucille was a customer at Youji Lu Grocery because on her desk she had a condolence gift basket Youji Lu sent to her when one of her cats died. The day I went to check out the dumpster in the alley behind the grocery, the owner of the boutique that shared the alley just happened to be hanging out, smoking a cigarette. I asked her if she was aware of a guy who rummaged through the grocery store's dumpster, and she verified that a Chinese guy did just that. I guessed from the boutique's address and the way the owner was dressed that she sold accessories with expensive labels, the kind of labels I noticed Lucille wore. Lucille had mentioned she shopped on North Michigan Avenue, so I asked the boutique owner if Lucille was one of her customers. It turned out they were quite friendly. Lucille often popped in before or after shopping for groceries at Youji Lu."

"You're right," Tamar said. "That was lucky. Okay, on to the fur. What made you suspicious that the fur on Manny's jacket wasn't dog fur?"

"That was purely a gut feeling. It just didn't seem right that a wealthy woman in her eighties, living in an apartment, would have a dog that shed."

The waiter brought dinner, which seemed to irritate Tamar. When he walked away she said, "What happened to Kate McCall?"

"She's back working at the Youji Lu Grocer," I said. "She has a lot of folksy knowledge about Kentucky mushrooms that's been passed down in her family. Mr. Chao wants her to become the grocery's mushroom expert, and is sending her to wild mushroom identification courses."

"How nice!" Tamar said. "How about telling me the story of DeWeldt's book getting into the hands of a Post reporter?"

"You're better off not knowing," I said. "That way, if you're tortured, you still won't reveal the truth."

"Is Ellis Knight going to get a real story out of this imaginary book?"

"I seriously doubt that book will ever see the light of day," I said, then tried to explain how DeWeldt's army of lawyers had filed injunctions against the Post, claiming the tabloid was in possession of stolen property belonging to DeWeldt, even though DeWeldt insisted the notebook had no identification markings linking it to him."

"But if there are real account numbers that Furry BFF's money was illegally put into—"

"Objection!" I said louder than I should have. "Investigating those account numbers would constitute a violation of DeWeldt's Fourth Amendment right prohibiting unreasonable search and seizure, blah, blah, blah."

"In other words," Tamar said, "if you're rich enough, you can afford lawyers who know how to interpret the law any way you pay them to. One more question."

"Good. I don't like my Persian food cold."

"The other night, when you mentioned genetic databases for dogs and cats. Why didn't you just tell me you were talking about cat fur and your murder suspects?"

"Oh, I don't know. I guess I wanted you to be surprised, like the public was when it all came out. And besides, the perp getting busted because he stepped in dog poop sounded much more realistic."

Chapter 38

Shortly after the resolution of Jackie Whitney's murder, a Partisan front page article ignited new interest in Kate McCall. Although better known for exposing Chicago's uninterrupted legacy of municipal corruption, The Partisan also took pride in championing the causes of common people. For this reason, the article focused primarily on Kate McCall's work with handicapped children, a mea culpa of sorts for encouraging images like the Chicago Post's depiction of Kate McCall as a farcical hillbilly sexpot. Thanks to the article, Kate's public image transformed from an ignorant hick suspected of murder to a sensitive young woman determined to help others despite the economic disadvantages of her upbringing. I purposely kept at arm's length from Kate's redemption, going as far as imposing a personal media blackout to ensure the focus stayed on her and not me.

Several weeks after the article's freshness had turned, I answered the phone to hear Kate's charming Kentucky timbre. We'd be right pleased, Kate said, if you would meet me and Debbie Lopez at Penguin House this very evening. Since the district attorney had updated Debbie on the developments of the Jackie Whitney case, we had not spoken since agreeing to have my illegally obtained evidence DNA tested before telling me to get the hell away from her. I could hardly wait to resume our fellowship.

They looked quite comfortable sitting across from each other in a booth, both grinning, both sipping from a cup of something. It was the first time I had seen Kate not wearing a tan jumpsuit.

"Well, now," Kate said. "Here he is." I slid in beside her. She draped her left arm over my shoulders and squeezed.

"You almost look happy," I said to Debbie.

"Smug as ever, aren't you, Landau?" Debbie said.

"What're you pissed off about? You had plenty of reasonable doubt to get Kate off. I just went a step farther and found the real killer."

"I wanted to get you'ns together so I could thank you both for what you done for me," Kate said. "No point in arguin'."

"It's your do-whatever-is-necessary attitude that bothers me," Debbie said. "Breaking into a man's house! You realize what would've happened—"

"So how're you feeling, Kate?" I said. "Looking back now with all the facts laid out. Must be hard to imagine being the sacrificial lamb in that whole mess."

"Yeah, it seems like a bad dream."

"I hear you're back working at Mr. Chao's grocery store," I said.

Kate gave Debbie a disbelieving look. "I would've thought you'd done told Mr. Landau 'bout what's been goin' on."

Debbie frowned. "Now that we're finished working together, we really have no use for each other."

"That's true," I said. "Debbie's more interested in half-truths than the whole truth."

"What the hell is that supposed to mean?" Debbie said.

"Don't take it that way," I said. "You said yourself that 'reasonable doubt' is all that mattered—"

"Oh, fuck you—"

"Hold on there, you two. It ain't doin' anyone any good carryin' on like that. Whyn't I tell Mr. Landau all the good things been happenin'? Yes, I am workin' for Mr. Chao . . ."

Kate went on to explain how the Partisan article inspired Mr. Chao to get in touch with the Chicago Botanic Garden, whose experienced volunteers were helping Kate organize and eventually run Nature's Child, a nonprofit organization dedicated to helping special needs children commune with the natural world.

When Kate finished talking, I offered her my sincere congratulations and wished her all the best. I had to go see another client, I lied, then walked out of Penguin House feeling a tremendous sense of satisfaction, as if I really helped make a difference in the life of someone who deserved to have good things come their way. I wanted to believe Debbie also felt great satisfaction hearing Kate talk about the future with such optimism. As a dedicated public defender, Debbie knew only too well that confidence in a brighter future was not an outlook often expressed by her clients. No doubt, a heavy toll had been exacted on Debbie's perspective on life, and, no doubt, she probably didn't appreciate my presence at the table. I really couldn't blame her.

Like his character Jules Landau, Marc Krulewitch, the author of Maxwell Street Blues, Windy City Blues, Gold Coast Blues, and Doubt in the 2nd Degree, is descended from an infamous Chicagoan. He grew up in Highland Park, Illinois, and now lives with his wife in Colorado.

Thank you for reading my book. If you enjoyed it, won't you please take a moment to leave me a review at your favorite retailer?

www.ingramcontent.com/pod-product-compliance
Lightning Source LLC
Chambersburg PA
CBHW021057110726
47900CB00007B/1913